HER FAVORITE FUMBLE

SHANNON STACEY

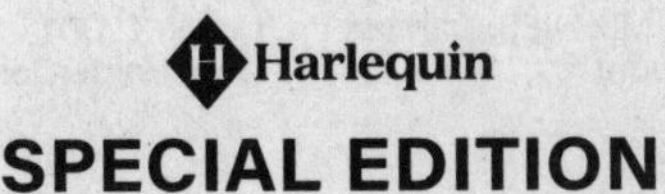

SPECIAL EDITION

Recycling programs for this product may not exist in your area.

ISBN-13: 978-1-335-47272-4

Her Favorite Fumble

For questions and comments about the quality of this book, please contact us at CustomerService@Harlequin.com.

Harlequin Enterprises ULC
22 Adelaide St. West, 41st Floor
Toronto, Ontario M5H 4E3, Canada
www.Harlequin.com

HarperCollins Publishers
Macken House, 39/40 Mayor Street Upper
Dublin 1, D01 C9W8, Ireland
www.HarperCollins.com

Printed in Lithuania

1 2 3 4 5 6 7 8 9 10 LIT 28 27 26 25

"I just can't wrap my head around why a person would drive all the way here," Nick said.

Lucy sighed. "It's the only place I remember feeling really happy."

"How old were you the last time you visited Wayward Harbor?"

She had to think about it. "I think I was maybe thirteen?"

"Okay," he said. "You know, I was pretty happy when I was thirteen, too, but it had a lot less to do with Wayward Harbor and more to do with having no real responsibilities. Being an adult is hard, no matter where you are."

"Listen, Nick. The only thing that's gotten me through the last week is the thought of being here in Maine. Don't ruin it for me."

He wasn't sure what to do next.

When it came to responsibilities and things he *should* be doing, Nick didn't just have a full plate. He had an entire formal place setting for twelve and every single dish was overflowing. Lucy from Las Vegas wasn't his responsibility.

Except she kind of was.

Dear Reader,

I'm so excited to be setting a new series in one of my favorite places—the rugged coast of Maine. I grew up exploring the sandy beaches of Cape Cod, Massachusetts, but there's something about exploring a rocky coastline that feeds my soul. New Hampshire has been my home for over three decades, but I've lived in Maine in the past, and I still have family there. It's one of my favorite places to be!

Lucy Macauley hasn't visited Wayward Harbor in years, but when her life falls apart, she packs up her car and drives three thousand miles to Maine, hoping to find comfort from her grandmother. Maybe she should have called first. Nick Slater's staying in her grandmother's cottage temporarily, and he's a little grumpy about a surprise roommate. After giving up his football career because his family needed him, Nick runs the family construction business, and he thought he was content. Then Lucy showed up in the middle of the night.

A man who's given up on dreaming, and a woman rebuilding her own dreams. A quirky town full of gossip, secrets and a long-buried scandal coming to light. Welcome to Wayward Harbor!

Happy reading!

Shannon

A *New York Times* and *USA TODAY* bestselling author of contemporary romance, **Shannon Stacey** grew up in a military family and lived in many places before landing in the small New Hampshire town where she's resided with her husband and sons for over thirty years. Her favorite activities are reading books and writing them, always with her dog at her side. She also loves coffee, Boston sports and watching too much TV. You can learn more about her books at shannonstacey.com.

Books by Shannon Stacey

Harlequin Special Edition

Wayward Harbor

Her Favorite Fumble

Blackberry Bay

More than Neighbors
Their Christmas Baby Contract
The Home They Built

Sutton's Place

Her Hometown Man
An Unexpected Cowboy
Expecting Her Ex's Baby
Falling for His Fake Girlfriend
Her Younger Man

Visit the Author Profile page
at Harlequin.com for more titles.

To anybody who's ever provided a soft place to land when things are hard. We all need a hug sometimes.

Chapter One

You can't get there from here.

—old Maine colloquialism

It was 2,915 miles from Las Vegas to the small coastal town in Maine that Lucy Macauley's grandmother called home.

Lucy rounded it up to an even three thousand miles, though, because some of those services weren't *right* off the highway exits as the signs led her to believe they'd be. There was a lot of backtracking.

Also, she'd panicked and gone the wrong way at a confusing interchange, ending up in Chicago traffic—a trauma already so embedded in her DNA, her future grandchildren would have a deep fear of the city they wouldn't be able to explain.

Three thousand miles was also about 2,990 miles too long to have nobody but herself and some easily tuned out podcasts for company. She had no job, no home, and everything that mattered to her was packed in her car.

It wasn't a great headspace to be in.

She wasn't broke, though. Thanks to a financially insecure upbringing driving her to squirrel away her money, and her former living arrangements not giving her the space to accumulate a lot of purchases, her savings account was healthy. It was earmarked for her dream of moving to Miami, though, so she'd rather not dip into it.

Lucy was turning thirty next month, and her current predicament was not where she'd seen herself when imagining that milestone. It wasn't the number she objected to, but the realization she had nothing to show for almost three decades of existence.

It wasn't something she'd thought a lot about until her life totally unraveled in the flash of a telephoto camera. She'd met a nice, down-to-earth guy in a coffee shop, which wasn't all that easy to do in Las Vegas, and they spent a lovely hour sitting at one of the tables in the window, getting to know each other. Lucy had dared to hope she might have finally found *the one.*

The next day, her face was all over the tabloids and social media. It turned out her nice guy was a football quarterback named Reese Noonan—he'd introduced himself as Andrew, which she later learned was his middle name—who was engaged to beloved actress Faith Lincoln.

Just like that, the "Fairee" fandom came for her, and Lucy became the most hated woman in the world.

And it reached a fever pitch when, a few days later, Noonan's football team lost the championship and Lucy got blamed for that, too. Apparently having coffee with her made him forget how to play the game he was paid nine figures to play.

Over the next several weeks, she lost her very lucrative cocktail waitressing job due to the attention, and then her roommate and landlord teamed up to tell her she had to leave because everybody in the building was being harassed. She tried hiding out in the home her mom shared with her next potential stepfather, but some destructive behavior from the quarterback and teary interviews from Faith Lincoln kept the attention from dying down. It only took six weeks before her mother watched in silence while the boyfriend told her she had to leave.

So now she was driving to the only place she remembered ever being truly happy—Wayward Harbor, Maine. She would get a strong, comforting hug from her grandmother and then she'd figure out what came next.

First, she had to figure out how to find Gran's cottage in the dark. Nostalgic childhood memories of a place didn't translate to navigating roads many years later. And dense cloud cover meant there was no moonlight, so she could only see what her headlights illuminated.

Luckily, her phone's navigation led her straight to the turn she needed, and tears prickled Lucy's eyes. Even though they were still bare from winter, the bushy tangles of beach roses along the white fence were finally a familiar sight.

A dark-colored pickup was parked in the driveway. Lucy had no idea what she'd expected her grandmother to drive, but a truck wouldn't have been high on the list. Lucy parked behind it and killed her engine. When her headlights clicked off, the world plunged into darkness.

That was what she got for not telling Gran she was coming. She should have. It was probably rude to show up unannounced, even for a granddaughter, but deep down, she'd been afraid Gran would have told her not to come. She wasn't sure she could handle another door being closed in her face right now.

After making sure the basics—phone charger, wallet, brush and a toothbrush—were in her tote, she slung it over her shoulder and grabbed her phone and keys. Then she got out of the car, closing the door as quietly as possible. Cold, damp air enveloped her, and she sucked in a breath as a chill immediately seeped into her bones.

Okay, so spring on the coast of Maine and spring in Las Vegas were apparently two entirely different seasons.

Using her phone's flashlight to navigate the uneven stones

of the walkway, Lucy made her way to the front door and breathed a sigh of relief when she found it unlocked.

Setting her tote by the door and slipping off her shoes, she tiptoed by flashlight through the living room, searching for a free outlet for her charger. While she looked, she wondered whether waking Gran now or letting her find her granddaughter on the couch in the morning would be the least alarming way to make her presence known.

"If you're one of those Airbnb folks, you've got the wrong—"

Lucy's high-pitched scream drowned out whatever else the deep, gruff voice was saying, and she whirled to throw her keys at the intruder as light flooded the room. She remembered too late she was supposed to clutch them in her hand with the keys between her fingers like metal claws.

The man caught her keys as easily as if she'd lobbed them to him so he could borrow her car. He was frowning, but his overall expression was more confused than menacing. "Are you okay?"

"No." That was an understatement. She looked around, panic rising. "Gran?"

"She's not here."

Lucy stared at the dark-haired man, registering his size first. He was tall, with broad shoulders and incredibly muscular arms. And those *abs*. All of which she could see because he was naked except for a pair of alarmingly low-slung gray sweatpants.

Even as some inner voice tried to reassure her it would be a ridiculous wardrobe choice for a home invasion, panic was coursing through her body. "What did you do with my grandmother?"

"She's traveling."

"Oh, she's just *traveling*? An elderly woman alone has gone running amok, just like that?"

"Elderly?" He barked out a laugh before shaking his head. "She's only sixty-nine, and she finished in the top ten of the food bank's 5k run last fall. Something you would probably know if you were really her granddaughter because it was the only thing she talked about for a solid two months."

"Of course I knew about the 5k run. We joked about how I can spend twelve hours walking in heels, but would only run if somebody was chasing me—and, honestly, maybe not even then. I'd probably give up. And Gran can run a 5k, but can't walk ten feet in high heels."

He stood there, arms folded across his chest. His eyes, which looked almost as dark as his hair, were narrowed, and he didn't seem to have anything else to add.

Lucy knew Gran had talked about the run on Facebook, though, which was as good as making it public knowledge. Did he really have proof of what he was saying? "Did you murder her and hide her body so you could squat in her home and tell anybody who asks that she's traveling?"

His eyebrow arched, and he scrubbed one hand over his scruffy jaw. "You might want to lay off the true crime podcasts."

Lucy opened her mouth to argue, but she *had* just driven three thousand miles with true crime podcasts playing as the background noise. She hadn't intended to tune them out, but even murder and mayhem couldn't distract her from thinking about the tattered mess her life had become practically overnight.

"Sorry," she muttered. "I'm somehow over-caffeinated and utterly exhausted at the same time. I'm Lucy Macauley. Helen's granddaughter."

The man nodded. "I'm Nick Slater. Helen didn't want the

cottage sitting empty while she was away and I needed a place to stay, so I'm staying here in exchange for doing some work around the property."

That made sense, and Lucy's pulse slowly settled into an only slightly higher than normal rhythm. "For how long?"

"She's visiting some friends in Florida, and then they're going on a cruise, and then she's staying with some other friends in one of the Carolinas on her way back through. She said it would be a couple of months, at least. And she just left four days ago."

"Two *months*?" Her heart rate kicked back into high gear. "I drove all the way from the West Coast, and I was planning to stay here with Gran."

"I'm staying here."

"I don't have anywhere else to go."

"Neither do I."

Her head tilted. "Are you from here?"

"Born and raised," he said.

"Then why don't you have anywhere else to go?"

When his annoyed expression deepened into an actual scowl, she realized that was a rude question. But she was exhausted and wanted him to go away so she could face-plant on that couch.

"Somebody else needed to use my place for a while, so this arrangement worked out for everybody."

"Except me."

"Except you," he admitted gruffly.

Lucy wasn't sure what the best move was, but she knew two things. When she'd said she was Helen's granddaughter, he hadn't mentioned the incident in Las Vegas, so maybe he didn't know the entire world hated her right now. And also, it was very late and she didn't have the physical or emotional strength to get back in her car and find someplace else to go.

"Maybe I can just stay here," she said. "I *really* need some sleep."

"There's only one bed."

"Of course there is. I read that book, mister."

The scowl deepened even further. "That is *definitely* not where I was going with that. What I meant was that the second bedroom's emptied out so I can work in there, but you can crash on the couch."

"That's very chivalrous of you," she said, relief fanning the dying embers of her sense of humor.

"I'm over six feet tall," he argued, and she arched her eyebrow. "Okay, I am six feet tall, though."

She waited.

He crossed his arms. "I'm closer to six feet tall than *you* are."

"I'll take the couch, of course. I was trying to be funny, but I probably missed because I just drove three thousand miles for a hug and now—"

She waved her hand around the room where her grandmother should have been and clearly wasn't, and then burst into tears.

Nick knew he should hug this woman he'd found in the living room.

She was crying. She'd driven three thousand miles for a hug. And, sure, she'd accused him of murdering Helen Griffin and hiding her body so he could squat in her cottage, but Lucy was clearly not having a good day.

Or a good week, more than likely, since she'd driven all the way across the country to get some comfort from her grandmother.

He took a step forward, but then stopped. "Do you want me to hug you?"

The good news was that the tears stopped. But he was a little insulted by the way her eyes widened as she took a step back. "No."

"Sorry," he muttered. "You were saying you needed a hug. That's all."

"I appreciate the thought, but—" She stopped wiping tears from her face to wave a hand at him. "You're definitely underdressed to be hugging women you don't know."

That was a valid point, so he shut his mouth, watching her while she walked over to pluck a few tissues from the box on an end table.

She didn't look much like her grandmother. Helen was shorter and more compact, with salt-and-pepper hair. Lucy was tall and lithe, like a dancer maybe. Black leggings and a tank top hugged curves in all the best places, and the long cardigan over them was so light, it didn't do much to cover her. It definitely wasn't designed for warmth, and between it and the slip-on canvas shoes, she had to be freezing.

But what Nick couldn't stop looking at was the cloud of red curls around the woman's face. It looked as if it had one of those plastic claw clips in it, but her hair really didn't want to be restrained. He couldn't help wondering what it looked like free, glistening in the sunshine.

And her eyes were the blue of a summer sky.

Annoyed with himself, Nick snorted, which drew Lucy's attention back to him. Since he didn't want to confess he'd been waxing poetic to himself about how pretty she was, he had to come up with a distraction. "Do you have a bag?"

"A bag?"

"In the car. You know, a bag with clothes in it? Hairbrush. Phone charger." He held up his hand. "Stuff for traveling. I can bring it in for you."

"I don't have a bag. I have *bags*—plural. And boxes." She

looked so forlorn he was afraid she might cry again. "Everything I own is in my car right now."

Dread and disbelief battled to take up the most space in his head. "That was information I didn't have when I agreed to let you crash on the couch."

She blew out a breath, shoving some of the unruly curls away from her face. "Can we talk about this tomorrow?"

Nick didn't really want to put off a conversation about whether or not this woman he'd known ten minutes actually intended to move in with him. But he also knew if he pushed, she was going to cry again. She was clearly out of gas, and maybe this would all make more sense after a good night's sleep.

"Sure," he agreed. "Do you need anything? Do you know where everything is?"

"I'm good. Thanks."

"Okay. Good night, then."

"Good night."

He went back into the bedroom and closed the door behind him before breathing out a sigh of relief.

His brothers weren't going to believe this, Nick thought as he slid back into bed. And they'd hear about it, one way or another, because everybody heard about everything eventually in Wayward Harbor.

He heard the toilet flush and then water running. Thanks to old floorboards and good hearing, he could track her movement around the cottage, until he finally heard the springs creak as she settled onto the couch.

Then he heard a low curse, followed by more movement around the living room. Finally, the band of light shining under the door went dark, and after some shifting around on the couch again, the cottage fell silent.

When, what felt like only a few hours later, daylight broke

through the split in the curtains, Nick crept into the kitchen and poured a mug of coffee from the machine he'd set to auto brew. The woman—Lucy, he reminded himself—was still asleep under a pile of what looked like every crocheted and knit throw she could find in the cottage. And Helen liked being cozy, so there were a lot of them to be found.

In a world where Nick had better luck, he'd be able to sneak out and deal with her later in the day. But her car was parked behind his truck in the dooryard and he'd returned the keys she'd thrown at him.

Before Lucy inevitably made her case for another night—or, Lord help him, more—in the cottage, he needed to call Helen. And that was a phone call he didn't want to make in front of Lucy. He didn't know Helen's granddaughter, but he'd heard some pretty unflattering whispers about Helen's daughter, Iris, over the years. And Iris had been an only child, which meant she was Lucy's mother.

Nick had no way of knowing how far that apple had fallen from the tree, but it was up to Helen to decide if she wanted Lucy in her home.

He was halfway through his first cup of coffee when the mountain of blankets on the couch began shifting. When a mass of curls popped out, like a bear emerging from hibernation, he had to bite back a laugh.

Lucy looked around, blinking. Then, with a groan, she swung her feet to the floor. Most of the blankets got pushed aside, though she did keep one knit throw wrapped around herself as she stumbled to the bathroom.

When she emerged a few minutes later with the blanket still wrapped around her, he took a mug out of the cabinet and slid it down the short counter so it came to rest next to the coffeepot. She smiled her thanks and grabbed the pot, while he wondered if she was going to want cream and sugar. But after pouring her coffee and replacing the carafe, she picked up her coffee and turned away.

Somehow she managed to get the mug to the table without tripping on the blanket, and then she wrapped it more tightly around herself before sitting down.

"Good morning," she said after taking her first sip.

"Morning."

She turned to look at him. "But not a good one?"

"What?"

"I said 'good morning' and you said 'morning,' so I'm wondering if it's not a good one."

He sighed from the depths of his soul. "Good morning, Lucy."

She smiled before pulling the blanket tighter around her shoulders. "Is the furnace one of the things you're working on?"

He shook his head. "The furnace is shut off because it's not winter anymore. I slept with my window open a crack, actually."

"Yay for you," she muttered.

"You said you drove from the West Coast. Don't you all live in air conditioning out there?"

"Yes, when it's hot *outside*. That's totally different than just letting the outside cold in. Also, air-conditioned air is *not* damp like this."

Nick didn't think it was damp at all, but he swallowed more coffee instead of arguing with her. He had a feeling he wouldn't win with her, and he'd need the caffeine to get through the day.

"I really should eat something with this coffee," she said suddenly. Before Nick could stop her, she was up and walking to the fridge with the blanket still clutched around her. "Gran used to make the most amazing blueberry pancakes."

He knew she wasn't going to find much in that refrigerator, and definitely not the ingredients for amazing blueberry pancakes. Helen had cleaned out the fridge before she left, and it was mostly condiments now, with one open quart of milk. He couldn't remember when he bought it, though, so he considered it highly suspect at this point.

"There's no actual food in here," she said.

"There's a package of bologna. And some tomatoes."

"That's weird."

"Hard to make bologna and tomato sandwiches without them."

"Gross," she muttered, though not quietly enough to keep him from hearing, before going back to her seat and picking up her coffee.

He tried not to be offended on behalf of his favorite sandwich. "If Helen had known you were coming, maybe we could have stocked up on your favorite foods."

The look she gave him over the rim of her mug might have set a lesser man on fire. "It's too early to be passive-aggressive."

"I just can't wrap my head around why a person would drive all the way across the country without at least talking to Helen first."

"We usually talk on Facebook, but I deleted all the apps off my phone and I need the password to put it back. I think I wrote it in a notebook that's, hopefully, at the bottom of one of the boxes in my car."

The mass deleting of apps was interesting because, as far as Nick could tell from people more online than him, that usually meant a person was having some kind of crisis the internet was making worse. "But you came anyway."

"I didn't really think it through, okay? I just… I went through some stuff and I needed to get away."

He wasn't sure what kind of "some stuff" would lead a person to put everything they owned in a car and drive all the way across the country, but it wasn't Nick's place to ask her. "Why here?"

"Because it's where Gran lives?" she asked, as though it was a ridiculous question. But he waited her out, and eventually she sighed. "It's the only place I remember feeling really happy."

"How old were you the last time you visited Wayward Harbor?"

She had to think about it, which didn't surprise him. He and Helen were pretty close, and he couldn't remember ever meeting Lucy. Since she seemed rather unforgettable, especially the hair, it wasn't likely they'd crossed paths. Or they had, but they'd been so young, he didn't remember.

"I think I was maybe thirteen? I'm not sure, but I remember we were going to go swimming, but I'd started my—"

She snapped her mouth closed, her cheeks flushing, as if Nick had reached thirty-five years of age without discovering women had menstrual cycles.

"Okay," he said. "You know, I was pretty happy when I was thirteen, too, but it had a lot less to do with Wayward Harbor and more to do with having no real responsibilities. Being an adult is hard, no matter where you are."

"Listen, Nick. The only thing that's gotten me through the last week is the thought of being here in Maine and getting a hug from Gran. Since Gran's not here, all I have is Wayward Harbor. Don't ruin it for me."

He knew he should mind his own business, but he couldn't help himself. "Do you want to tell me what happened?"

"No."

"Okay." He wasn't sure what to do next.

The easiest path was to get her keys from her, move her

car, and then drive himself into town for breakfast. When it came to responsibilities and things he *should* be doing, Nick didn't just have a full plate. He had an entire formal place setting for twelve, and every single dish was overflowing. Lucy from Las Vegas wasn't his responsibility.

Except she kind of was.

This cottage was his responsibility because, in exchange for staying there, Nick was housesitting and doing some construction odd jobs that needed doing. And leaving a woman he didn't know and who Helen hadn't known was coming alone in the cottage didn't feel like a responsible thing to do.

It was too early to call Helen, though. The woman was a night owl by nature and was also on vacation with friends, so Nick felt as if he should wait until at least nine. And that meant he wasn't getting breakfast until at least ten, which wasn't an option.

As far as he could tell, he had two choices. He could leave this woman claiming to be Helen's granddaughter alone in the cottage and drive himself into town.

Or he could take her with him.

"I'm going into town. Come with me and I'll buy you a hearty breakfast, and then we'll stop at the market."

She looked down at the outfit she'd traveled *and* slept in. "I need to go get my bag and take a shower."

"I can wait five minutes." When she glared at him again, he shrugged. "Or ten."

A few minutes later, when the shower started, Nick tried not to think about the woman standing naked under the spray. He was less than twelve hours into the awareness he might have a thing for blue-eyed redheads, though, and also that dating hadn't been a priority in his life for a while.

To drag his mind out of places it had no business being, he focused on the problem at hand—still Lucy, but the fully clothed version who'd invaded the cottage and thrown a wrench in his plans.

After breakfast, one way or another, he was going to talk to Helen. And if she didn't have the heart to turn away her granddaughter, he was going to find himself in a bind.

The only thing he knew for sure was that sharing a cottage with Iris Macauley's daughter was going to put him smack in the middle of one of the juiciest stories to go around the Wayward Harbor grapevine in three decades.

Chapter Two

The sign-up sheet to volunteer for spring cleanup is on the bulletin board in the town hall. We'll be cleaning up winter debris in the parks and around town, getting Wayward Harbor ready for the upcoming summer season. Please bring gloves and rakes, and the town will be providing trash bags, as well as lunch for the volunteers. Come for community pride and stay for the free pizza!

—Wayward Harbor Online Community Group

In a continuation of the theme of not recognizing her own life, Lucy sat silently in the passenger seat of a pickup driven by a man she didn't know.

She'd taken closer to twenty minutes than ten, even with simply gathering her wet hair into a bun, but she'd been smart and taken her keys with her into the bathroom. He couldn't leave without her if he couldn't get his truck out. And even if he had, she could drive herself into town and buy her own breakfast.

But even though she didn't know him, it beat going by herself. Walking into a restaurant alone and finding a place to sit felt too daunting in her current mindset, and she might have just continued living on coffee and whatever road snacks were left in her car.

Because she had no clue what to say and Nick didn't seem

inclined to initiate a conversation, she stared out her window at the choppy gray water crashing against the rocky shore. Her memories of Wayward Harbor were full of blue skies and sparkling water. Humid air and digging for sea glass. The tangy smell of sunscreen and the taste of ice cream dipped in chocolate jimmies.

Apparently, those memories hadn't been made in April.

If there had been anything to eat in the cottage, she would have turned down the invitation to breakfast. Not that it was much of an invitation—he simply told her she was going.

She wanted to talk to Gran, and she *really* didn't want an audience for that, so it would have been a good time to call. *But* she wouldn't be able to do that until she'd rummaged through all the stuff in her car to find the notebook she'd scribbled her passwords in so she could sign into Facebook and ask Gran for her cell number.

Just thinking about putting any social media apps back onto her phone made her stomach hurt, and she sighed so deeply, Nick glanced in her direction.

He was still frowning, of course. Sure, she'd barged into his life with no warning, but he'd chosen to invite her to breakfast. If he was that annoyed, he could have left her to rummage between her car seats for snacks. Or, because she was a grown woman—even if she was currently in crisis—she could have driven her own damn car into town and bought her own damn breakfast. If he didn't want her company, he shouldn't have told her to come with him.

She was about to tell him that when he rounded a corner and Wayward Harbor came into view.

The town followed the curve of the shore, the buildings a historical mix of white siding, faded gray shingles and brick. Piers jutted out, smaller ones for the tourists and, off in the distance, the larger commercial piers. Boats bobbed in the water, masts swaying against the sky.

Lucy had forgotten how ruggedly gorgeous the coastline was here.

After they'd passed the park with the statue of Cricket—a poodle who saved a toddler from a strong current in the fifties, according to legend—Nick took a left and navigated through the much narrower streets of the small downtown. There were a couple of places, with cars parked on both sides, that she wasn't sure his truck and the vehicles coming the other way would both fit, but they did.

"This is the closest spot we'll get," he said, parallel parking the extended cab truck so smoothly she wanted to ask him to do it again, but more slowly, so she could figure out how he did it. Her car was half the length of his truck and it would have taken her at least two tries. In Las Vegas, she often walked or called an Uber because it was easier than finding and paying for parking, so her parking skills were a little rusty.

After he turned off the engine, Lucy pulled the hood up over her hair and slid her sunglasses on. He stopped to frown at her. "What?"

"Are you on the run? From the law, I mean?"

"Am I a fugitive from justice?" She laughed. Maybe she *was* on the run, but it wasn't from law enforcement. "No. I'm just cold, thank you very much."

That didn't exactly explain the sunglasses, but she guessed he didn't care all that much because he didn't ask any more questions. When he opened his door and got out, she did the same, and he met her on the sidewalk.

For a moment, she had to hustle to keep up, but then he noticed and slowed his pace so she could match it. She didn't see any signs advertising food, and when he turned down an alley between two buildings, she started to wonder if just blindly following this guy was a good idea.

On the backside of the building was a door next to a large window that had Pete's Place written across it in uneven window paint. The white clapboards needed repainting, and she couldn't help wondering when they'd last taken a squeegee to the glass in the door and window.

"This looks like the kind of place you go to plan bank robberies," she told him. "Or to pick up prescriptions that have somebody else's name on the labels."

"At least you're dressed for it," he said.

She rolled her eyes, then realized he wouldn't be able to see her reaction through the sunglasses. "You're a funny guy."

"Pete likes the look of the place. He says it keeps the tourists away."

"Isn't the point to attract tourist dollars?"

He shrugged. "That's probably true for most of the businesses, but Pete's said more than once that he'd flip burgers on a hibachi on the sidewalk for pocket change before he'll cater to people who think the entire world wants to see pictures of their scrambled eggs."

"Ah. So he's grumpy, like you."

Nick, who'd been about to pull open the door, frowned at her. "I'm not grumpy."

"You're scowling at me right now."

"Because you called me grumpy."

She sighed. "You haven't smiled a single time since I met you."

"You met me maybe a whole twelve hours ago, when a strange woman who doesn't like bologna and tomato sandwiches had broken in and woken me up."

He'd clearly taken her rejection of his sandwich choice personally. "I didn't break in. The door was unlocked."

"Lesson learned," he said mostly under his breath before yanking the door open and waving for her to enter.

Pete's Place was small, but it was a lot nicer than the exterior had led her to expect. The pale blue walls and light wood tables and booths were welcoming, and a coffee counter ran almost the length of the dining room. There were several men sitting there, as well as a few in booths.

They all turned to look when the door opened. The man behind the counter, who might or might not have been Pete, nodded. "Morning, Nick."

"Morning, Pete."

Pete, along with several other guys, looked curiously at Lucy, but Nick didn't introduce her. She didn't mind at all and followed him silently to an empty booth. He chose the one all the way in the back, farthest from any other diners. Breathing a sigh of relief when he chose to sit facing the front, she slid into the booth with her back to the room. With her hood up, nobody could see her, and she took off the sunglasses.

Pete walked over and set two mugs of coffee on the end of the table. "You want coffee, or do you want something else?"

"Coffee, please."

"Menu's behind the condiments. I'll give you a minute."

She pulled one out and studied the offerings, suddenly famished. "What's good here?"

"Everything. Best breakfast in Maine."

"How many different places have you *had* breakfast in Maine?"

He shrugged. "Hard to say."

Lucy assumed that was a grumpy man's way of admitting he was working with a small sample set and returned her attention to the menu.

Nick cleared his throat. "Is there an angry ex or almost ex who's going to show up on the doorstep looking for you?"

"No," Lucy said, but she lowered her gaze to the spoon she was fiddling with as she wondered if she should warn him no angry exes were going to knock on the door, but paparazzi might. Or a sobbing mob of Faith Lincoln fans. Or maybe angry football fans.

Telling him was probably the right thing to do, but that confession came with the risk he'd toss her out the same way her roommate and then her mother's boyfriend had. She was out of places to go.

"You can tell me," he said, and she startled before realizing he was still talking about angry exes. "You *should* tell me, actually, because if there's a possibility I'll have to defend you in the middle of the night, I'll wear sleep pants with a stronger drawstring."

Was that humor? His expression hadn't changed, but she laughed and shook her head. "No exes. No almost exes. No need for combat sleep pants."

An image of him last night, wearing the sweats with the weak drawstring so low on his hips, flashed through her mind, and she had to set down the menu so she wouldn't use it to fan her face.

Pete appeared about thirty seconds after she dropped the menu. "What are you having?"

"I think I'll have whatever Nick is ordering," she said rather than admitting she couldn't make a decision.

"Usual?" he asked, and Nick nodded.

"Be right up."

Lucy shook her head, putting the menu back in the stand behind the condiments. "Are we getting something good?"

"Guess you'll see," he said, and though he didn't smile, she could hear the amusement in his voice.

If it was a sign he was in a good mood—on the inside, at least—now might be a good time to hit him up for Gran's number. "If you're staying in the cottage and doing work, you must have a way to contact Helen. Stuff always comes up during renovations."

"Yup."

"Okay. Since I haven't found my passwords yet, if you just give me her cell phone number, I can call her. The only number in my phone is an old landline, but I never cared because we just talked on Facebook." He didn't even blink, but he gave an almost imperceptible shake of his head, as if he was silently talking to himself. "You're seriously not going to give me my own grandmother's number?"

As soon as the words were out of her mouth, she heard how they sounded. Hopefully, he wouldn't throw back in her face the fact that if she was a good granddaughter, she wouldn't need to get the number from a veritable stranger.

"I'd like to talk to her first," he said.

"Why? I mean, we could talk to her together if you want, on speakerphone." He was quiet so long, she put the pieces together. "You don't trust me."

"I don't *know* you."

That was fair. "Whether she tells you to tell me I can't stay or I hear it from her directly, it'll still suck."

"The difference is that she'll be honest with me. She might not be able to bring herself to tell *you* no."

Her eyes narrowed. "*Or* you want a chance to convince her you can't work on the cottage with me there. And since you've already torn apart the second bedroom, she can't really tell *you* no."

"That's not the conversation that's going to happen."

She crossed her arms, her eyebrow arching. "Maybe I don't trust you, either."

"Okay."

Frustrated, Lucy took a sip of her coffee. Then she watched

Nick pull the salt, pepper and ketchup bottle from the condiment rack. *Ketchup?*

"I can't believe I blindly ordered the same breakfast as a man who likes bologna and tomato sandwiches."

He *almost* smiled.

Nick should have told Lucy she hadn't grabbed one of her grandmother's hooded sweatshirts.

The hoodie was his. Her first clue should have been the size. Helen would have to wear it like a belted dress. And also, the Slater & Sons Construction printed on it could have been a clue, but she might not have remembered he'd given her his last name in the confusion last night.

In the moment, he hadn't had the heart to mention it. She looked warm and cozy, and it was better than the possible alternative of her walking into Pete's wrapped in blankets.

What he hadn't foreseen was how distracting it would be to sit across from a beautiful woman wearing a hoodie that belonged to him. It even had his last name on it. That particular sweatshirt was his favorite, actually, because it was the last of their original order. His brother had found a cheaper supplier and though he insisted the fabric and fit were the same, Nick disagreed.

"You're staring at me," she muttered.

Because you're wearing my favorite hoodie. "You're sitting across from me. It would be weird if I sat here staring at the ceiling. Hard to drink my coffee that way, too."

"See? Grumpy."

He pulled the trifold menu out of the holder and stood it up between them. It wasn't quite tall enough, but he scrunched down in his seat until it blocked their eye contact.

She laughed as she grabbed the menu and folded it back up. He almost laughed with her, but his phone vibrated in his pocket, and he pulled it out to see Helen's name on the screen. There was no way she'd already heard he was at Pete's with a redhead who might be her granddaughter.

Then again, news traveled fast in Wayward Harbor.

"It's my brother," he lied, sliding toward the end of the booth. "I need to step out and take this really quick."

She nodded, and he accepted the call when he was halfway to the door so it wouldn't go to voicemail. "Hey, I was going to call you later."

"I beat you to it," she said, and the warmth in her voice made his lips curve a little as he slipped outside. "I just wanted to check in and see how you're doing and if you have everything you need in the cottage."

He had everything he needed, plus some. "I'm good. But your granddaughter showed up late last night. She slept on the couch because I've already torn into the second bedroom."

"Lucy's with you?" He heard the rush of a relieved breath. "I've been so worried. I heard about some nonsense online, and I've sent her several Facebook messages, but she hasn't responded. That's when I realized I don't have her cell number."

Nonsense online? "She said something about deleting all the apps off her phone and she hasn't found her passwords yet."

"Honestly, I called you because I'm putting off working up the energy to call Iris and see if she has Lucy's number. One would assume she'd know how to reach her daughter, but…it's Iris."

"Lucy asked me for your number, but I wanted to talk to you first. I can send her down the road if you're not comfortable with her being here."

"I'm not sending my granddaughter down the road, Nick Slater. Not without a reason, anyway. Give her my number and tell her to call me. She can video call if she wants because we're having a stay-home day. But you have to be okay with it, too. I already told you the cottage was yours for the summer."

Nick stifled the weary sigh and settled for closing his eyes for a few seconds. "It's your cottage, and she's your granddaughter. I can make it work if that's what you want."

"For now, if you're sure. The poor girl needs a safe place to land right now. You'll keep an eye on her, right? Make sure she's okay?"

Nick pinched the bridge of his nose. "I won't let you down, Helen."

The promise landed like a boulder on top of the weight his shoulders already carried, but he wouldn't let her down. He didn't let *anybody* down.

Not anymore.

"And Nick? Don't say anything about those old Iris rumors, okay? I don't think the poor child needs anything else on her plate right now."

"I understand." He wasn't sure he agreed, but he'd follow Helen's lead.

Once they hung up, he went back inside, just in time to watch Pete set their plates on the table. He nodded his thanks and, after Pete was done, slid into his seat and looked at his plate. Two blueberry pancakes, two scrambled eggs, bacon and home fries. Just the way he liked them.

Lucy already had a chunk of pancake on her fork. "You make good breakfast choices. Though I should have asked for a half order of whatever you got because this is a lot of food for somebody who's not—"

When she waved her hand toward him, he frowned. "Somebody who's not what?"

"You know, *almost* six feet tall."

He snorted and grabbed the ketchup to squeeze some on

his scrambled eggs. Lucy wrinkled her nose, but thankfully kept her opinions to herself this time.

They ate in complete silence, and when Pete brought the check, he waved off her attempt to pay for his breakfast. He wasn't sure what her financial situation was and, until he knew more about her, he wasn't going to let her spend money on him.

"You can owe me one," was all he said, and then—nodding to Pete and ignoring all the curious looks sent their way—they left and walked back to the truck.

"We can stop at the market," he said. "Just grab what you need for now. At some point, if necessary, there's a bigger—and cheaper—grocery store a few towns over."

The hood and sunglasses were firmly in place when they walked into the small local market, and they stayed in place, which amused him because the lighting wasn't great in some of the aisles.

He made sure to buy more bologna and several tomatoes, just because it made her laugh again. They got some staples, like bread and a new jug of milk. She was big into fruits and vegetables, and she grabbed several packages of chicken to divide up and freeze.

By the time they reached the register, she'd tucked the sunglasses into the pocket of her—actually *his*—sweatshirt and dropped the hood. The curls captured in the bun were still damp, but the wisps around her face were frizzy from having the hood up all morning, and he wondered if they were as soft as they looked.

They split the cost of groceries in half, with Lucy giving him cash to cover her portion, and when they got back to his truck, she took each bag out of the cart so he could put it in the back seat.

They'd just finished when a girl whose parents he knew

pretty well spotted them and stopped in her tracks, staring at Lucy.

"Ohmigosh," the teen said breathlessly. "You're her!"

Lucy shrank back as the girl pulled her phone out of her back pocket, and Nick stepped forward. "Felicity, don't do that."

"But, I just—"

"This is Helen Griffin's granddaughter, and I just know you're not going to violate her privacy in any way."

He didn't like bringing Helen's name into whatever was going on, but it was the only way he could think of to keep Felicity from taking a selfie or a video or whatever else she was going to do that had drained the color from Lucy's face.

He watched the teen walk away, and though she looked back a couple of times, her phone stayed in her pocket. Lucy was already in the passenger seat of his truck, hood up and sunglasses on. She'd told him she wasn't a fugitive and she wasn't running from an ex, but if Felicity recognized her on the street in a town Lucy hadn't been to since around the time the girl was born, it had to be something big.

"Thank you," she said in a quiet voice when he climbed into the driver's seat and shut his door. "I guess I should have left the hood up, but I was getting hot."

"We're going home," he said as he turned the key, immediately regretting the harsh tone. "And you're going to tell me everything."

Chapter Three

It's Amnesty Week at the library! You can return those overdue books with no fines! And if you bring in a canned food or any other items for the local food pantry's list on our website, any past fines will go away. Remember, if you don't have any overdue fines, you can still donate and the library staff will forgive the fines of your neighbors!

—Wayward Harbor Online Community Group

Lucy gave Nick the abridged version of how her life had fallen apart while they put the groceries away. She talked fast in a steady voice, just wanting to get through it.

She told him about meeting a nice guy and sharing a coffee and some conversation. About her face being all over the tabloids and the internet the next day. About being blamed for destroying a fairy-tale romance and making Faith Lincoln cry. For costing a football team and their fans a fancy trophy. About how the toxicity chipped away at everything until she had nothing left.

"Don't these things blow over pretty fast?" he asked when she stopped talking. "Some other celebrity will get arrested for a DUI or one of them will say something they shouldn't in an interview and you're forgotten."

"That's what usually happens. I happened to get sucked

into a drama with a very dedicated fanbase, so it hasn't really died down. They'll get distracted by something else eventually, I guess. I *hope*."

"I can understand wanting to get away for a few days, but packing your life into your car seems extreme."

"When everything blew up, I told myself the same thing you said—it'll blow over soon. But then the team lost and it blew up again. And Faith Lincoln did interviews and it blew up again. Even though I was one of the best servers he had, my boss fired me because crowds were coming in to get photos or videos of me. My roommate threw me out. My friends tried to be supportive, but then they got caught up in the likes and the views and cared more about going viral talking *about* me than actually talking *to* me. Once my mom let her boyfriend throw me out, I felt really alone."

"That sounds hard," he said in a soft voice. "I'm sorry you didn't have the support you should have."

Tears blurred Lucy's vision, and she blinked a few times. "Thank you. I'm not trying to get sympathy, I promise. I just wanted you to know that I didn't come here to hide, really. Sure, I wanted to hide for a few days and get some love and blueberry pancakes from my grandmother, but I brought everything I own because I know I don't want to be in Las Vegas anymore."

"I went there once, for a friend's bachelor party, and I don't ever want to be in Las Vegas again, either."

That made her laugh because she hadn't known him long, but she could have guessed that about him. "I liked the city itself, honestly. I thought I had my mom and a lot of good friends, but then, when I really needed them, I found out my circle was quantity, and not quality."

"So you're not running away from anything. You're running *to* something."

She smiled, trying to pretend she didn't have an escaped tear running down her cheek. "Thank you for understanding."

"Also, Noonan's a mediocre quarterback at best, but he's got good receivers able to catch the junk passes he throws. And they wouldn't even have made postseason if they didn't have one of the best defenses in the league."

"I don't know what all of that means, but thank you for thinking he's mediocre. That actually makes me feel better."

Nick handed her a slip of paper with a phone number on it. "That wasn't my brother who called while we were at Pete's. It was Helen. She was worried about you and has been trying to reach you, so I told her why you hadn't responded."

"So she knows, then."

"It seems so. She said you could video call her because they're having a quiet day in today."

"Thank you," she whispered, looking at the digits on the paper. It wasn't the way she'd wanted to be reunited with Gran, but it would have to do.

"I was going to do some work on the bedroom, but I can do some yard work so you have privacy."

She shook her head. "You already know everything, anyway, but I appreciate the offer."

Once he'd gone into the small bedroom and closed the door, Lucy sat on the couch and took a few deep breaths. If Gran wanted her out of the cottage, Nick probably would have delivered the bad news on her behalf, but she couldn't be sure. Maybe her grandmother wanted to let her down gently, and not through a third party.

Before she could talk herself into burrowing back into her blanket cocoon and calling later, Lucy saved the number into her contacts and then hit the button for a video call.

Her grandmother's smiling face filled the screen a moment later, getting a little blurry when tears shimmered in Lucy's eyes.

"Lucy! How are you, honey?"

"Better now," she said honestly.

"Look at you in my cottage! I'm sorry I'm not there to hug you, but it makes me so happy seeing you there. Are you settling in okay?"

Lucy shook off the dismay she'd felt at being recognized in town. "I am. Nick took me to breakfast at Pete's and then we went to the market."

Even though she deliberately kept her voice light, Helen peered closer at the screen. "Did it go okay? Are you and Nick getting on okay?"

"Yes. He's great, actually." If a little on the grumpy side. "One of the girls in town—Felicity, I think her name was—recognized me, but Nick didn't let her take a picture or video. I'm afraid I'm going to bring all that toxicity here."

"Don't even worry about it. Word will get around town you're my granddaughter and they'll watch over you, and that mess will all blow over."

Lucy had been telling herself that for weeks and it hadn't yet, but she nodded. Then she heard voices in the background on Helen's end, and her grandmother held up a finger to tell somebody off camera to wait.

"Sorry about that. We're supposed to have an at-home day to relax after all that driving, but there's a big flea market a couple of towns over, and you know how it is."

"I won't keep you. I just wanted to talk to you and make sure it's really okay if I stay here while you're gone."

"Of course it is! I've missed you so much, honey. Video chats and phone calls aren't the same, but coming to visit you or having you come here for a holiday would have meant maintaining a relationship with Iris, and...well, we're not close."

Lucy wasn't sure why, exactly, but she didn't push. "I'm here now, and I promise I'll stay until you get back. But don't cut your vacation short for me. I'm looking forward to relaxing in Wayward Harbor for a while."

Once they'd disconnected, Lucy flopped against the back of the couch and blew out a long breath. Until she'd felt the warmth and love coming through the video call, she'd been afraid Gran would be upset by having a relative she hadn't seen in over fifteen years just show up without invitation.

It was going to be okay.

Probably. A lot hinged on how quickly the Fairee debacle faded away and, if it flared up again, how much Nick was willing to tolerate.

"I'm done," she called to him. "You know, just in case you were being quiet because I was on the phone."

Rather than firing up a power tool, Nick left the bedroom and walked over to the fridge for a soda before turning to face her. "How'd it go?"

"Really good. I convinced her not to change her plans, but she said I could stay for as long as I need to, and she said you'd already agreed?"

He nodded, though he didn't look all that happy about it. But Lucy couldn't tell if he regretted agreeing or if it was just his Resting Grumpy Face.

"It'll be fun," she promised. "I know you haven't seen me at my best, but I'm actually a very happy, positive person, and I'll be an awesome roommate."

"That's great to hear." He looked at her for a few seconds and then gestured back toward the bedroom. "I'm just going to go…pound nails with a hammer or something."

"Okay, I'll probably—" She looked around the cottage. She'd been about to say she'd clean something, but everything was already very tidy. "I should start going through the stuff in my car."

"If you need a hand carrying anything in, just shout."

She nodded and watched him disappear into the small bedroom, closing the door behind him. Then she poured herself a glass of water, leaning against the counter to drink it.

It was time to unpack her car and start sorting out a new life for herself. She wasn't sure what it would look like, but for now it was sleeping on the couch that belonged to her grandmother who wasn't around. And sharing the cottage with a very attractive, but also very grumpy, man who was barely tolerating her presence.

Maybe she'd go through the stuff in her car and bring in the things she needed for now, but she decided against totally unpacking. That girl in town had recognized her. And Nick might have kept her from taking a picture, but she was going to tell all of her friends—and probably the entire internet—and word would spread.

Gran and Nick might claim they were willing to put up with it, but they didn't know how bad it could actually get, and she wouldn't do that to either of them.

She might have to leave, and the idea was so exhausting, Lucy decided to put off the car for now. Instead, she grabbed a random cozy mystery paperback from Gran's bookshelf and curled up in a blanket on the couch.

Tomorrow she would unpack the car and find her passwords so she could put the apps back on her phone. She didn't want to, but it was the only way to see if the world had finally moved on, or if the ugliness was going to follow her to Wayward Harbor.

Tomorrow, she thought, opening the book to chapter one.

It was too quiet.

Nick set the coping saw on his makeshift workbench and

listened. A woman dragging bags and boxes into the house should lead to some screen door banging, if nothing else.

He opened the door a crack and peeked out. For a few seconds, he thought the cottage was empty, but then he heard the faint creak of the couch springs. There were no boxes piled up or bags for him to trip over.

Lucy hadn't brought anything in from her car that he could see.

He told himself it wasn't his problem, but maybe she needed help and didn't feel comfortable asking him. Or maybe she was second-guessing the wisdom of moving in with a total stranger. He couldn't say he'd blame her, but he'd promised Helen he'd look after her, so if push came to shove, he was going to be the one to leave. He'd still do the work of course, because it wasn't Helen's fault some quarterback blew up her granddaughter's life, but it would be seriously inconvenient.

Nick crept into the living room, not wanting to wake her if she'd decided to nap. Driving alone from Nevada to Maine was a lot, even when it was a *fun* road trip, so it would probably take her a few days to bounce back. But she lowered the book she was reading and blinked at him from her crocheted nest.

"Good book?" he asked instead of asking her why she was reading instead of dealing with the stuff in her car.

"It is." She sat up, shoving off all but one blanket. "I decided not to unpack my car."

"I know it'll be a bit of a mess, having it stacked in here, but it's more convenient than going outside every time you need something."

"It's not that."

Something about the nervous way she picked at the fringe on the blanket made Nick want to sit next to her and hold that hand in his. "What's going on?"

"I probably won't be here long enough to make it worthwhile."

Nick frowned, sitting in the very old and uncomfortable armchair that was the only place to sit other than on the couch with Lucy. "I thought you wanted to stay until Helen gets back."

"I do."

So it *was* about sharing the space with him, he thought. "If you're not comfortable with me here, I can find someplace else to crash."

She shook her head, finally looking at him. "No, that's not it. And you're helping Gran, so if one of us was staying somewhere else, it would be me."

"You might want to check out some prices before you say that," he said. "There's a reason my brother and his kids are staying in my house and not a short-term rental."

"You really just moved out of your home and let your brother move in?"

"He had a small fire, and his house was saved, but the water damage was a problem. He needed a place to go temporarily and the only rental available was a one-bedroom, third-floor apartment over the bank, and they wanted him to sign a one-year lease. Helen and I had talked about some work she needed done and I knew she was traveling, so I offered to do the work in exchange for staying here so Beck and the kids can stay at my place while the insurance company does its thing."

"What are you going to do when Gran comes back?"

She probably wanted to know if he'd been intending to use the smaller bedroom, so he shrugged. "Hopefully, Beck's going to get everything sorted and find a place, but if not, I'll crash on the couch."

"Or if your mother's boyfriend isn't a jerk," she muttered.

"And I wasn't even couch surfing. The man has *two* guest bedrooms."

Anger rose up in Nick, sharp and hot, and not entirely explainable. He barely knew this woman. But he *did* know that he couldn't like a man who turned his back on a family member in crisis. And if the boyfriend was sharing a home with Lucy's mother, she was basically family to him.

His opinion of Iris Macauley was even lower, but he swallowed it down and took a calming breath. "Okay, back to why you're not bringing your stuff in because you don't think you'll be here very long, even though that's the plan."

She sighed, flopping back against the couch and staring up at the ceiling. "That girl recognized me in town, and even though you didn't let her take a picture or anything, it's going to get around and the whole world will find out I'm in Wayward Harbor."

"And?"

Lucy stopped staring at the ceiling long enough to roll her eyes at him. "And people will start harassing me and also harassing everybody else to get to me, and I'll have to go."

"You think people are going to come all the way to Wayward Harbor to give you a hard time?"

"Trust me, Maine has Fairee fans, too."

Nick had no idea what she was talking about. "What do fairies have to do with it?"

"No, like when fandoms combine a couple's names. Faith and Reese? Fairee. And trust me, their fans are everywhere." She sighed. "Maybe I should dye my hair."

"No." The word came out with more force than he intended, and his cheeks warmed when she gave him a questioning look. He wasn't about to confess to being low-key obsessed with the color of her hair, and he also hated the idea of her dying it because of some mouthy jerks on the internet. "That stuff stains bathroom fixtures. Especially older ones."

"Okay."

"As for these Fairee people, they can stand in the street and carry on as much as they want, but they can't come on this property. This is Helen's home and you're her granddaughter. That makes it your home, too, and nobody's driving you out of here."

Her smile was shaky, and Nick watched the tears gather in her eyes. She was going to cry again.

He grabbed the box of tissues off the table, intending to toss it to her. But it would have bounced off the blankets, so he had to hold it while she disentangled herself as tears ran unchecked down her cheeks.

"If you keep crying, people are going to think I'm being mean to you," he said, using a deliberately grumbly voice to make her smile.

Thankfully, it worked and she was smiling as she dried her face. "You're not mean. Grumpy? Yes. But not mean."

Again with the grumpy thing. "How about I give you a hand and we can at least bring in what you need for now."

Maybe he'd get lucky and Lucy had some sweatshirts buried in her car. Once she'd unpacked them, he'd be free to take his favorite hoodie back without feeling guilty.

"I have a big weekender bag on the back seat that's packed with the important stuff," she said as she pushed herself to her feet. "And I have one box of important stuff I need to bring in. But a lot of it can stay in the car so we're not tripping over it, and I'll go through it a bit at a time."

"Whatever works for you," he said, gesturing for her to lead the way. "But I really think you should take the bedroom."

"I appreciate the chivalry, but honestly, I'm a side sleeper anyway. I'll have an easier time on the couch. And you have to get up and go to work all day. I insist."

"If you change your mind at some point, let me know."

"I will, though I won't. Trust me, you'll barely know I'm here."

Of course, he wasn't even a little bit surprised when, twenty minutes later, he could barely walk through the living room because there was "oh, just one thing" in each box or bag that Lucy needed.

This was going to be fun.

Chapter Four

Free: Trash bag full of pre-wrecked play clothes for boys, sizes 2T to six, passed down through all three of my boys. If you know them, you know why it's a whole bag for free.

First comment: Can you post photos of each individual item?

—Wayward Harbor Online Community Group

"So what's this we hear about you having breakfast at Pete's with a woman nobody's ever seen before?"

Nick glared at his brother before closing the door of his truck with a little more force than necessary. Gray could have waited until he was in the house, at least. But all three of his brothers had beat him to the jobsite, and they were standing around waiting for gossip instead of getting to work. And of course it was Gray who'd jumped right into a conversation they knew Nick wouldn't welcome.

Four years younger than Nick, Gray had been pushing his older brother's buttons since he was a toddler. Two years after Gray, Beck was born. He was the quietest and most thoughtful of them, though he could push buttons, too, if the mood struck him. And a year after him was Theo, who was barely restrained chaos. They'd all gotten their dad's dark hair and dark eyes, and they could easily be picked out of a crowd as brothers. When it came to personality, though, the differences were obvious.

Nick wanted to work more than he wanted to explain Lucy to his brothers. "You know how it is at Pete's. There's always someone to talk to and nobody eats alone."

Theo laughed. "Sure. I mean, she got out of your truck and then got back into your truck. Oh, and you went grocery shopping together, but okay."

As a rule, Nick loved Wayward Harbor. But there were times, like when the gossip kicked into high gear, that he wouldn't mind seeing the community in his rearview mirror. He'd much rather work than talk, but he also didn't want his brothers' imaginations running away with them. They were going to have way too much fun with his situation as it was, but at least they wouldn't think he was *dating* her.

"Lucy Macauley is Helen's granddaughter," he said brusquely. "She didn't know Helen was traveling and showed up at the cottage Saturday night."

"Iris Macauley's daughter is in town?" Gray asked, eyebrows raised.

"Wait. *The* Lucy Macauley?" Theo asked, and they all turned to look at him. "You know, the woman that Reese Noonan cheated on Faith Lincoln with?"

"It was one coffee in public," Nick said. "And Lucy didn't know who he was."

Theo scoffed. "Okay, you're telling me she didn't know who Reese freakin' Noonan was?"

"Not everybody follows sports," Nick said. "And it's possible to know a name and recognize a guy in uniform, but not make the connection to a guy you run into in a coffee shop. How do you know so much about it, anyway?"

"When it happened, it was impossible *not* to see it. I just scrolled or swiped past it because I didn't care, but I saw it. Didn't realize she's Helen's granddaughter, though."

"Wait," Beck said. "She's Helen's granddaughter. You're staying at Helen's cottage. Breakfast at Pete's. Grocery shopping. This woman lives with you now?"

"From a top five NFL quarterback to a former college running back," Gray said before he could respond. "Hell of a downgrade."

Even as his body tensed and anger urged him to lash out, Nick forced himself not to react. His brother was joking—taking a shot at his brother the way they all did—and it wasn't their fault they didn't know how deeply the words cut him.

He'd given up his dream for *them*, but he never let them see how much it had hurt because he didn't want them to carry the guilt around with them.

"She's crashing on the couch because she didn't have anywhere else to go," he said in a tone more harsh than he'd intended.

Okay, so maybe Lucy wasn't totally wrong about him being a little grumpy now and then. Sometimes.

"And we don't get paid to stand around gossiping," he continued, before casting a dark glance at Theo, who was scrolling on his phone. "Or being online."

There was a lot of grumbling, but his brothers stopped talking about Lucy and got to work, which was all Nick cared about. This was a big job, and they were already slightly behind schedule.

The historic colonial home was set off from the road by a tall, dense row of hedges. And from the back, a long and sweeping lawn sloped down to the water's edge. It was a gorgeous property, and some rich family from Vermont had bought it.

They'd hired Slater & Sons to totally gut the interior. From a distance it would still be a majestic, historic home. On the inside it would be sleek and modern, with much of the back wall replaced with glass so they could sit in the air conditioning and look out over the water.

As much as Nick and his brothers—and most of Wayward Harbor—hated out-of-staters buying up property and making summer homes, he appreciated that they were preserving the exterior.

And he *really* appreciated the amounts on the checks the guy from Vermont was writing out to Slater & Sons.

A few hours later, Nick had to make a quick run into town to buy some more pencils because they had a way of disappearing that drove him mad. He wasn't surprised to find his brothers lounging on the back lawn, eating lunch.

Gray, whose turn it was to supply the food, tossed him a sandwich from the cooler. It was ham, which wasn't his favorite, but it had extra Swiss, so not bad.

Theo gestured him over, so he caught the soda Gray tossed after the sandwich and went to join him. The others were enjoying the warm spring sun, but Theo was under a tree in the shade. Probably so he could see his phone screen.

"While I'm eating my lunch and *not getting paid*," Theo said once he'd sat down and unwrapped the sandwich. "I've been doing a deep dive on some of the social media platforms."

Nick gave his youngest brother a flat look. He didn't think his constant nagging about phones during working hours was unreasonable. "Don't even get started with the forklift fail videos because we get hooked in. Then it goes to funny snowmobile fails and then cute animals being goofy and then it's almost quitting time and nobody's even picked up a hammer."

"No, that's not what I'm talking about." He paused, and then chuckled. "But remind me to show you the one with the guy who tried to ride a full-dresser Harley up a two-by-six into the back of his truck."

"Theo."

"I looked up Lucy," he said quietly. A scary calm settled through Nick as he glared at his brother, waiting for an explanation. "I mean, we all know what happened, of course. But I was just curious about how bad it could be to make a woman drive all the way across the country to live with *you*."

"She didn't drive out here to live with me, and you know it. She came to visit Helen." But that wasn't the point. "How bad is it?"

"Bad. The internet really hates her. Looking at the time stamps and stuff, it's kind of dying down, but..." He handed Nick his phone. "Those are screenshots in my photo app, so you can just swipe through them. And it's not even a fraction of what's out there."

Nick flipped through the screenshots of posts and comments, his blood pressure rising with each swipe of his thumb. The stuff being said about her. The names she was being called.

The threats.

"Can you find out where these people live?" he demanded, looking up at Theo.

"Whoa." His brother snatched the phone back. "No, I can't. And even if I could, I definitely wouldn't tell you because if you go to prison, we all have to work harder and that would suck."

If he did go off on a Lucy Macauley revenge tour, his first stop would be the house with the two guest bedrooms where Iris was living with some guy. Throwing Lucy out to face these wolves was unforgivable, in his book.

"I skimmed through Lucy's accounts, and there were two women she was clearly good friends with," Theo continued.

"One of them went viral with videos talking about Lucy while also mentioning some ugly jewelry the woman made. Her other *friend* did the podcast and interview rounds with titles like 'Lucy Macauley's best friend tells all' and the like."

"She had nobody." Nick glared at the phone in Theo's hand, trying to get his temper under control. "All that hate and abuse coming at her for something a *man* did, and not a single person had her back."

"That sucks. And look, it's pretty unlikely any of these keyboard warriors actually come looking for her, but I wanted you to know what's out there."

"Thanks."

He finished his sandwich so they could get back to work, but all afternoon, his mind was on Lucy and the toxic ugliness he'd seen directed at her. And that was just a small sampling.

No wonder she'd pulled a hood over her remarkable hair and hidden part of her face with the sunglasses.

But she was here now, and he barely listened to Gray drone on about the logistics of the number of outlets the homeowner wanted. As a rule, Nick hated gossip, but with a few well-targeted comments, he could get the word out that Wayward Harbor needed to rally around Helen Griffin's granddaughter.

He'd do it for Lucy.

With Nick at work for the day, Lucy decided it was a good time to sort through the mess she'd made of her grandmother's living room.

While packing up her belongings in Las Vegas, she'd tried to be deliberate about grouping things in boxes and bags, but the more upset she'd gotten, the more she'd just tossed things in wherever they fit. And when she'd loaded everything into her car, she'd been struck by how little she appeared to own.

But piled up in Gran's living room, it looked like a lot. Most of the clothes she repackaged to return to her car. She wasn't going to need little black dresses or strappy heels here. Those would wait until she reached Miami.

The box of her important documents she'd keep inside because she didn't think Wayward Harbor was a hub of crime, but it wasn't smart to keep them in the car. To that box, she added the notebook in which she'd scribbled all kinds of random information. Half of the papers, old receipts and torn envelopes shoved between the pages had passwords written on them. Someday she'd make a better system, but for now it worked.

Lucy also dug her small sketchbook out of the bottom of a bag and added it to the box. It was where she brainstormed fun cocktail ideas—whether the liquors or fun add-ons, like glitter or rim sugars. While she was most creative with pen and paper, she always took photos of the pages and uploaded them to a digital notebook.

She condensed the towels and sheets in the bathroom's linen closet and took the resulting empty shelf for herself. Her core wardrobe—jeans, leggings and simple tops—fit on the shelf, along with a lingerie bag she filled with underthings. Other items, like her cardigans and pajamas, could stay in a duffel, but she didn't want to dress in bag-rumpled clothes every day.

Once she'd pulled what she needed for daily life, she was down to a duffel bag, two boxes and her tote in the living room. The rest she was able to pack back into her trunk.

It felt good to have that done, but there was one more thing she had to do before she could fully relax, and that was call her mother. Maybe Iris Macauley wasn't the most maternal of figures, but Lucy hadn't told her where she was going. For all Iris knew, her daughter was staying with a friend in Las Vegas.

And whether she deserved it or not, Lucy didn't feel right

about her mother not knowing she'd actually driven to the opposite coast.

It was late enough in the afternoon that the time difference wouldn't be an issue, so she went out to the front porch. For some reason she didn't want to be *in* Gran's cottage while she talked to Iris—as if her mother's toxic energy could infect the place through the phone. After wrapping herself in blankets because the wind never let up here, she sat down and dialed.

Iris answered on the third ring. "Hi, Lucy. I only have a few minutes because I'm on my way out. What's up?"

No asking where her daughter was. Or if she was okay. Definitely no apologies for doing nothing while her boyfriend threw her out. Typical Iris.

"I just wanted to let you know I'm in Maine."

"Maine? What are you doing in Maine?"

"I'm visiting Gran." The ensuing silence stretched on for so long, Lucy pulled the phone away from her ear to see if the call timer was still running. "Mom?"

"You're visiting my mother? Why?"

Because my life blew up and you chose your boyfriend over me, so I had nowhere else to go. "I wanted to get away."

"How is Mom?"

Lucy forced herself to relax her jaw and her grip on her phone. Iris wasn't going to even broach the subject of the Fairee debacle because, deep down, she was ashamed of not sticking up for her daughter and wouldn't want to admit it out loud.

"She's great." She wasn't sure why, but she kept the fact Helen was off on an adventure to herself.

"Good. I worry about her living in that cottage all by herself."

Not worried enough to actually call, Lucy thought. "Mom,

she does 5k charity runs. I think it's going to be a long time before Gran's worried about living in the cottage alone."

"She may not be worried, but I am. It's hard to have an aging mother so far away. I really wish she'd sell it and move into a retirement home where people can keep an eye on her."

Lucy wondered if Iris would be so worried if Helen lived in a plain old house in the woods somewhere in the middle of the state. The uncharitable thought *should* make her feel guilty, but her mother's attraction to men grew stronger with every dollar in their bank accounts. It wasn't far-fetched to suspect Iris's concern for Helen was driven by the property's value.

But she also knew if she pointed out Iris hadn't given a thought to Helen's welfare until Lucy was in a position to potentially manipulate her grandmother, there would be raging and tears that wouldn't end until Lucy apologized just to make it stop. She wasn't in the mood to hear it, especially from a woman who'd chosen her boyfriend—who was noticeably dragging his feet on engagement ring shopping—over her own daughter in crisis.

"I'll bring it up," she said finally. "If I have concerns."

"You don't want to leave it too late, honey. You'd never be able to live with yourself if something happens to her and you could have prevented it."

Lucy blinked away the angry tears filling her eyes. Iris didn't used to be so…toxic. They'd been incredibly close during Lucy's teen years, but her mother seemed to get more desperate with every passing year.

Desperate for what, she didn't know. Security? Love? Money? But Iris was always chasing something, and that something was usually a man with the means and desire to take care of her.

"I have to go, Mom," she said once she was sure she could speak. "My battery's almost dead, but I'll call you soon."

Once she was off the phone, Lucy snuggled deeper into the fleece blankets. She left an opening around her eyes and nose, though, so she could breathe. And also so she could look out over the water.

A few minutes later, she heard a truck pull into the driveway and peeked out of the blanket burrito to see Nick walking toward her.

"You okay?" he asked. "You were so still I thought you'd dumped a pile of blankets in the chair, but then I saw your feet and was afraid you'd actually suffocated yourself this time."

"Very funny," she said as he dropped into the other chair. "I called my mom to let her know where I am."

He nodded, his gaze locked on the horizon. "Did she know you were coming here?"

"No."

"So you left Las Vegas and drove all the way here, and you've been here for a couple of days, and she still hadn't called *you*?"

Lucy shrugged one shoulder, which he probably couldn't see because the gesture barely shifted the blankets. "I'm an adult, and she's not exactly the helicopter mom type."

"Did she ask how long you're staying?"

She snorted, seeing right through the attempt to get that information for himself. "No, but she did ask me to convince Gran to sell this place and move into a retirement home."

She wasn't sure why she told him that. Talking about some of her mother's less attractive personality traits wasn't her style, and it certainly wouldn't improve Nick's view of the situation any. But there was something about sitting on the porch with him that made her comfortable sharing.

Nick looked at her, and she held her breath because it looked like his lips *might* curve into an actual smile. "I'd like to be in earshot when you suggest that to Helen."

"Great way to pay her back for her hospitality, right?"

"Honestly, it's probably something she'd expect from her daughter." He cleared his throat. "Everybody knows they're not close."

"It just feels so gross." When he turned so he was looking at her, that familiar neutral expression on his face, she tilted her head. "What?"

"Trust me when I tell you I do *not* want to wade into your family business, but…there's Helen, you know? So I'm just trying to figure out where your head is on this before I say anything."

"Where my head is? I'm angry that I have a mother whose only reaction to finding out I've driven all the way across the country is to realize she might have an opportunity to grow Gran's bank account, which I guess she thinks she'll inherit. I'm offended she thought I'd just go along with it. I'm sad for Gran. And because I'm mad, I'm getting hot in these blankets, but I know if I throw one off, then I'll be cold. That's where my head is."

Was it just her imagination, or did his face actually soften? "I'm sorry your mother's putting you in this position, but the important thing is that you *know* she's doing it. Will you tell Helen?"

"I don't think so. It would only be hurtful, I think." She unwrapped the top blanket and pushed it behind her. "Unless Iris starts reaching out to her directly, thinking my being here will be an opportunity for them to reconnect. I'd rather not be confrontational with Iris, but I won't let her take advantage of Gran, either."

"Good." He pushed up out of the chair. "I'm starving, so I'm going to rustle up something to eat."

Lucy stood abruptly, almost falling over as the blankets tangled around her legs. "I'm sorry. I had to wait to call my mom because of the time difference and I didn't realize it was so late. I should have made something."

Nick paused with the screen door half open to look at her. "I don't expect you to make me supper, Lucy."

He was so close she could see his eyes weren't as dark as she'd originally thought. The lighter shades of brown captured her attention, and she might have stood there staring if he hadn't cocked an eyebrow.

"Sure," she said, trying to gather herself. "But even if you don't *expect* it, I should make dinner. I mean, you're letting me stay here and you work all day and I'm doing…nothing."

"You're not doing *nothing*. You've been through a lot and you drove a long way. Taking a few days to rest is not a bad thing." He stepped inside and held the screen door for her. "Let's go throw something on the grill."

"There's a grill?"

"Of course there's a grill. Who doesn't own a grill?"

Lucy just rolled her eyes and followed him inside. At least he hadn't offered to make her a bologna and tomato sandwich.

Chapter Five

Looking for a recommendation for a local-to-you builder who can remove my parents' front steps and put in a wheelchair ramp. They estimate my dad will clear physical rehab in three weeks. I'm in Vermont, but I can do Zoom meetings because my mom has her hands full. I know it's a tight timeline. Thanks in advance!

First comment: They might be too busy but you won't get many recs besides Slater & Sons Construction if you want local to Wayward Harbor.

—Wayward Harbor Online Community Group

Four days later, Nick stopped by the cottage during his lunch break to grab a list he'd left on the nightstand. He thought he'd typed it into his phone, but that particular list of measurements he'd written on a notepad. He tended to bounce between the two, knowing his life would be easier if he just chose between digital and analog, but old habits were hard to break.

As soon as he stepped through the door, he spotted Lucy on the couch. She'd been stretched out—wrapped in a blanket, of course—and she sat up immediately. Judging by her confusion, she'd been asleep.

"Oh, I must have nodded off," she said over the sound of the television.

He wasn't sure what she was watching, but a lot of rich women appeared to be yelling at each other about something. There was an empty bowl on the table, along with two candy bar wrappers and an open bag of chips.

Lucy was wallowing again.

A day or two of wallowing was one thing. Everybody needed to wallow once in a while, especially after a long drive that ended in disappointment. But Helen wasn't going to be back for weeks and, at the rate she was going, Lucy would be one with the couch by then.

"Oh good, you're up," he said with a pointed look at the antique clock on the wall. It was purely decorative, but he made his point. "I have to do some errands, and you're going to help me."

Lucy clawed her way out of the blanket and then ran a hand over her hair. It didn't help. "I don't know what kind of errands builders do, but I'm pretty sure I wouldn't be very good at them."

"Think of it like this—while Helen's away, she rented the cottage to me in exchange for labor. The way I see it, since I'm the one who let you stay—because I'm a glutton for chaos, apparently—you're also bound by that contract. So it's time to get to work."

"I think you're underestimating how bad I am at building things, or anything DIY, really."

"I didn't say I was giving you a nail gun or a power saw." He might be a glutton for chaos, but he wasn't reckless. "Five minutes."

She laughed. "Has anybody ever told you you're very bossy?"

"I'm not only the oldest of four boys, but I run the company we all work for. Being bossy is pretty much my entire personality at this point." He went into the bedroom and grabbed the list he needed from the nightstand. Lucy was carrying her dishes to the sink when he passed back through the living room. "I'll wait for you outside. Four minutes."

She was laughing when he closed the door behind him, which probably didn't bode well for her appearing anytime soon. He didn't mind, though, because he really enjoyed her laugh. If it wasn't so warm inside, he would have been tempted to stand in the living room and count down the minutes.

But he was wearing one of the newer Slater & Sons Construction hoodies, and he didn't care what Beck said, they weren't the same fabric. The one he was wearing didn't breathe as well, and he overheated too easily.

Fifteen minutes later, he had regrets. He'd left the jobsite intending to grab the list, hit the hardware store, and then go straight back to work.

Now he was waiting for Lucy. Again. And, unless he wanted to bring her to work with him—which he did not—he'd have to bring her back to the cottage after.

At the twenty minute mark, he was about to get in his truck and leave without her, but then she stepped out onto the front porch.

Wearing his sweatshirt.

Why did seeing this woman wearing his hoodie make him want to pull her into his arms? His fingers practically itched to slide up under the fabric and glide over her bare skin.

"I said five minutes," he said gruffly, trying to muster irritation to douse the heat pounding through his veins. "Not five minutes times four."

"I decided jeans were a better choice," she said cheerfully, ignoring his scowl as she climbed into his truck. "And then I thought it might get warm enough so I want to take the sweatshirt off, so I had to put a shirt under it."

He did *not* need to think about what she was or was not

wearing under the hoodie. "Riding in the truck doesn't require a wardrobe change."

Lucy just laughed and turned away to watch the waves breaking over the rocks as he navigated along the shoreline.

It was worth losing time on the job to hear her laugh. It worried him when she hid away in the blankets because he hadn't known her all that long, but he thought she was generally a positive, upbeat person.

Sure, she'd been let down by every single person who mattered to her, but she was here now. Even if she couldn't get a hug yet, she had Helen.

And she had Nick. He hadn't asked for Lucy to barge into his life, and he wasn't sure exactly what to do with her, but he wasn't the kind of guy who could sit back and do nothing while a person needed a hand up.

"So where are we going, anyway?" she asked when they reached the outskirts of town.

"The hardware store. Unfortunately, due to economic reality, we have to buy the bulk of our supplies from the box stores in the city, but we always end up needing random things, and we get those from Smith's Hardware."

"And is the owner a Smith?"

"Yes, but—" He paused while navigating a particularly tight turn. It was so fun living in a quaint historic town with brick structures built while they were still designing roads for horses. "He's not from around here. Back in the sixties, I guess, the Smith who was the third generation to own the hardware store decided to sell. Don Smith owned a small, struggling hardware store a little ways inland. He decided to sell his, and when he bought our Smith's, he didn't have to change the sign."

"That was very practical of him. A good quality in a business owner."

Nick parked and made sure he had the list before turning the engine off. "Are you going to wait here or go in?"

"I'm not going to sit in the truck while you do all the work."

He was about to tell her going inside and grabbing a few things wasn't exactly work, but she was already out of the truck.

Smith's Hardware was a sprawling old building with multiple rooms and wooden floors that squeaked. It had almost anything a person could need, but good luck finding it. Don, though, knew where almost everything was in the layers of merchandise that was organized mainly by decade.

The fact it took so long to get to one of the big box stores—a time that could be doubled or even tripled by tourist traffic during the summer—and being able to dig up a fitting for a washing machine from the 1990s kept him in business.

"Oh wow," Lucy breathed as she stepped into the dim, cool interior of the building. "There is literally *everything* here. Like, if you have a leaf blower, scented candles and a baking pan on your list, this is the place to go."

"Feel free to look around while I take care of this."

She actually looked offended. "I'm not shopping on company time. Lead the way."

Nick clenched his jaw and headed for the counter, where Don was chatting with a couple of old-timers. He'd been joking when he told Lucy she was bound by his agreement with Helen, but maybe she'd missed that.

To be fair, he was probably frowning at the time. According to her, he did that a lot.

"Mornin'," Don said as the other two guys wandered off to poke around the dusty back shelves. "Who's this with you today?"

"I'm Lucy. I work for Nick."

"You don't work for me." He looked at Don. "She doesn't work for me."

"You said—"

"Lucy's Helen's granddaughter. She's visiting for a while and wanted to get out of the house."

"Ah." Don nodded slowly, but his expression when he looked at Lucy told Nick he'd heard all about it already. "Welcome back."

"Thank you."

Before Don could ask any not-so-subtle questions that might earn him some gossip currency, Nick slid the list across the counter. "I just need to grab a few things."

It felt good to be out and about, Lucy admitted to herself while Nick dropped the tailgate and threw his purchases in the bed of the truck.

It was so easy to put on the TV or pick up a book and sink into the comforting pile of throw blankets. Being disconnected from social media left a lot of open space in her time, but she needed to find better ways to fill it than napping.

As she looked around, she could see the corner of the market down the block. "I know you have to get back, but would you mind if I walk over to the market really quick and grab a few things?"

He closed the tailgate with a thud that didn't mask his exasperated sigh. "Be quicker to drive over."

"True. But it's not as windy today and it's almost warm."

"Fine. We'll walk."

"I can find my way, seeing as how I can literally see the building from here."

He looked at her in a way that suggested he was considering how to phrase what he wanted to say. "It'll be faster if we both go."

Lucy laughed because it was very clear he thought she'd wander off to window-shop or take too long squeezing the produce.

Nick didn't hurry her, though, as they walked down the sidewalk side by side. She noted the businesses they passed, but soon became distracted by a large ginger cat shadowing them on the other side of the street. Every time she stopped, the cat stopped.

"What are you doing?" Nick demanded the third time she stopped walking to test her theory.

"Playing with that cat over there. It's stalking us, and every time I stop, it stops."

When she pointed across the street, he nodded. "That's Dolly. She's the town cat."

"She belongs to the whole town?"

He considered that for a moment. "I wouldn't say she belongs to the whole town. It's more like the whole town belongs to her."

"Who takes care of her, though?"

"Everybody. She's spayed, and there's always a collection jar at the market for people to drop in change. It adds up pretty quickly and takes care of her routine medical care. If she needs a little extra, more jars go out with a note from the vet detailing what she needs. Like, recently she had a procedure to have a lump checked out, which is expensive. And there are folks who feed their own cats on their porches and Dolly has a rotation of who she visits, and she gets her preventatives every month with a little tuna from old Bob."

"What about during the winter?" She started walking again—Nick really did have to get back to work—and so did Dolly.

"She's got plenty of places to go, and during a bad cold spell, she usually goes to the Bergeron house. They've got a dog door for their pair of goldens, and the Bergerons will wake up to find Dolly curled up with the dogs." He nudged Lucy with his elbow and took her attention away from the cat in time to keep her from walking into a sign.

"And in the summer," he continued, "you can tell when a storm's going to be a bad one because she always goes to Edna's. She lost her husband years ago when a tree fell on him during a wicked storm, and I think Dolly knows she needs the comfort."

"She's a lucky cat."

"We're a lucky town. Dolly has some kind of relationship with almost everybody here, and if she doesn't like you? You might not be our kind of people."

Lucy stopped at the edge of the market's parking lot. "So if I don't pass the scrutiny of a stray cat, the good people of Wayward Harbor won't like me?"

"I wouldn't lead with calling her a stray."

"I'm already Iris Macauley's daughter. What chance do I have if Dolly doesn't like me?"

"None really. You'd probably just have to put all your stuff back in your car and head on down the road."

When she laughed, he laughed with her, and the impact of the low, warm sound made her start walking again so she wouldn't stare at him. The man really needed to laugh more often because it was incredibly sexy.

Lucy made quick work of grabbing the things she needed at the market. Usually, she liked to wander through stores, looking for anything that might strike her fancy in the moment, but with Nick hovering next to her like a rain cloud, she kept to the things she'd come for.

They'd barely gone ten feet from the door when a woman grabbed her arm. "Hey, are you going to the—"

When Lucy turned her head to look at the woman, she gasped and retracted her hand.

"Oh, I'm sorry, I thought you were—" The woman paused, the quick shake of her head not clearing the confusion wrinkling her forehead. "Somebody else. Sorry."

"No problem." The woman was moving before she could say anything else, though she did look over her shoulder once.

"Let's go," Nick said, sounding tense again as he frowned at the departing woman, which Lucy didn't understand. Stuff like that happened to people all the time. "I actually do have to go back to work."

Once they'd gotten back to the truck and were on the road, Lucy got tired of the silence. The man needed to turn his radio on. "What kind of work are you doing on the cottage, anyway?"

"Nothing major, except for the small bedroom and the back deck. The original structure only had the one bedroom, like a box, I guess. It was built to last, and it has. The second bedroom is an addition put on shortly before your grandparents bought it, built by somebody who probably didn't make his living as a builder."

"That doesn't sound good."

He shrugged. "The hard part was already done. A friend of your grandparents jacked up the addition and put a proper footing under it. He reframed the window, and Helen had professionals come in and fix the way the roof tied into the main cottage. Unfortunately, her friend passed away with some loose ends left undone, and I'm taking care of them."

"That's nice of you."

"We take care of our neighbors around here."

"The ones Dolly approves of, anyway."

"Of course."

"What are you doing to the back deck?" she asked.

"You might have noticed, when we grilled outside, that it's not in great shape and the steps are pretty much a hazard? I'm going to rebuild the deck and steps, but also add a ramp off the end."

"Does Gran need a ramp? I thought she was running 5ks."

"She doesn't need a ramp right now and maybe she won't. But it doesn't hurt to add one while I'm doing the work. Plus, when she puts stuff in the shed for the winter, she can use a dolly and roll it down the ramp rather than carrying things down the steps."

She nodded, relieved. "I bet I can help with building a deck."

To her surprise, he didn't scoff at her. Instead, he appeared to think about it for a minute. "There will probably be times I could use a hand. Add checking in the shed to see if Helen has any work gloves that'll fit you to your list."

"What list?"

Nick glanced over at her, but only for a second because the shoreline—and therefore the road—was particularly curvy. "Your list. You know, your ongoing list of things you need to do and buy and take care of in general."

She shrugged. "Okay."

"You don't have a list, do you?"

"That can't be a surprise to you." When he snorted, she laughed. "Just like it's not a surprise to me that you *do* have a list. Probably plural. I bet you have multiple lists."

When he didn't respond to that, she laughed again. They were pulling into Gran's drive, so she gathered her phone and her bag.

"I can grab the groceries, so you don't have to get out," she said as he pulled to a stop. "I know you're already late getting back to work."

"I'll run them in, and you can put them away," he told her.

Since she was in the driveway already, Lucy took the time to walk out to the end and grab Helen's mail. She'd put the junk mail in recycling and the important stuff in a basket on the bookshelf where Nick had been putting it.

He was on his way out when she passed him. "Have a good rest of your day. And thank you."

He stopped with his hand on his truck's door handle. "For what?"

She smiled. "For getting me out from under the blankets."

The smile he gave her in return was like the sun breaking through a dense morning fog. A real smile, with white teeth and crinkling eyes that made it hard for her to breathe. "Anytime."

And when she walked inside, the first thing she saw was a sheet of paper stuck to the front of the fridge with one of Gran's magnets. *House List* it said across the top. And under that, in neat block letters: *Find Lucy some gloves.*

Chapter Six

I'm looking for a local diver willing to search for a diamond ring. My fiancé proposed to me at the end of the town pier, and he dropped the ring. Please be nice in the comments. He feels really bad. We might be able to scrape up a little payment, but he spent the rent on the ring, so we're hoping for an act of kindness here.

First comment: Your fiancé? You mean you said yes after all that?

—Wayward Harbor Online Community Group

Lucy was curled up in a porch rocker, thankful the furniture was large enough to accommodate her *and* her nest of blankets. It had been two days since she'd gone into town with Nick, and she was bored.

Sitting around the cottage alone while he was working all day wasn't cutting it anymore. She'd cleaned everything that could be cleaned. She'd even puttered around outside. Though she didn't know enough about plants to pull anything that might be a weed or might be a perennial waiting for warmer weather, she'd cleaned up the obvious stuff. Dead leaves. Sticks blown in by winter storms.

She'd even cleaned and reorganized the gardening shed while hunting for a pair of gloves so she could cross it off the list. Unfortunately, Gran's hands were smaller than Lucy's, so that task remained pending.

Lucy wanted to find a job. Though money wouldn't be an issue for a while yet, she needed something to occupy her time. And even though her anxiety spiked at the thought, she needed to meet people and socialize. She wasn't wired to spend so much time with her own thoughts.

And besides going door-to-door, the best way to find out if anybody was hiring locally was with Facebook.

Now the passwords for her social media apps were in one hand and her phone was in the other, but she hadn't done anything with them yet. She knew she couldn't keep her head in the sand forever—she needed to know if the scandal was dying down or if the Fairee fandom still wanted to destroy her.

But the idea of letting the world back in had her stomach tied in so many knots, she wasn't even sipping the coffee sitting on the side table next to her—in an insulated mug with a lid, of course, to keep it hot.

She could call her mom. Iris hadn't followed up at all, checking to see if she was still in Maine. Or if she was doing well. But she knew if she called Iris—just seeking the comfort of a familiar voice, if nothing else—she'd just end up fending off questions about Gran's property.

Gran had sent her photos that morning from the entrance of some kind of theme park centered around alligators, so Lucy didn't want to interrupt her fun, possibly dangerous adventure.

It was time to rip the bandage off, she told herself.

The internet wasn't the fastest she'd ever used, though she was grateful to have it, so it took her almost an hour to redownload and sign in to the apps she wanted back on her phone. For several of them, she'd deleted her accounts entirely, and she didn't bother with those. Maybe once she was in Miami and wanted to build up her new brand, she'd make fresh accounts.

If Miami was still on the table.

She still hadn't sent a message to her friend Sydney, down in Miami. Lucy had been squirreling away money for a solid two years or more, planning to join her and make the dream of designing signature cocktails for a living come true.

When her coffee date lit up the tabloid world, Sydney had reached out, asking if she was okay. Already burned by so-called friends and in a dark emotional place, Lucy had told her she was okay, but needed space and didn't want to talk. That had been a mistake.

But as the weeks passed, Lucy had put off reaching out to Sydney, afraid her friend would want no part of the Fairee circus. Lucy would have been crushed, and she hadn't felt ready for that kind of risk. She still needed hope on her horizon.

Now she sent Sydney a long overdue text message, apologizing for disappearing and promising to call within the next few days to explain everything.

Facebook was the hard one. She'd kept on top of her privacy settings, so there wasn't a lot of negativity. But there were a *lot* of people who'd taught her there was a difference between being a friend and being somebody you knew socially and who'd hit the Like button on the photo of the cute shoes you scored on sale.

By the time she'd deleted all of the insincere messages fishing for details poorly disguised as concern, and unfriended everybody who wouldn't be a part of her life going forward, she was left with five people.

Gran. Iris, who she would unfriend if not for the drama that would ensue. Sydney. And Sydney's husband and sister.

That was depressing, she thought as she carried the blankets back into the cottage. It was tempting to turn on the television and lose herself in blankets and mindless entertainment for a while, but she actually wanted to *move*.

It only took five minutes to clean the bathroom. At first, having never shared a bathroom with a man before, she'd been expecting the worst. She'd heard a lot of horror stories over the years. But Nick was very neat and good at cleaning up after himself, so it hadn't been a problem.

There was a sweatshirt in the tub, though, and she remembered him saying he'd gotten caught in the rain yesterday, and that he'd do a wash when he got home today. Lucy had a few things, so she added the wet sweatshirt to make a load and started the washer.

Gloves, she thought.

She'd run to Smith's Hardware and buy herself some gloves. And she'd have some time to browse the eclectic offerings and maybe find something else she needed.

When she walked into Smith's Hardware and the old-fashioned bell over the door rang, Don looked up from the counter. He didn't smile and call out a greeting the way he had when she was with Nick.

He just stared at her for a moment, gave a curt nod and went back to whatever he'd been doing.

Maybe he was just busy, she told herself as she wandered the aisles. Not customer busy, since she was the only one in the store as far as she could tell, but paperwork busy.

She found a good pair of leather work gloves, along with a lighter pair of gardening gloves. There was also a cute, pink-handled hammer she couldn't resist, but Don's cold reception had sapped the idea of exploring the store of its charm.

When she set the gloves and hammer on the counter, he looked up again. This time his eyes narrowed slightly. "You don't look much like your mother."

"No, not really," she said, taken aback by his abrupt tone.

She hoped he wouldn't follow it up by asking if she looked like her father because she had no idea. She'd always assumed she must.

"Helen's good people," he said. "We look after her in this town."

Heat prickled across Lucy's chest and up her neck. The man didn't care who she looked like. He just wanted her aware he knew she was Iris Macauley's daughter and they'd be keeping an eye on her.

She forced her lips into a stiff smile. "I'm glad Gran lives in such a great community. Have a good day."

Before he could say more, she headed for the door. Between the Facebook culling and being reminded this town would hold her mother against her, she wasn't in the mood to explore any of the other businesses.

When she got back to the cottage, she left the gloves and hammer on the counter. After throwing the load of laundry into the dryer, she put some chicken breasts in marinade for supper later. And she took great satisfaction in crossing gloves off the list.

She read until the dryer buzzed, and then made quick work of folding and putting away her laundry. She wasn't sure what to do with Nick's sweatshirt, but he probably wouldn't mind if she just set it on the bed.

It felt slightly wrong to open the door, but when Lucy stepped inside the room, it was still very much her grandmother's space.

Like the rest of the cottage, the bedroom had a warm, comfortable vibe without a lot of clutter. An old maple dresser Lucy knew was older than Iris. A matching bedside table with a lamp and a short stack of paperbacks. A gorgeous wooden rocking chair she knew her grandfather had bought for Helen when she was pregnant with Iris. A soft braided rug covered much of the hardwood floor, and a large window looked over the backyard.

Lucy could remember sitting in that window, watching the birds and butterflies in the garden with Gran, and the memory made her smile. As did the framed photo of Helen and Lucy walking the beach together when she was maybe twelve years old. It was the only photo on the dresser besides Helen's wedding photo.

There were no photos of Iris anywhere in the cottage that Lucy had seen, which was sad.

And there was very little sign Nick had been sleeping in this room. The phone charging cord on the nightstand. Two duffel bags on the floor next to the rocker, which held a stack of folded blue sweatshirts. A pair of sneakers sat under the rocking chair, though Lucy had never seen Nick wear them. He usually stepped in and out of his work boots at the door, not bothering with tying them.

And there was the fact the quilt that was meant to cover the bed had been folded down out of the way, and was currently half shoved between the mattress and the maple footboard.

Since Nick seemed to never be cold, it didn't surprise her the flannel sheet was enough of a cover for him at night. And even though she spent a lot of time awake at night, unable to sleep, she rarely heard the mattress creaking or shifting. He was probably a heavy sleeper.

Maybe because that bed looked incredibly comfortable.

And she was tired after an emotional day.

Nick probably wouldn't be home for hours. She could stretch out and take a comfortable nap. Just a short one, and then she'd smooth the covers and feel ready to make a plan.

And Nick would never know she'd been in his bed.

There wasn't a single soul Nick would admit it to, but he'd spent some time over the last week imagining what it would be like to have Lucy in his bed.

Of course, when he was in the shower or trying to sleep at night, Lucy wasn't wearing his favorite hoodie—or anything at all—and he was in the bed with her.

Nick looked at her, stretched out on his bed and so soundly sleeping she hadn't heard him come in, and felt a pang of sympathy. The couch was reasonably comfortable to sit on, but Nick had tried stretching out on it once while watching a movie, and it wasn't great. Sleeping on it night after night had to be getting to her, and he couldn't blame Lucy for sneaking a decent nap while he was out.

He needed to stop dragging his feet and finish up the small bedroom. Because he was usually tired after a workday, he'd been picking and choosing from the variety of tasks he wanted to complete for Helen, but he had to get Lucy off that couch so she could get a decent night's sleep.

He thought about sending a text to the group chat with his brothers, asking for help. The four of them could have Lucy moved into the bedroom in no time.

But Beck would have his hands full with the kids. Theo would be doing water training with the fire department this week and would be exhausted. And Gray was already stressed about them falling behind on the Brock remodel. He'd be in a mood and Nick didn't want to hear it.

Rather than bother any of them, he'd just work harder. If he hustled during the day, maybe he could cut out a little early. And he could work on it longer after supper each night.

Nick was about to back out of the room and quietly close the door when he realized Lucy's pretty blue eyes were staring at him. She was awake, but barely, and she blinked a few times before her eyes widened and she sat up.

"Sorry. I wasn't hiding under the blankets, though. I haven't been sleeping well at night, and I was just going to put your sweatshirt on the bed and…it was too tempting to resist."

"It's not the most comfortable couch ever."

"It's the quiet, mostly. It's so dark and quiet here, like being smothered by a thick, dark blanket."

"Wouldn't you like that?"

She laughed, shaking her head. "It's different—almost like claustrophobia."

"Have you tried leaving the TV on? It's got noise, flickering lights. Put on a movie set in Vegas and you'll probably be asleep in no time."

"I don't want to disturb your sleep, since you're the one with a job and a reason to get up in the morning."

"Once I'm out, it takes a lot to wake me up. I'm a heavy sleeper."

"Unless a woman sneaks into the cottage in the middle of the night."

He snorted. "It is reassuring to know I won't sleep through a little breaking and entering."

"For the record, I didn't break anything. I just entered."

"That's valid. I grabbed a steak and some potatoes to grill on my way home."

"Sounds good." She smoothed the wrinkles out of the sheets and put the sweatshirt she must have laundered on top of the rocking chair pile.

"Your car was here, so I thought you might be out back, but when I went to fire up the grill, you weren't there. I thought you might be walking out on the beach, but when I came in to plug in my phone, you were all Goldilocks in the bed."

She laughed as she followed him to the kitchen. "It was definitely just right."

Lucy washed and diced the potatoes while Nick seasoned the steak. Then, after she'd loaded the potatoes into a tin foil packet along with a probably unhealthy amount of butter and garlic salt, they took it all outside.

Before Helen left, Nick had brought out her patio furniture, though it was in the yard and not on the rickety deck he'd be replacing. It was one of the ornate, black metal sets, with an umbrella that went through the center of the table, and four café-style chairs. He hadn't bothered bringing out the umbrella or chair cushions because spring was still happening, but it worked as is.

Since it would be a bit before they needed plates and everything else, he sat in one of the chairs across from Lucy while the steak and potatoes worked up a good sizzle.

"Since a ton of tourists come here in the summer, there must be a lot of seasonal jobs, right?" she asked him.

"Some, yeah. It works out well for the high school kids and the college kids who come home for the summer."

"Oh."

Her brow furrowed, and he realized something about his answer had disappointed her. "Are you looking for a seasonal job?"

"I don't know how long I'll stay after Gran comes home, but I won't leave until we've had a nice visit. I need to work, but I don't want to take a permanent position from somebody who's looking for long-term employment, you know?"

"That makes sense." He wasn't sure if a woman who'd been working in Las Vegas understood the pay scale for the jobs typically held by young people in a small town in Maine, coastal or not. It was tempting to ask about her financial situation, but he was afraid to open that door to another person who'd expect to rely on him. "What are your skills?"

She thought about it for a moment. "Remembering drink orders. Carrying trays loaded with cocktails while dodging handsy men. Deescalating angry customers. Oh, and doing it all in high heels while smiling, of course."

"Okay." She wasn't giving him a lot to work with. "Anything else?"

"Some random miscellaneous skills, I guess, but those are the relevant ones."

"Did you have a long-term goal? Were you planning to do that job forever?"

"Of course not." Her mouth twisted as anger flared, surprising him. "Even though I was one of the best on the floor, my boss was already making some noise about transitioning me to the management team because of my age."

"Being promoted is usually a good thing. It means you're good at your job, and wouldn't that mean more money?"

"Not with the tips I made. I probably would have made less in the long run. And I don't want to manage people. I *liked* what I was doing."

He could believe that. "So if you didn't plan to be a server forever, but you didn't want to be a manager, what was the plan?"

Pink flooded her cheeks and neck. "I've been saving up to move to Miami."

Nick was proud of himself for holding back a full-body shudder. "Miami?"

"Is there anything better than sunshine, beaches and a big city?"

When it came to cities, Nick could think of a lot of things that were better. Muscle cramps. Burgers with no cheese. The fridge and dryer dying in the same month.

"But Miami?"

"My friend Sydney—who I worked with for years—moved there when she got married. She's an event planner, and she's been after me to join her business as a mixologist to design signature cocktails for the events. I'm really good at it, actually."

If he was lucky, maybe Lucy would head for Miami before

the heat crackling between them sparked something they'd both regret. "Have you told Sydney you're currently unemployed and on the road, so it's the perfect time for a fresh start?"

Lucy looked down, suddenly obsessed with making sure the strings of her hoodie were hanging equally on each side." No."

"Are you not excited about it?"

"Sure. But I came all this way to see Gran, you know? It would be wrong to leave without seeing her, especially since Miami's far away and I'll be finding a place to live and jumping into business. Who knows how long it'll be before I come back."

That made sense, but he could tell by the way she wouldn't meet his eyes there was more. "And?"

"And I want to let the whole Vegas thing die down a little first."

"Confirming that job is still a viable option is the logical first step in a plan."

She glared at him, blowing out a breath. "Thank you, Mister Action Steps, but I've had a lot of doors slammed in my face over the last almost two months and I can't… If I reach out to Sydney and she wants nothing to do with my mess, I'll have nothing. I just need a little time."

"It's not *your* mess," Nick said firmly, anger flaring as he thought of all the people who should have had her back but didn't.

"It *is* my mess because the one thing that guy *didn't* do was tell the world I didn't know who he was and that I'm just an innocent bystander. He'd rather they assume poor Reese was seduced by some woman they should target all of their rage at, instead."

Nick made a growling sound but said nothing as he got up and flipped the steak. Then he flipped over the potato packet and gave it a good shake before closing the lid of the grill again.

"What about you? If you didn't have to live here and keep the family business going, what would you do?" she asked.

He shrugged, not liking to talk about his dead dreams, but he knew she wouldn't give up that easily. "I *don't* have to live here. I choose to, and it's a good life."

"But did you always want to take over the construction company? I know you're the oldest, but you do have brothers. Was there something else you wanted to be when you grew up?"

"Football." The word slipped out before he could stop it.

"A football player? Like a professional one?" She scowled. "I'm not really a fan of football players."

Nick had forgotten a quarterback was the reason she was in Wayward Harbor right now, and he winced. "What did *you* want to be?"

"When I was little, I wanted to be a penguinologist in Antarctica."

"Is penguinologist actually a word?"

"Yes, it is, thank you very much."

He cast a pointed glance at the way she was snuggled into *his* hoodie. "Do you know how cold it is in Antarctica?"

"Hey, I'm acclimating. I'm not even wrapped in a blanket right now." She sighed. "Anyway, back to you. I think most boys want to be athletes when they grow up. Football. Baseball. All the other sports balls."

Nick wasn't sure why it mattered, but he wanted to tell her what football had meant to him once. Not because he wanted to convince her not all football players were like the dirtbag she'd met in Las Vegas, but because he wanted her to know he'd had big dreams once—was compelled to show her he wasn't always so…serious. He was *not* grumpy, but he'd accept too serious.

"I made it, actually," he said quietly, keeping his gaze on the smoke sneaking out from under the grill's lid. "I got a scholarship to a D1 school in Texas, and by the end of my junior year, I was already considered a top draft prospect."

"Were you a quarterback?" she asked, nose wrinkling. "You seem like a quarterback type."

"I was a running back. And I'm a little offended by that comparison due to your recent and, as far as I know, *only* interaction with a quarterback."

She scoffed and flicked her hand, as if swatting thoughts of that other guy away. "I just meant serious and bossy. You seem like a guy who'd want to be in charge of the team."

"The coaches are in charge of the team."

"Whatever. But why football?"

He sighed, resigned to talking about it now that he'd opened the door. "I was obsessed with football for as long as I can remember. I also loved running. My mom was convinced I'd be a track star, but then my dad signed me up for the local football league for kids and that was it."

"Admittedly, I know very little about sports, but I know you have to be *really* good to be high in the draft."

"I was. And for the first time, I had my own identity. I wasn't just Sully Slater's oldest kid, destined to pound nails for a living. I wasn't lumped in with my brothers as 'one of those Slater boys.' By the time I was varsity, I was the pride and joy not only of Wayward Harbor, but the entire region. And by high school graduation, nobody in Maine talked about football without saying my name."

Her eyebrow arched. "You must have been insufferable."

"Probably. But I was also disciplined and focused, and shared a common goal with a team of guys who were like brothers. Being in that locker room and on the field felt like *home* to me."

"You're not much older than me." She frowned. "Right?"

"I'm thirty-five."

"Okay. Again, don't know sports, but did you retirc already?" She covered her mouth. "Oh no, did you get hurt?"

"I never played pro ball."

Lucy dropped her hand. "Wait, after all that, you didn't get drafted?"

"My dad passed away suddenly, right before I started my senior year."

"Oh. I'm so sorry." Her eyes softened, and he got up to check the steak just so he didn't drown in them.

"I came home for the funeral, and it was a mess, of course." He shook the potato packet and closed the lid again, though he didn't turn around. "Gray was a senior in high school. Beck was fifteen and Theo fourteen. We'd not only lost Dad, but he had jobs in the works. Some were unfinished. Some he'd scheduled and taken deposits for. Mom hadn't worked outside the home since I was born—she mostly helped Dad with the office part of the business. This was before college athletes could earn money on their merch and stuff, so I couldn't do that. But I told her if she could hire somebody to keep the jobs going and keep the roof over their heads, I'd be able to send money when I signed my rookie contract."

Nick stopped to breathe for a minute because he hadn't even gotten to the hardest part yet. Lucy was quiet, seeming to know there was more, but not pushing him to continue.

"I went back to Texas, but my mom—she couldn't get her feet under her. She called me every night, crying about how difficult it was to manage my brothers. My mom was dealing with depression and my brothers were acting out. It was pretty obvious they were falling apart and needed *me*, and it doesn't matter what the choice is—I'll always choose my family."

"That had to be devastating," Lucy said softly. "I'm sorry you lost football. It obviously meant a lot to you."

"It did. But time went by, and Gray and Beck had things pretty well in hand, with Theo…being Theo. He was a handful, but he was making good choices, so I started thinking about football again. I interviewed around and was offered a position as a JV coach just outside of Boston. Two weeks before I was supposed to start, our mom was diagnosed with cancer."

He heard her gasp. "Nick. I'm sorry."

"She was one of those stubborn, skeptical women who avoided doctors and hospitals, so by the time it was bad enough to get her in there, there wasn't a lot they could do. But I couldn't leave her and my brothers. And after she passed… well, here I am."

Because the chairs were on grass, Nick didn't realize Lucy had gotten up until she was standing next to him. He turned, intending to tell her it was fine and send her in for a platter, but she wrapped her arms around him and the words stuck in his throat.

She was the perfect height for hugging. Her arms went around his waist, and he wrapped his arms around her back, holding her close enough so his face was buried in the neck of the blue hoodie.

He knew he should keep it short, but he couldn't remember the last time he'd been hugged. It was probably when he and his brothers had to line up after their mother's funeral service and accept handshakes and hugs from what felt like the entire population of Wayward Harbor. He'd been numb, and the hugs had been awkward and rushed.

Not Lucy's hug, though. She held him until his body relaxed. His heart rate slowed. Even his breathing slowed, until he felt more at peace than he'd felt for a long time.

Only then did she back away and give him a smile. "I'm going to start bringing out the stuff we need. Don't let those potatoes burn."

So along with the gorgeous hair and eyes, and looking damn good in his favorite sweatshirt, the fact she could offer comfort and then let him be went on the list of things he *really* liked about Lucy Macauley.

By the time the steak and potatoes were on the table, the mood had lightened, though the breeze was kicking up as the sun went down. The light next to the door and the solar light topping the deck posts gave the meal a nice ambience.

He laughed when the wind kept blowing her hair in her face as she tried to lift her fork to her mouth. With an exasperated sigh, she pulled the hood up and tucked the hair in.

"You should make a list," he said between bites. "The steps you have to take to make the Miami thing happen."

"I just have to drive there," she said with a shrug. "I can figure out the rest when I get there."

"Yeah, just driving to Maine with no plan worked out so well for you."

She grinned at him across the table, and it took his breath away. "It hasn't really worked out that bad, actually. And if I have to make a list of serious things I need to do, then you should make a fun list. Like a shenanigans list."

"A shenanigans list?"

"Yeah, you know—a list of fun shenanigans you want to get up to."

"I don't get *up to* shenanigans."

"And there's your problem."

"I don't think we've established I actually *have* a problem."

"Haven't we, though?" She flashed him another smile.

"What's something you've always wanted to do for no other reason than it seems like a cool thing to do?"

"Sunrise on Cadillac Mountain," he said without thinking.

"I don't know what that means. Where is Cadillac Mountain?"

"About two hours up the coast, give or take. It's in Acadia National Park, and because of the elevation, it's the first place in the United States you see the sun rise."

"Two hours?" She held up her hands. "Put it on your shenanigans list and we'll do it."

He chuckled, appreciating the enthusiasm. "To go during the season, you have to make a reservation. You can't get near it on the weekends and holidays, but getting up and out of here at like two in the morning isn't really feasible on a workday. It's not worth the effort."

"Something you've wanted to do for so long it was the first thing that came to mind when I asked you means it's absolutely worth the effort." She pointed her fork at him. "I'm putting it on the list."

And sure enough, when he'd finished cleaning the grill and went in to help her with the kitchen cleanup, he saw a fresh sticky note on the fridge.

Under the heading of *Our Shenanigans* were two bullet point items. Sunrise at Cadillac Mountain. And going out in a boat.

Our. The word echoed through his mind and he smiled. He liked the sound of that.

Chapter Seven

Dolly's test results are back and that little lump is totally benign and nothing to worry about! Thank you to everybody who donated to help cover the cost of the testing. We know she's grateful, too, but fair warning: She's a little cranky right now.

—Wayward Harbor Online Community Group

Buoyed by the fresh pot of coffee Nick had set up for her to brew before he quietly left for work without waking her—he really *was* a great guy—Lucy parked her car in the public parking lot, ready to walk the town and find a job.

First, though, she was going to visit Cricket's statue for luck. It was something she remembered doing as a child sometimes. Her memories of Wayward Harbor were always hazy, but she recalled Gran telling her how a toddler had been torn from his mother's arms by a big wave during the fifties, and how the dog had swum out and hauled the baby to shore.

She also remembered Iris's snarky comment about how the dog probably half drowned the kid rescuing it and the town just wanted a quirky statue like all the other coastal towns had. But Lucy didn't care. She loved dogs and she'd need the luck.

The statue stood at the center of the town green, which abutted the rocky shore of what passed as the public beach. Shoes definitely recommended. Lucy knew in the summer the place would be bustling with tourists and ice cream carts and artists. But right now, it was quiet as she leaned across the metal chain to rub Cricket's nose for luck.

With her hood up in a vain attempt to hide her hair, Lucy strolled along the sidewalks of Wayward Harbor. She skipped the street that followed the shoreline as most of those businesses catered to the tourists and probably weren't even open yet. Plus, those were the most likely spots to be filled by local teens and college kids.

So far the only business she'd seen with a Help Wanted sign in the window was a hair salon looking for a stylist. Reception, she might have been able to pull off, but nobody wanted Lucy cutting their hair.

When she turned a corner, a huge oval sign with a storm blue background and gold lettering caught her eye. In fancy script, the sign read Scuttlebutt, Spirits* & Scones. And underneath, in smaller block letters, *Ghosts, Not Liquor.

Lucy could use a little sugar fortification, and she was a sucker for a good sense of humor—and also for scones, of course—so she pulled her hood off and stepped through the door into what smelled like carb heaven.

The front of the shop was adorable. A lot of wood, but accented with a pale yellow that, combined with the large front window, made for a light, cheerful atmosphere.

The woman behind the pastry case that doubled as a counter turned when she came in, and something pinged in Lucy's memory. Straight dark hair pulled up in a ponytail, with bangs. Warm honey-brown eyes, and dimples when she smiled.

A name rose from the dusty depths of her mind and spilled out of her mouth. "Willow?"

"Lucy! Welcome back, stranger."

"Wow, we used to hang out on the beach all the time. We climbed all over the rocks and explored the tidal pools." They'd been summertime best friends, so long ago Lucy couldn't believe she recognized her.

"I remember! My great-aunt owned the house two up from your grandmother's. And my aunt ran this as a bakery, but it was called Brown's Bakery, then. I spiced up the sign a bit when I bought it from her."

"Yeah, you certainly did. So, you sell scuttlebutt now?"

Willow laughed. "We don't sell scuttlebutt, but it often comes free with the scones."

"I know I've heard that word before, but I've never seen it on a sign."

"It's gossip, basically. Back in the day, the drinking water on a ship was kept in a scuttlebutt and the sailors would gather there to chat over a drink."

"There are a lot of nautical terms in this town."

"Yeah. Some of the puns are a little out there, but the tourists *love* that sort of thing."

"And the spirits?"

"Well, there's Jacob, right there in the middle of his brothers." She pointed to a grainy monochrome photograph on the wall, and Lucy stepped closer to see the three young men standing in front of this building. The sign, which was much smaller than the current one, simply read Cobblers. "They weren't very good at cobbling shoes, but they made a lot of money smuggling bootleg liquor from Canada by boat. They kept the booze in the cellar, and one night in 1853, whether he was helping himself to the product or going down the steps in the dark to avoid the light being seen, he fell down the cellar stairs and broke his neck."

"Poor Jacob. But 1853? Wasn't Prohibition later than that?"

"For most of the country, yes. But Maine outlawed alcohol in 1851." She pointed to a black-and-white photo of an apple-cheeked woman holding up a whoopie pie. "And that's Lavinia. She was poisoned by a jealous wife in 1932."

"Wow. That must have been quite the scandal."

"Truly. Her husband owned this building then and ran it as an apothecary. She supplemented their income by selling baked goods that people came from miles around to get their hands on. Especially the whoopie pies."

Lucy didn't have a lot of memories from her visits to Wayward Harbor, but she definitely remembered the time Gran made whoopie pies with a whipped raspberry filling.

"There was a man named John who was always first in line for Lavinia's whoopie pies. He loved those things, and his wife, whose name was Mary, wasn't happy about that because she considered herself quite the whoopie pie maker. So she poisoned Lavinia."

"Wait." Lucy sank onto one of the stools because she wasn't going anywhere anytime soon. "The jealous wife was about the whoopie pies? Lavinia wasn't having an affair with her husband?"

"Oh, there was no affair. Just the sweet temptation of baked goods."

"I probably listen to too many true crime podcasts, but the obvious move there is blaming the husband. One, he's the husband. And two, an apothecary is like a pharmacy, right? Lots of poison lying around the place."

"Lavinia's husband probably would have gone to prison for murder, but this all happened during high summer, when everybody's windows were open, so half the town heard Mary yelling at John that she'd gotten rid of Lavinia, so now he could stay home and eat the whoopie pies she made for him."

"Oh yeah, you gotta close the windows before you confess to murder."

Willow laughed. "Definitely. And a crowd was gathering,

so almost the *entire* town heard John tell Mary he'd rather strip naked, coat himself all over with chum and throw himself off a boat into shark-infested waters before he'd eat anything she baked."

"That's very…vivid."

Willow nodded, eyes gleaming with amusement. "I'd tell you the story was embellished over the generations, but Abigail, the teenage daughter of John and Mary's neighbors, fancied herself a writer and kept *very* detailed diaries. They're kept in a locked case at the library, as a matter of fact."

Lucy laughed, but then she noticed the photo of Lavinia looked as if it was hanging slightly crooked now and stopped. "Have you ever contacted one of those ghost hunting shows to come in and do an investigation?"

"Nope." Willow waved her hand at the wall with the photos. "I know what I know, and people who come in either believe or they don't. But if some so-called experts disproved it, I'd probably have to change my sign because somebody would come in who'd seen the show and scoff, and Lavinia would make one hell of a mess."

Lucy looked around, puzzled. "I remember we used to come here and your aunt would give us day-old stuff for free. But I don't remember ever hearing about Jacob and Lavinia."

"We were very strictly forbidden to talk about them because she was afraid it would be bad for business. I found those pictures in an old safe in the cellar." She sighed. "Sadly, Jacob's rum running money was not still in it."

"Speaking of rum running money, you don't happen to need any temporary help, do you? I promised Gran I'd stay until she gets back, and I need something to keep me busy."

"I wish I did, honey. But this business can only support one person—that being me—because I own the building and live upstairs. It won't support two." She drummed her fingers on the counter for a moment, until they heard a sound like something falling over in the kitchen. "Sorry. Lavinia hates when I do that."

"Is she destructive?" Lucy didn't like the idea of objects being hurled at her if she made an annoying sound.

"No. Lavinia's just opinionated. I do have to label everything, though. A lot of bakers reach for ingredients from muscle memory, but I have to check labels because things get moved around sometimes. She'll switch the sugar and salt containers if she's in a mood. And she tried to switch the cinnamon and chili powder on me once, but I was paying attention."

"It sounds like she keeps you on your toes."

"For sure. You know, Billy Loring over at the Uneven Keel might need some help."

"If the Uneven Keel is a bar, that's a five-star nautical pun."

Willow laughed. "Yes on both counts. I heard he's supposed to have some kind of surgery on his hand soon, and the woman who usually fills in for him is a teacher, so she's not available until school lets out mid-June."

"I can try it, I guess." She sighed. "It seems being Iris Macauley's daughter's not great for the résumé."

Pink darkened Willow's cheeks. "Yeah, she came up a lot when that whole thing… You know. In Las Vegas."

"I didn't know who he was. I didn't recognize him because I don't care about sports, and he gave me his middle name."

Willow's smile was genuine. "I believe you."

It was so nice to hear those words, Lucy was afraid she'd cry, so she stood up. "Okay, I'll go see if Billy Loring holds my mother against me. But I'll definitely be back. A *lot*."

"I'm here from four thirty in the morning to two in the afternoon, every day, though I don't unlock the front door until six."

Lucy laughed. "I will *not* be here at six o'clock."

"Good luck," Willow called to her as she left.

The Uneven Keel didn't look like much, even though it was right on the water in the touristy part of town. A long rectangle of a building with gray shake siding, and a sign with its name wrapped around a crooked anchor. But it was right on the shore, and a dock extended out into the water to offer parking for customers who arrived by boat.

Inside, it looked like every ocean-themed bar she'd ever seen on her television screen. A long bar. A bunch of square tables with cheap chairs. A row of booths along the wall opposite the bar. The back wall looked out over the water, with a massive window flanked by two doors. The one on the right led to a small deck that extended to the pier. She assumed the large deck to the left would offer outdoor seating during the season.

Some fishing nets and other sea-related items hung on the walls, and there weren't too many customers. Not surprising, probably, in the lull between lunch and the end of the workday. There were several men at the bar. A couple of guys in utility company sweatshirts took up one table, and there was a group of women at another. Watching her from behind the bar was a man about Gran's age, with a long, silver ponytail and a scruffy beard to match.

Lucy smiled and walked to the bar, aiming for the widest gap between customers. "Are you Billy Loring?"

"Ayuh." He squinted at her. "Who's asking?"

"I'm Lucy." There was no sense in offering the Macauley surname—changed from Griffin by her mother and stepfather during the eight-month marriage that had landed them all in Nevada—unless he asked. "I'm looking for temporary work."

"Do you have any references?"

She didn't really think him calling a Las Vegas nightclub that thought she was getting old and also fired her for breaking up Fairee would get her very far. "Willow Brown liked me well enough to send me your way. And I guess Nick Slater would vouch for me."

Maybe.

He tilted his head. "How do you know Nick?"

"We live together." The words were out of her mouth before she considered a better way to phrase their relationship.

"Ah." He nodded once and went back to checking for water spots. "You're Iris Macauley's daughter."

Ouch. "I prefer to think of myself as Helen Griffin's granddaughter."

That earned her a rusty chuckle and some eye contact. "Helen's good people. You got experience?"

"I was a cocktail waitress in Las Vegas casinos and nightclubs for eight years, and I worked in various restaurants before I turned twenty-one."

In her peripheral vision, she saw a woman's head turn, and her eyes narrowed as she looked Lucy up and down. Lucy wasn't sure if the woman didn't like cocktail waitresses from Las Vegas or if she'd made the connection and recognized her as the sinker of the Fairee ship, but she tensed.

"I've never been to Vegas," Billy said, nodding his head toward the grizzled man who smelled like low tide sitting three stools down, "but I bet Bones over there don't tip like those high rollers."

Lucy wasn't sure she wanted to know why the man went by Bones. "I'm not looking to get rich—just something to keep me busy until Gran gets home from her travels."

Snatches of whispered conversation from the table where the woman was sitting reached her.

Iris Macauley.

Reese Noonan.

Poor Faith.

Great. A trifecta of Lucy Macauley's shame. Her face and neck heated, but she didn't turn her head to look at them. Even before she blew up on the internet, she knew engaging usually only made things worse.

"And did Willow tell you I'm having surgery and Nicole can't cover for me until school lets out sometime the middle of June?" Billy asked.

"It might have come up."

"Can you make drinks, or do you just carry them on a tray?" He cringed and slapped his hand down on the counter. "That didn't come out right at all. Didn't mean to disrespect the job."

"It's all good." Lucy wanted to tell him about some of the signature cocktails she'd designed because, honestly, she *loved* talking about them. But this didn't seem like that kind of place. "I can make any mixed drink you can think of and some you've never heard of. And I can pull a draft with a perfect head."

That got his attention. "Even a stout beer?"

"Just the right amount of foam, every time."

"We're not going to have any of that nonsense I heard about in Vegas, are we?"

And there it was. "I can't guarantee nobody will ever show up to harass me or sneak videos of me while I'm working."

He snorted. "I don't care about folks like that showing up here. They wouldn't be the first to find themselves out on their asses. I'm talking about the nonsense that started it all."

Lucy lifted her chin and looked him in the eye. "I didn't do anything in Las Vegas but have a cup of coffee with a man who lied to me about his name."

She said it loudly enough for the chatty women at the table to hear, speaking clearly.

"I'm not looking for any kind of attention, and I don't want it," she continued. "I just want to serve drinks."

He considered for a moment, then nodded once. "We're open eleven thirty to nine until the season starts, then we're open to ten."

Lucy struggled to keep a straight face. Where she came from a lot of people were just heading out for a night on the town at ten.

"We're closed on Tuesdays," Billy continued. "Come in Wednesday night and we'll see how it goes. Jeans and any shirt you want as long as I can't see your nipples, armpits or belly button. And wear flat shoes. I don't want to listen to those heels clacking around behind my bar all night."

Lucy smiled. "So I should save the stilettos I like to wear when I'm on my feet all night for when you're out recovering, then?"

His booming laugh turned heads. "Oh, I'm not going anywhere. They're cutting on some tendon in my hand, so I can't pour. But I'll be here."

"Okay." Lucy had won over one grump in Wayward Harbor. She could do it again. "I'm looking forward to it because I bet you've got the best stories."

He laughed again. "You know it. See you Wednesday."

"You got a minute?" Beck asked while Nick was clearly in the middle of figuring out why he'd cut a board a sixteenth of an inch short when he was confident he'd measured it twice. Maybe.

"Well, it's been about forty-five minutes since the homeowner's called me for something ridiculous, so I've got ten to fifteen before the next one. What's up?"

"I saw you try that board and then I heard all the swear words you managed to string together without even taking a breath. That's not really like you, so I'm checking in to see how things are going with you and Lucy Macauley."

Startled, Nick dropped his pencil. At least bending over to pick it up gave him a few seconds to blank out his expression before facing Beck again. "With me and Lucy? No clue what you're talking about, dude."

Beck looked confused, and he wondered if he'd overdone it. "You're just off in some way, and I realized it's been like two weeks living with some woman you don't even know. So I wanted to say, if it's an issue, you can come home. I can sleep on the couch, you know."

Nick breathed out a subtle sigh of relief. His brother thought Lucy was annoying him and had no idea the real reason her presence was costing him sleep.

"Lucy's fine. We get along fine, so there's no reason for any of us to sleep on a couch." *Except Lucy*, his guilty conscience coughed up.

"Are you sure? We can make it work if you staying at Helen's is a problem."

"I said I'm fine." When Beck just kept staring at him, he frowned. "What?"

"I don't know if I believe you."

"What the hell's that supposed to mean?"

"It means you'll be miserable if you think it's best for me, and for my kids. So I can't really trust that when you say you're fine, you're actually fine."

He wasn't wrong, but Nick hated that doing the right thing by his family seemed to be making his brother feel even worse about it. "I'm really fine. Lucy and I get along well enough. But I hate that *she's* sleeping on a couch even though she says it's fine. If we could all focus and maybe get on track, I could leave a little early each day. I can use the extra time to get the smaller bedroom done so she can sleep in a proper bed."

"We'll do that, then. And if you need help at the cottage, just shout. We can figure that out, too."

Nick nodded, although he probably wouldn't just shout. His brothers had enough going on. "I'll have to grab Gray at some point for the electrical finish work."

"Okay. I better get back to it, then."

"Hey, I left the specs for the hallway arch in the pocket of my sweatshirt, which is over by the door. Can you grab it for me before you go?"

Beck walked over and picked up the sweatshirt, shaking some sawdust off before digging in the pocket. "You finally getting used to these new hoodies? I thought you'd wear the one old one you have until it literally falls apart in the washer."

Nick scowled down at the obviously inferior sweatshirt he'd thrown on that morning. "Next time we place an order, I want the old ones back. I don't care if I have to pay the difference out of my own pocket."

"Come to think of it, you've been wearing the new ones for like the last week or so. Something happen to the other one?"

Yes, something happened to his favorite hoodie. A redheaded hurricane blew into his life and laid claim to it, and he liked seeing her wear it too much to take it back.

But there was a zero percent chance he'd be sharing *that* with his brothers.

"Don't you have anything better to do than worry about my clothes?"

Beck was laughing when he walked away.

Nick was measuring a fresh board for a third time when his phone, which he'd tossed on a makeshift worktable nearby, started ringing, and he swore under his breath. It was no wonder he cut the board wrong.

Since the three people he generally answered calls from 24/7 were in the building with him, and he'd spoken to the overly anxious homeowner less than an hour ago, he was tempted to ignore it. But the possibility it might be Lucy made him put down the level and pick up the phone.

When he glanced at the screen, though, he saw his insurance agent's name flashing at him. Dreading a new problem to solve, he answered the call.

Ten minutes later, Nick parked his truck as close to Barnett Insurance as he could find a spot and started walking. The redhead in his favorite hoodie sitting in the center of the sidewalk wasn't hard to spot.

When he reached her and stopped, she looked up at him and smiled as if sitting on the sidewalk with a cat in her lap was a totally typical thing to do in the middle of a workday.

"What's going on?" he asked when she didn't say anything.

Lucy shrugged. "I'm doing an errand."

"According to Keith Barnett, who owns the insurance company behind you and called me because he's worried about you, your errand has consisted of sitting in the middle of the sidewalk for over half an hour."

"Dolly wanted to say hi, so I bent over to pet her, but she wanted more and more pets. My back started to hurt, so I sat down to pet her, and then she crawled into my lap and went to sleep." She shrugged. "You can't move if a cat's sleeping on you. It's the rules."

Nick arched an eyebrow at the cat, who was side-eyeing him without moving her head. "She's not asleep."

"Probably because some guy came and blocked out her sun and woke her up with his deep, grumpy voice."

"If my voice is grumpy—and I don't think it is—maybe it's because I had to leave the jobsite early because Keith was worried about you, but you're just here being a cat bed."

"If Keith was so worried, why didn't he come out himself and just ask *me* if I'm okay?"

"We mind our own business around here."

"Oh, clearly." She snorted out a laugh, earning an annoyed glance from Dolly.

Lucy had a valid point, of course. But what she didn't seem to understand—and what Nick didn't want to explain to her—was that Keith had probably watched her long enough to determine she wasn't ill or injured. No, she'd clearly been going through something that wasn't Keith's business. But out of concern, he'd called Nick.

Because everybody in Wayward Harbor knew that Lucy was staying with Nick. That she was his responsibility.

Sighing, he extended a hand to help her up. When she grimaced and didn't take it, he folded his arms and waited.

"So, my foot fell asleep a while ago," she admitted. "And I'm afraid when I try to get up, I'm going to fall over and, one, that would be embarrassing. And two, it might actually hurt."

"Do you think that would be more or less embarrassing than being the woman who was sitting in the middle of the sidewalk with a cat in her lap for more than half an hour?"

"I don't believe for a second I'm the first person to ever sit and visit with Dolly for a while."

"I'll give you that," he said as the cat stepped out of Lucy's lap, stretched in a way Nick envied, and then sauntered away. "Though most people sit on one of the park benches so pedestrians don't trip over them."

This time, when Nick extended his hand, she took it. He hauled her to her feet, and after a few seconds, he thought she was steady, so he released her hand.

Then her leg caved—maybe it was her feet not having feeling back or maybe it was the heel on her boot twisting—but suddenly he had an armful of Lucy.

Her entire body was pressed to his, and his arms wrapped around her, holding her close. Heat shot through him, and he knew he should let her go and step back, but he was afraid she'd fall.

Everything around him faded away until all that remained was Lucy in his arms. The warmth of her body. The red curls tickling the side of his face. Her fingers clutching his arms.

When she started shaking, he got scared for a second, but then he realized she was laughing. She pulled away enough so he could see her face, though she was still clutching his sweatshirt. Her face was flushed, her eyes sparkling with humor, and she'd never looked more beautiful to him.

"I told you it would be embarrassing," she said breathlessly.

He couldn't say any of the things he wanted to say to her in that moment, so he just shook his head. "Why are you wearing heels?"

"These? They're not even high heels." After a few test stomps of her feet, she backed away, and every muscle in his body mourned the loss of contact. "And I wanted to look nice today."

"Where did you park? I'll walk you back to your car."

"I'm parked over by Cricket, but I'll be fine. You probably have to go back to work."

He shrugged. "It's a nice day."

"It's actually pretty cold."

"Come on. I'd hate for you to fall down again and get hyperthermia. People might leave you there because you've established a reputation for randomly plopping down on the sidewalks."

"A reputation?" She laughed and slapped his arm. "It was one time."

"That's all it takes sometimes."

They walked in comfortable silence for a few minutes before she glanced over at him. "Speaking of reputations, you know all the stories in Wayward Harbor, right?"

"I don't know a fraction of the stories in Wayward Harbor, but I do know a few, yes."

"Do you know why some old guy I saw at the Uneven Keel would be called Bones?"

"Yup." He nodded. "But first off, if you want to blend in at all, the locals just call it the Keel."

"So noted, though I don't think it's possible for me to blend in. But back to Bones—did he find a skeleton in a cave? Pull up a skull on his fishing line? Does he have a weird hobby building things out of fish bones?"

"He choked on a chicken bone in third grade."

"Oh."

"Also, he's only, like, fifty-five."

"*Oh.* No. Really?"

"Yeah. He went to school with my dad—same class—so he's roughly the same age my dad would have been today."

"I'm sorry. Does it bother you to talk about him?"

"Not really. It used to, in the beginning. But now, I guess it hurts less to remember him than it would to forget him." It was true, but he didn't want to go *too* deep into it. "What about your dad?"

She shrugged. "Unknown."

"You don't know where he is?"

"I don't even know *who* he is." Her easy smile and shrug let him know it was something that didn't bother her. "His name is *unknown* on my birth certificate."

Old rumors about Iris ran through his mind, but he was *not* going there, so his brain circled back in the conversation, and he glanced at her again. "Why were you at the Keel?"

"Oh, I got a job there."

"Of course you did. Tell me, did you actually *meet* Billy?"

"I did." In his peripheral vision, he saw her turn and give

him a brilliant grin. "It'll be fine. I have a way with grumpy dudes."

But Nick, still off-kilter from the feel of Lucy in his arms, imagined coming home after work to an empty cottage because she was working, and he didn't even crack a smile.

Chapter Eight

I moved to Wayward Harbor last month. We bought a home on Seacrest Lane, but somebody on our road lets their chickens roam free. They can be quite aggressive, and they make it difficult to drive by constantly being in the road. I'm attaching a photo so you can see how large they are. Why don't they have to be fenced in?

First comment: I'm not sure where you're from, but those are turkeys.

Second comment: If you grab the big one that looks like a rooster with the feathers on the back end instead of the front and move him, the others will follow.

Theo Slater: Ma'am, as one of the first responders who will have to patch you up, do not *try to engage with wild turkeys. There's nothing you can do but be patient until they're out of the road. Wildlife has the right of way.*

—Wayward Harbor Online Community Group

By the time Nick got home from work, Lucy was practically glowing. She had a job. She'd reconnected with an old friend. Dolly liked her enough to take a nap on her lap.

And, while she was trying not to think about it *too* much,

remembering the feel of Nick's arms around her for the second time was hard to resist.

Even though it only happened because he was much too nice of a guy to let her fall on her face, Lucy was *almost* sure Nick had thought about kissing her.

She'd definitely thought about kissing *him*. For a moment, with her body so close to his, with their gazes locked and her hand on him, it would have been so easy to bring her mouth to his.

The sound of his truck door closing jerked her thoughts back from the delicious detour they'd been taking, and she pulled the lasagna out of the oven. She hadn't made it from scratch, but since she'd found it in the freezer, she assumed it was one he liked.

"That smells good," he said as he stepped out of his boots at the door.

"Perfect timing," she said. "It's almost time to eat."

"Sounds good. I'll just go wash up really quick."

The lasagna looked good, as frozen foods went, and she hadn't burned the bread she slathered with butter and garlic salt and stuck in the oven. And Nick responded to her attempts at small talk while they set the table, mostly about Helen because they'd exchanged text messages about her new job after Lucy got home, but she could tell something was bothering him.

"I'm sorry I embarrassed you in front of the whole town," she said when it was time to put the lasagna on the table, but she couldn't take it anymore.

His brow furrowed and he tilted his head. "What are you talking about?"

"When I…stumbled on the sidewalk earlier. I know I embarrassed you, and you seem kind of angry." She frowned.

"Or maybe you're upset because we were talking about your dad. Either way, I'm sorry."

"I'm not angry, Lucy." He scrubbed a hand through his hair, messing it up in that way she loved so much. "I don't really want to talk about this, but I also don't want you thinking you did something wrong and that I'm mad about it. I'm not angry or upset. I'm just…tense, I guess."

"Tense?"

"I wanted to kiss you."

"Oh."

"And I'm tense because I've spent pretty much the entire time between then and now thinking about what it would have been like to do it."

As if the words weren't enough, his dark eyes were locked on her face with an intensity that made it hard to swallow. To even think, really. Vulnerability felt like such a risk, her fingernails bit into her palms. But if he could confess he'd wanted to kiss her, she could admit she'd wanted him to.

"I…wouldn't have minded."

"I would have minded," he bit out, and she winced at the belated realization he might not be too thrilled about being attracted to her. "When I finally kiss you, it's not going to be in the middle of the sidewalk with the entire town gawking at us out the windows."

When I finally kiss you.

When.

Finally.

The words echoed through Lucy's mind in time with her racing pulse. She wanted to move—to close the distance between them—but he was still scowling, so she kept her feet still. "Do you have any idea when that might be?"

The question startled a chuckle out of him, clearing away

the frown lines. "Maybe when I can wrap my head around why it's not a bad idea."

"Oh, it's totally a bad idea. We live together, so if it's a bad kiss, it'll be incredibly awkward. One of us will have to sleep on a pile of blankets in the shed."

Nick's mouth quirked up at the corners, making him look almost smug. She hadn't seen that expression on him before. "It won't be a bad kiss."

"You sound very sure of yourself."

"I am. Partially because if one of us has to sleep in the shed, you know it'll be me. And there's no way you're going to let me take all the blankets, so that's a lot of pressure on me to succeed. I'm good under pressure. But mostly because I've spent enough time thinking about kissing you to know it's going to be good."

"But it's still a bad idea."

"Absolutely."

Her resolve was crumbling like a stale cookie. "I'm the one who drove three thousand miles to see my grandmother without calling first, so if one of us is going to respect an idea being bad, it'll have to be you."

Nick was so close to her now, she was afraid he'd be able to hear her pounding heartbeat, and his dark eyes gleamed with promise. "Do you *want* me to kiss you?"

"Yes," she whispered.

Nick put one hand on her waist, and with the other, he cupped her cheek. He watched his thumb stroke over her bottom lip, and a shiver went down her spine. Then his hand slid to the back of her neck and he lowered his mouth to hers.

Lucy melted against him, her hands sliding up his back as his fingers bit into her waist. His other hand slid from her neck into her hairline as his tongue dipped between her lips.

She lost all sense of time as Nick kissed her with a hunger

that matched her own. It was even better than the kisses he'd given her in her daydreams, and she never wanted it to end.

But eventually, Nick released her hair and broke off the kiss. His hand still at her waist, he rested his forehead against hers. They were both breathing too fast, clearly wanting more.

"Thank goodness we finally got that out of our systems," she whispered, and he actually laughed before standing straight.

"Totally out of our systems," he repeated, the lie as obvious as hers had been.

"The lasagna's getting cold," Lucy said, because she didn't know what else to do. Going in for another kiss before ripping off his clothes would have been preferable, but pasta was a decent consolation prize.

"Right." He pulled out his chair but didn't sit down. "You know there are only two of us here, right?"

She considered the huge pan of lasagna. "We'll definitely be having leftovers tomorrow. But I can freeze it in portions, too, so we don't have to eat it for the next three days."

"I won't be here for supper tomorrow, actually. I'm going out."

Going out? Lucy wasn't sure what that meant. If he was going out with his brothers, wouldn't he just say, "Hey, I'm going out with my brothers tomorrow," or something like that? He'd said going *out*, not going *home*.

But he couldn't be going on a date. He'd just kissed her, and he might have said it was a bad idea, but he hadn't said it was a bad idea because he had a date lined up for the next night. She wouldn't have kissed him if he had, no matter how much she wanted to.

"Okay," she said when she realized she had to say *something*. "Thanks for letting me know."

"My brothers want to cook out in the backyard," he told

her while he held up a plate so she could drop a chunk of lasagna onto it. Then he set that plate in front of her chair and lifted his own. “You want to go? It’s just burgers and dogs, but there’s no sense in you making something for just yourself when we always grill too much.”

“I’d love to go,” Lucy said without hesitation. She wasn’t about to pass up an opportunity to meet Nick’s family.

“This is delicious,” he told her after taking his second or third bite. “Thank you for making it. I know lasagnas are a lot of work.”

“I’d love to take all the credit, but it was a frozen one.” She chuckled. “And it gave me a good excuse to warm up the cottage without touching the thermostat.”

“Oh, I noticed,” he said, and his voice was grumpy, but the corners of his mouth twitched.

They ate in silence for a few minutes, but Lucy could practically see him worrying about something. His shoulders were tensing again. The furrow in his brow was deepening. And the way his gaze kept flicking to her and then bouncing away told her he might have something he wanted to say, but wasn’t sure she was going to like it.

“Maybe while we’re at my place tomorrow,” he finally said, “we could not say anything about…anything.”

Nick looked so uncomfortable, Lucy couldn’t stop the laughter that bubbled up. “So are we just ignoring your brothers? Or should we act out the conversations, like charades? Are we betting on which of us can make it through the whole cookout without saying anything?”

He dropped his fork onto his plate, that exasperated sigh she loved so much making her smile. “You know what I’m talking about.”

“Yes, I do,” she admitted. Toying with him was fun, but she didn’t want him to rescind the invitation. “I mean, we agreed it was a bad idea ahead of time. We just needed to get it out of our systems, so there's no sense in telling anybody. I've been the subject of enough gossip in this town, thank you very much."

"Exactly. I'm glad we're on the same page."

"And look at the bright side." She waited for him to look at her, and then smiled. "At least neither of us will have to sleep in the shed."

The most alarming thing about Lucy Macauley, as far as Nick was concerned, was how quickly he'd gotten used to living with her.

The second most alarming thing about Lucy was how much Nick had enjoyed kissing her and how much he wanted to do it again. And how much time he spent thinking about it.

Right now, sitting next to her in his truck on his way to the family home for a cookout, was *not* the time. But remembering the feel of her lips against his had a way of sneaking up on him at inopportune times.

Minutes from introducing Lucy to all three of his brothers was *definitely* an inopportune time.

He should have waited to kiss her until *after* she'd met his brothers. They knew him too well, and he wasn't going to be able to hide the chemistry between him and Lucy. Actually, the harder he tried, the more they would notice something was up, and they'd start paying attention.

"Why are you antsy?" she asked from the passenger seat, breaking into his thoughts.

"I'm not."

"You're drumming your fingers on the steering wheel, and you never do that." She pointed a finger in his direction. "You know, Lavinia hates that. Don't do that at the Scuttlebutt."

Nick was so confused. He was often around Lucy, but this was next level. "Who is Lavinia?"

"The ghost. At the bakery." She scoffed and rolled her eyes. "Her picture's right there on the wall."

"Right, the whoopie pie lady."

He took a right turn onto a dirt road, and then a left into his driveway. Four trucks made parking tight, but he pulled into his usual spot—farthest from the door because he was nice like that.

"Wow, what a pretty house. It's not what I was expecting."

He looked at the classic sage green Cape with the deep porch, trying to see it through her eyes. The early-season perennials were starting to bloom in the beds around the foundation, and he thought it looked pretty. "Should I be offended?"

"I thought it would be like a square house, probably painted gray, with lots of… I don't know—man stuff."

"I don't even know what that means, but we do have a grill in the backyard and a riding mower in the shed." He glanced sideways at her. "Don't ever assume the toilet seat's down, though. My mom gave up nagging about that by the time Theo was out of diapers."

"It must be really cool to have a home you grew up in. I guess Gran's cottage is the closest thing for me, and, well, you know how often I got to come here."

"It felt pretty small for a while. It's a three bedroom with a full bathroom upstairs and a half bath downstairs. Sometimes, especially during our teen years, it didn't even feel like we had elbow room." He chuckled, shaking his head. "We did bunk beds, with me and Gray in one room and Beck and Theo in the other. Me leaving for college was one of the best days of Gray's life."

But he didn't want to keep going down that conversational road because it dead-ended with Nick getting called home—

and back to the room he shared with his brother—and realizing immediately they needed him to stick around.

"I've never shared a room," Lucy told him.

And Nick's mind started spinning. Like *ever*? Obviously she'd had relationships in the past, but had she ever lived with anybody? Hell, had she been married in the past? He wanted to ask, but it was also none of his business.

"I don't remember having my own room, which I did until I was six," he said instead. "But I remember the day they moved Gray into my room because Mom was about to have Beck."

She nodded, and then gave him a thoughtful look. "Are you putting off getting out of the truck for some reason?"

Busted. To be fair, it wasn't only a matter of putting off introductions. It also felt good to reminisce about his younger days, when the house was full.

They got out of the truck, and he led her around the house to the backyard, where everybody was already gathered. Nobody was at the grill yet, though, so they weren't running as late as he'd hoped. The less time they spent here, the better.

Their parents had loved cookouts and had many friends, so a large patio made from paving stones extended from the deck steps. The grill was massive, and there were several tables with chairs, along with Adirondack chairs in conversational groupings.

It was overkill for how they used the space now—just whoever happened to be home throwing some meat on the grill—but so far none of them had suggested selling any of it.

"Okay, so the resemblance is strong in this family," Lucy said as soon as they turned the corner.

"Yeah. Not only is it pretty obvious we're brothers, but it was very obvious who our dad was, too. Mom always griped about how she had to carry and deliver us, but we got nothing from her." He shrugged. "But I see her in my brothers' facial expressions all the time."

Lucy smiled at him, but he caught a glimpse of sadness in her eyes and wondered what it must feel like to have no siblings. And to have what sounded like a pretty terrible mother.

And for a second, he was tempted to tell her something that might help, but it wasn't his secret to tell. And he'd promised Helen he wouldn't say a word.

"Okay," he said as his brothers approached. "These are my brothers, in order down from me—Gray, Beck and Theo. Everybody, this is Lucy Macauley."

He deliberately said her last name because he trusted his brothers to greet her with warm smiles, which they did. She shouldn't have to shy away from using her name, even in Wayward Harbor.

He stroked the dark hair of the little girl who ran up and wrapped her arms around his legs. "This is the best niece in the whole world, Sierra. She's four. And the best nephew in the whole world, Jeremy—over there in the sandbox—is two. They belong to Beck."

"It's a good thing he had one of each," she said, her eyes sparkling with humor.

"It did work out well for me. I'd hate to have to rank two nephews or two nieces," he said.

"We were just about to fire up the grill," Theo said. "You want something to drink, Lucy?"

"Just water would be great."

"I'll show you around inside," Nick said. "I'll grab her one while we're in there."

He could practically feel his brothers' nosy stares boring into his back as he led Lucy across the deck and through the slider into the dining room. Giving her a brief tour of the downstairs—pretty basic dining room and kitchen area, living room and what had been a playroom before being turned into the home office for Slater & Sons—he tried to see it through her eyes.

It looked a lot like it had before their parents passed, with simple, solid furniture and very little clutter. Cream walls lightly decorated with family photos and a lighthouse painting from a yard sale. Hardwood floors with throw rugs. But it didn't feel the same to him since their mother died. It was functional, but the heart had gone out of the home.

"The half bath is here," he said, pushing open the door a bit. "So you'll know where it is. And I'll save you the upstairs tour since I have no idea what condition the bedrooms are in. It looks a lot like down here, except with furniture for clothes and sleeping instead of sitting and eating."

"It's a lovely home," she said. "You must miss being here."

Not really. "I have to run over here now and again because the office is here, but it's actually been nice at the cottage. We tend to have a hard time leaving work at work in this house."

He'd grabbed two bottles of water from the fridge and was about to open the slider when he realized Lucy had stopped in front of his parents' wedding photo, which hung in the living room.

"You're right," she said. "For a second, I thought it was you in this photo."

He chuckled. "I'm not *that* old, and I've never been married, but I know what you mean. I am, however, just old enough so our childhoods were captured with print photos, and there's a shoebox of them in a closet. My mom wished us luck figuring out who's who, and she wrote Collective Childhood on the label."

Lucy was laughing when they stepped out onto the deck, so of course they all looked. Nick was trying so hard not to be tense, but he was afraid one of them was going to make a bad joke about them living together. Or ask her about Las Vegas, or—even worse—reference the old rumors about Iris Macauley. They didn't know as much as he did, because they didn't spend as much time with Helen, but even the basic gossip could be hurtful.

He wasn't surprised Lucy had no trouble relaxing and fitting right in. She was personable and warm and so many things Nick wasn't, and soon he was enjoying himself. She asked them all questions about Wayward Harbor and what they did for fun. Theo told her about his work with the fire department before she had a deep discussion with Sierra about their favorite movie princesses.

He noticed she never asked any of them about work and the family business, which he appreciated.

"Oh, I meant to ask you about one of the signs I saw," she said to Nick after setting her empty plate on the table. "I know this town loves some nautical puns, but it can be hard to tell what a business sells before it opens for the season. What is Dinghy Doodads?"

All four of them laughed, but it was Gray who answered. "It's…a gift shop, I guess you'd call it?"

"That makes sense," she said.

"It's kind of a co-op thing," Beck added. "Basically the community can make things to sell there, and the shop takes a cut and the crafter gets the rest. It's definitely targeted toward tourists."

"That's an understatement," Nick said. "We have some true artisans in the community, so there's pottery and art and jewelry. All ocean related, of course, and mostly specific to Wayward Harbor. But tourists will buy anything, honestly."

"One lady buys these little teddy bears in bulk, and her daughter makes them T-shirts that say Wayward Harbor, and they get obscene amounts for them. Some of the kids collect driftwood, and they have a stencil for using a wood-burning tool to do a silhouette of a lighthouse on some rocks with a sailboat. People buy them like they're museum pieces."

"My favorite, though," Theo said, "is Doreen, who uses molds to make tons of small chocolate balls. She sells them in clear little baggies with a tag that says Moose Poop, and she literally can't make them fast enough to keep them in stock."

"And tourists will buy anything that is made from any part of an old lobster trap," Beck added. "Brooke, my best friend's wife—well, ex-wife, I guess—is part owner of the place, and she's said she'd feel bad for taking their money, but they're practically throwing it at her."

Lucy, who had been laughing through their tales of tourists being easily parted with their money, held up her hand. "That's settled. I will *definitely* be visiting Dinghy Doodads when she opens."

"Probably two weeks from today," Beck said. "She usually opens mid-May to catch the retirees who want it to be warm enough to enjoy the outdoors but before Memorial Day kicks off the summer season."

"Remind me to add it to our shenanigans list," she told Nick.

He nodded, knowing his smile didn't quite make his eyes because he caught the questioning glances from his brothers. Nick having anything to do with shenanigans would surprise them. His sharing a joint shenanigans list with a woman they'd just met would make them ask questions.

"We should get going," he said, so abruptly Lucy frowned at him. "I hate to eat and run, but I want to finish trimming out the window in that bedroom today. Gray, I'll need to get with you about the electrical finish work soon."

"We should help clean up," Lucy said, standing and picking up her plate.

"We'll take care of it," Beck told her. Nick could tell by the way Beck had been watching him that he'd sensed the shift in his brother's mood. "Thanks for coming with Nick. It was great to meet you."

"Thank you for dinner. I hope I'll get to see you all again soon."

Once they were back in his truck, Nick's guilt over the forced departure seeped in. Lucy had been having a good time, and he'd rushed her out of there. And telling himself it was so one of his brothers couldn't say something that would embarrass her didn't change the fact he was actually afraid they'd back him into a conversational corner. He'd either have to tell them he was falling for a woman who intended to leave Wayward Harbor in her rearview mirror, or he'd have to say that, yes, she was attractive, but there was nothing between them.

And Nick wasn't prepared to say either of those things out loud.

Chapter Nine

We love books as much as anybody, but please stop donating books that should be recycled. It's okay to let them go if they're old and musty or missing covers and chunks of pages. Try sharing the love of reading with your friends and family. If they don't want the books, our patrons probably won't, either. And if you're donating them by leaving them on our front step in the darkness because you're embarrassed to bring them inside during library hours, please take them to recycling. Your friendly local librarian thanks you.

—Wayward Harbor Online Community Group

"Don't you take any sass from Billy Loring."

Lucy laughed at her grandmother's stern words. "I won't."

"And you better call me in the morning and tell me how it went."

"I will." She glanced at the clock on the stove to make sure she didn't lose track of time. She suspected Billy Loring wasn't the kind of boss to laugh off being late on day one. "When do you leave for your cruise?"

"We depart in six days, so not for a while yet. I can't wait, though. I've wanted to do a two-week cruise for *years*."

The joy on her grandmother's face was infectious. "Nick put the itinerary and your list of excursions on the fridge because the man *loves* to put lists on refrigerators, and it's going to be such an adventure. Take lots of pictures!"

"You know I will. Now, you should get going, but make sure you let me know how it goes."

At eleven, buoyed by her conversation with her grandmother and a sweet text message from Nick wishing her luck, Lucy parked in one of the four spaces marked for employees of the Uneven Keel only. They were at the far end of a long, skinny parking area that had a bit of a slope to it, but a business having its own lot in Wayward Harbor was a blessing.

Lucy went in the back door, assuming the front door would still be locked, and a dark-haired woman in her forties, wearing an apron and hairnet, looked up as she walked through the kitchen. Lucy smiled and waved, and the woman nodded before going back to work.

When she pushed through the swinging door into the front of the house, she didn't see Billy anywhere. But a curvy blonde woman who also looked to be in her forties, wearing jeans, an Uneven Keel T-shirt and her hair in a french braid, was rolling silverware into napkins at one of the tables that overlooked the water.

"Good morning," Lucy said. "Billy told me to come in and try out a shift."

"Lucy, right? Iris Macauley's daughter?" When Lucy reluctantly nodded, the woman snorted. "You really break up that actress and football player?"

"No. The football player did that. I just had coffee with a guy I met in a coffee shop." She was really tired of saying that.

"Cool." The woman got up and set the tray of silverware on the end of the bar. "I'm Mattie. And since you'll have to write it on slips now and again, it's spelled with a double *t*, not a double *d*, because it's not short for Madeline."

"People must get that wrong a lot. What *is* it short for?"

Mattie sighed so hard, her shoulders actually rolled. "We'll do this once and then I don't want to hear about it again."

"Okay." That sounded ominous.

"My mother named me Clematis, after the vine because it's her favorite. As soon as I started school, the kids started shortening it to Clem and that didn't work for me, so I had to come up with something on my own really quick. I've been Mattie ever since, but if a woman comes in and asks for Clematis, it's either my mother or my aunt, so keep a straight face and point her in my direction."

"Got it."

"Good. I take care of the tables and you take care of the bar. When I give the slip to the kitchen, I'll tell you what booze I need. If you can't remember the drinks, write them down because I won't. Tips are pooled and split at the end of shift because sometimes I'll get more families and you'll get more drinkers, and that's how we make it fair. And then it doesn't matter if we have to cover for each other for a few minutes or if you have to run food from the pass for me. Clean aprons are under the bar, and dirty ones go in the laundry bag hanging in the break room."

"Sounds good."

Mattie started walking, but then she stopped and turned back so quickly, Lucy almost ran into her. "Oh, one more thing. Sasha, the cook, is my wife. She's also Billy's daughter."

"Oh. That's good to know."

"Yeah. One big happy family, but we're loud and all three of us can be short-tempered. Sometimes there's yelling—usually when we're putting up with flatlanders overrunning the place—but don't take it personally and feel free to yell back. Don't take any crap, even from me."

It was one of the more interesting job orientations Lucy

had been through. And also the shortest, because Mattie just waved her hand toward the bar and then went out back.

With no instructions on how she could help with the opening process, Lucy pulled an apron from the stack behind the bar. It was short and red, with two pockets and a white Uneven Keel logo, so she was glad she'd worn a black shirt with her jeans instead of the red one that was a very different shade. T-shirts weren't really part of her wardrobe—she preferred tank tops with light cardigans or blouses over them—so she was wearing a long-sleeved black jersey top that was as close as she owned. White sneakers completed the uniform.

After tying the apron around her waist, she plucked an order pad and two pens from the basket next to the aprons. She slipped them into one of the pockets and got to work familiarizing herself with the area behind the bar. Glasses, ice. How the liquor was arranged on the shelves behind her. Memorizing the different beers on tap. Then she skimmed over the menu, paying special attention to the small section of familiar cocktails with nautical pun names.

The Gone Overboard made her smile. It was probably a better name for the cocktail with five different kinds of alcohol than Long Island iced tea, which is what it was usually called.

Satisfied there were no drinks on the specials list she didn't already know by a more generic name, she looked at the clock. Five more minutes.

She poked her head through the door to the kitchen, where Mattie was helping Sasha prep for the day. "Is there something I should be doing? Can I help?"

"Hi, Lucy," Sasha said. "I'm Sasha, by the way. Good to meet you."

"You, too."

"I don't think there's much left to be done," she continued. "But do me a favor and make sure Dad does paperwork with you before the end of your shift. He's not great at remembering things like legally required documents."

"Gotcha."

Billy Loring emerged from a door at the far end of the kitchen at eleven twenty-nine and, after doing a visual sweep of his restaurant, unlocked the door.

There were no customers waiting to get in.

But as the clock ticked toward noon, customers began trickling in. Several guys sat at the bar, wanting burgers and beer for lunch. A family sat at a corner table, and, much to Lucy's dismay, the judgmental woman and her friends were back.

Because Mattie handled the tables, Lucy did her best to ignore them, but Billy kept forgetting he was supposed to be letting her take a trial run at the bar, so she didn't have much to keep her mind off the whispers. And those women weren't the only ones.

There was a lot of whispering and a lot of sideways glances in Lucy's direction over the course of the afternoon. She couldn't tell if they were stemming from the Las Vegas disaster or because she was Iris Macauley's daughter, but she kept her chin up and did her best to pretend it wasn't happening.

There was a time midafternoon when there were no customers, and Mattie disappeared out back. Lucy was trying to figure out a way to remind Billy about the paperwork without sounding sure she was coming back. It was supposed to be a trial shift, as far as she knew.

"You coming back tomorrow?" he asked before she could broach the subject.

"If you want me. I don't feel like I've done a lot to prove I can do the job."

"I've been doing this a long time, and you're a natural. Mostly, I wanted to see how you'd deal with people not being as warm and welcoming as they should be."

She shrugged. "Nothing I can do about it. But right now they're talking about me. If they start talking *to* me, no guarantees. But I've never actually hit anybody, so there is that."

"Good enough."

"So…is there some paperwork I should fill out?"

With much grumbling, Billy eventually produced the documents she needed to fill out. While she wrote, he poured himself a soda water and leaned against the bar.

"We'll be opening the outdoor seating soon, and then it starts getting busier. The big deck's gonna be closed for a private event Wednesday night, though. One of the summer people wants to host a get-together to toast the opening of the season, and they'll be up here getting their summer homes ready. It'll be just women, I guess."

Lucy was surprised they wouldn't go up to the restaurant and bar at the resort hotel. She hadn't been there, but Iris had driven her by it a lot when she was a kid, talking about how she'd stay there someday. "Okay."

"She said something about fancy shots," Billy grumbled. "What's fancy about shots? You pour the booze in the shot glass and you knock it back."

Lucy lit up so hard inside, she was surprised she wasn't literally glowing. "I can handle the fancy shots. I know what she wants."

He looked over at her, frowning—but in his contemplative way, not the angry way. "You do?"

"It's kind of my thing, actually. Designing signature cocktails and shots for events." She smiled when his eyebrows shot up. "I told you I can do mixed drinks and drafts, which I can, obviously. But my true passion is…art with alcohol, I guess you could call it?"

"Huh. And you got an idea for these women?"

"I do." It was inspired by spending a lot of time thinking

about Miami, though she didn't want to share that and get into a whole discussion about it. "A layered shot that looks like sand, water and sky. Like the ocean, to kick off their summer weekends by the sea. I just need to know how many women."

He nodded, looking impressed. "Ten is what she said. I charge a fee for private events on top of the bill. You take care of them for the night so I don't have to think about them and I'll split the fee portion with you. And you and Mattie split the tips, of course."

"It's a deal."

Lucy would have done it for free, but she kept that to herself.

With her job secured, her paperwork done and a fun party where she could really show off her talents on the horizon, she sailed through the rest of the shift. She didn't even mind the increase in whispers and furtive glances when the dinner crowd filled the place.

She couldn't wait to get home and tell Nick.

Lucy's first shift at the Keel seemed like a good time to finish off the second bedroom, so Nick left work early and roped Gray into leaving with him.

When they pulled into the driveway, he was slightly surprised her car wasn't there, though. Billy Loring had a big personality, and he wasn't sure it would vibe with Lucy's. Also, she was going to be the center of attention, surrounded by sideways glances and whispers, and it wouldn't have shocked him to find her on the couch, under the blankets. He'd figured there was a fifty-fifty chance she wouldn't make it the full shift.

"It must be awkward, having a woman you barely know sleeping on the couch every night," Gray said as he took his tools into the smaller bedroom.

"Not really. She's easy to get along with." He was going

to say more—about how he enjoyed her company and looked forward to coming home at night to see her—but he shut his mouth.

"Glad to hear it, though I'm surprised you didn't give her the bed and sleep on the couch. That would be a very *you* thing to do."

"I tried, actually. But since I have a job and she didn't, she said I needed a better night's sleep."

Gray nodded. "Then let's get this room done so she can get some sleep, too."

It took them two hours to hang the ceiling fan light and smoke detector, and then install the outlet and switch covers on the electrical boxes Gray had installed earlier in the process. After giving the room a thorough cleaning, it took them two trips to bring back the furnishings being stored in a neighbor's barn.

His brother helped him reassemble the bed frame, which was the same maple as the rest of the furniture in the cottage. It was all heavy and possibly older than him, but a quality it would cost a fortune to replace nowadays.

"I can help you bring in the dresser and nightstand," Gray said after checking the time on his phone. "But then I'll have to run. Cory signed tonight and he's looking to drown his sorrows."

"Damn."

Cory Weston had been Gray's best friend since kindergarten, and he'd been going through a tough divorce that nobody in Wayward Harbor had seen coming. Rumor had it he'd cheated on Brooke, though Nick had never asked Gray to confirm or deny it.

"How's he doing?" he asked as they walked out to the truck to get the dresser.

"Not great. Pretty wrecked, actually."

"And Brooke?"

Gray sighed. "I don't know. I've been giving her space, you know?"

It had to be messy for his brother, Nick thought. Gray and Brooke had dated for a long time in high school, but their relationship hadn't survived Gray going off the rails after their dad died. Things had been rocky when she started dating his best friend, but after some time passed, Gray had chosen his friendship with Cory over nursing a grudge.

But, though he'd never say it aloud, Nick thought Gray had always stayed a little bit in love with his best friend's wife.

"You guys need a driver?" Nick asked once the stuff he needed Gray for was done.

"We're just going to hang at his place, but I appreciate the offer."

Nick nodded, turning to pick up the curtain rod left to hang so his brother wouldn't see the disappointment on his face. He had too much to get done here to justify spending the evening at the Keel, but it would have been a good excuse to see Lucy.

"Thanks for the help."

"Anytime. Fair warning, tomorrow morning might be a little rough," Gray said as he grabbed his bucket of tools from the corner.

Nick chuckled. "Take the time you need. Nobody wants you running a nail gun with a hangover."

Once his brother was gone, Nick threw on some music and got to work putting the finishing touches on the room. He hung the curtains first, and then rummaged around for bedding. Some of it got moved to make room for Lucy's clothes in the linen closet, but he'd let her move those to the dresser. He found some cozy flannel sheets and a warm quilt. Then he draped two fleece throws at the end of the bed so she'd be able to nest.

After moving the bags and boxes from the living room into a corner of the bedroom, he grabbed a knit blanket from her couch pile and draped it over the armchair they'd set in the corner next to the dresser.

Once that was done, he went to the kitchen and opened the box Gray had brought with him from the house, where it was delivered. By the time he'd unpacked the gift and set it up on her bedside table, he was starving.

Throwing some chicken breasts on the grill was easy enough, and Lucy could easily throw it on bread or a make a salad if she didn't grab anything at work.

Eating alone didn't feel great, though. He'd loved it for the few nights between Helen leaving and Lucy showing up. Supper with his brothers always meant talking about work, and sometimes he needed a break from the pressure. Especially if he was trying to enjoy a burger.

But he liked sharing meals with Lucy. They talked about anything and everything *but* work. Books. Movies. Television shows. Music. Their favorite amusement park rides. Who got the most scars learning to ride a bicycle. Their conversations went off on random tangents, almost all of which ended with laughter.

Even turning the television on while he ate didn't help. Scripted banter and laugh tracks couldn't replace Lucy, so he ate quickly and cleaned up after himself. Then he worked on tearing apart the old back deck until he heard her car pull into the driveway.

He went through the back door seconds before Lucy walked through the front door, getting inside just in time to watch her face light up when she saw him.

"How'd it go?" he asked, as if the huge smile wasn't answer enough.

"It was awesome. Mattie and Sasha are both very cool, and

Billy—well, he wants me to come back, so I assume he liked me well enough."

"No problems with the customers?" If somebody was going to do a deep dive on just why Iris was a sore subject in Wayward Harbor, it would probably be somebody who'd had too much to drink.

"Nope. I mean, I could tell they were giving me looks and talking about me sometimes, but trust me when I tell you that's nothing compared to what it used to be."

"Good. Did you eat? There's extra grilled chicken in the fridge."

"I did, but I'll eat it for lunch tomorrow before I go in if you're not planning to."

"It's all yours."

Nick made himself wait while she took off her shoes and the coat she'd borrowed from Helen's closet. And while she poured herself a glass of water and drained half of it.

Then she looked at the couch, frowning. "Did you steal one of my blankets?"

He crossed his arms, eyes narrowed. "Did you actually count them?"

"Of course not." Her sheepish glance in his direction made him chuckle. "But I have favorites, and one of my favorites is not where I left it."

"I took it," he said without smiling, curious to know how she'd take that information.

"Oh." She took another sip of her water, staring at the couch over the rim of the glass.

He waited her out, knowing she wasn't going to leave it at that. At the very least, she'd try to get him to return one of her favorites for one of the blankets that didn't make the cut.

"You're *never* cold," she pointed out. Then she jerked her gaze to him as she gasped. "You didn't use it to…like, put in the bed of your truck to protect the paint or use it as a drop cloth or anything like that, did you?"

"Even if I needed a cloth for some reason and was willing to sneak one from your dragon's lair of hoarded blankets, I would never use something of Helen's for that purpose."

"To be honest, I'd believe that before I believed you were cold and needed a throw blanket."

"Fine. Come on." He walked to the door of the second bedroom and turned to make sure she'd followed before opening it and flipping on the light.

This time her gasp was one of surprise and not outrage, and he stepped aside so she could enter.

"You finished it!"

"Gray came over and finished off the electrical, and then he helped me put the furniture back in." He shoved his hands into his front pockets. "Didn't seem right for you to sleep on the couch after being on your feet all day."

"Thank you, Nick." She looked around, her hand on her chest. "It's so pretty. And you even made the bed."

"Now close the door and turn the light off." When her eyebrow arched, he laughed. "Yeah, I hear it now. But trust me."

Once the door was closed and she hit the switch, plunging the room into darkness, he turned on the machine on the bedside table. Soft white noise filled the room as the lights on the tiny branches of a wire tree sculpture twinkled in a random pattern.

The tree's branches gave off just enough of a glow so he could see the joy in her face as she watched the lights.

Suddenly, all the time he'd spent looking up items and reading reviews on the retailer sites was worth it. "I thought it might help you sleep."

"It's perfect. I love it."

"It has a little remote control, and I put the instructions in the drawer of the nightstand. You can have the noise on and the lights off, and vice versa. And there's different settings for the lights."

"I love it so much." Before he had time to brace himself, she threw herself into his arms. "Thank you."

The hug broke through the scraps of willpower he was able to summon, and when she pulled back and her gaze went to his mouth and her lips parted, he couldn't help himself.

It was the kiss of a parched man who'd finally been given water, and she moaned as her body arched against his. Her mouth was demanding, and he gave until his knees were weak and he wasn't sure if he even remembered how to breathe.

He wanted to back her up to that bed, lay her down, and then take his time stripping her clothes off as he got to know every inch of her.

But then what, the voice in his head that still had reason wanted to know. This thing between them was a dead-end road—she was leaving town—and every mile they went down this path would just make it harder to turn around.

"Still a bad idea," she said softly when their lips parted and their breathing had slowed.

"A very bad idea," he agreed. "I should go to bed. *My* bed. The bed in the other room."

"Probably." Her fingers still rested on his shoulders. "Definitely."

He forced himself to step back, and her hands fell to her sides. "I replaced the doorknob, by the way. It has a twist lock now."

She laughed, her expression softening. "To keep you out or keep me in?"

"Both probably," he said. "Whatever keeps us from messing up this good thing we've got going on."

She nodded. “Good night, Nick. And thank you again for my gift.”

The smile he gave her was tight, but it was the best he could do. “Good night, Lucy.”

When he was stretched out on the bed, staring up the ceiling, Nick had to admit to himself that he was worried about messing up this good thing. But every day he grew more certain kissing Lucy *was* the good thing.

Chapter Ten

Is anybody missing a dog? Looks like a shorthair breed mixed with a husky maybe? No collar. Very skittish and not friendly at all. We had a hard time getting him in the crate and had to use meat to trap him. Please spread the word because he's very unhappy.

—Wayward Harbor Online Community Group

Eight days later, Lucy was such a tangled mess of nerves that, if her nerves were yarn, even the most experienced and frugal knitter would toss the skein and knit something else.

Helen was only one day into her two-week cruise, and Lucy hadn't anticipated how much anxiety she'd have about her grandmother being on a floating resort out in the ocean.

She didn't know *what* was going on with Nick. Since the night they'd come very close to crossing the line from kissing to making out in her bedroom, he seemed to have retreated back across the friend zone line. There was laughing and joking and conversation, but he hadn't initiated another kiss, and she wasn't brave enough to do it.

The whispers and looks around Wayward Harbor, especially at the Keel, weren't dying down. If anything, there were more, and she didn't understand that. The Las Vegas thing should definitely be dying down, and since Iris hadn't followed her daughter to town, it felt as if people should be getting over Lucy's last name by now.

And she was about to serve her "fancy shots," as Billy called them, to ten obviously wealthy women on the deck. They were friendly enough, but clearly used to the best, and Lucy wanted desperately to deliver.

The shot had three layers—from the bottom up Kahlúa, then Bailey's Irish Cream carefully tinted a pale blue, and at the top, a more intense blue made of blue curaçao and vodka—resembling the beach, the ocean and the sky. She set each shot glass on its own little saucer of sand. Billy had grumbled about buying play sand when they lived on the ocean, but she'd curtly told him that good old Maine sand was full of bugs and bacteria and who knew what else, which shut him up. The little shells she'd collected and cleaned with Nick. When she'd explained what they were for, he'd taken the task seriously, and the shells were perfect.

She used tweezers to set a tiny floating candle in the center of each shot. Then, when she'd signaled Mattie and gotten the nod to indicate she was free to carry a tray, Lucy lit each candle and took a picture with her phone for her digital scrapbook.

Luckily, it was a still night, with no wind to blow out the candles. She'd obsessed over the weather forecast so much Nick had threatened to take her phone away, but Mother Nature had cut her a break.

Lucy and Mattie carried the two trays out to the deck and set a saucer in front of each woman. Their gasps and the way they scrambled for their phones to take pictures earned Lucy a smile from Mattie before she took the empty trays and went back to her customers.

"Get one of all of us, please," the hostess said, handing over her phone.

Lucy took a deep breath and took a step back so she could

fit them all in the frame. "This is a wish from all of us at the Uneven Keel, that all of you have a magical, wonderful summer. Now, three…two…"

She was ready when they blew out the candles and captured more of them laughing and clapping. After setting down the phone, Lucy quickly and efficiently went around the table and used the tweezers to remove the candles and drop them onto an empty saucer. She set it out of the photo frame and picked up the phone to take pictures of them downing the shots.

Then she returned the phone and went back inside, leaving them to their revelry.

"Pretty slick," Billy said, giving her what she thought was a nod of approval. "You got a little sweat around your hairline there. They'll be content for a few minutes, so go take a quick break."

Lucy nodded, pulling her phone from her pocket as she went through the kitchen and out the back door. While the joy and triumph were still pumping through her system, she was going to call Sydney. And since the clock was ticking, she couldn't think too long about it or second-guess herself. She skimmed through her contacts and hit the button to call.

"Lucy!" Sydney's greeting was so loud, she pulled the phone away from her ear for a second. "I've been so worried about you."

"I know, and I'm sorry. I just… I was hiding from the world."

"Where are you?" her friend demanded. "Are you still in Vegas?"

"I'm in Maine, actually."

"Instead of coming right here, you went to *Maine*? Girl, it's cold as hell there. Why would you do that?"

Lucy didn't want to confess she was afraid Sydney would do like everybody else in her life and turn her back. "My

Gran's here and it felt like a good time to visit with her. During the transition, you know?"

"Oh, that's right. I forgot you had family there. How's she doing?"

Lucy laughed. "Good, from what I can tell. She's not actually here."

"You need to start at the beginning and tell me everything."

"Okay, but I'm on break, so I have to talk fast."

Lucy told Sydney everything, from having coffee with Reese Noonan to her job at the Uneven Keel. She even told Sydney about Nick, though she left out the kissing. She wasn't sure why, but she didn't want to talk about that.

"So you're in Maine, freezing your ass off, while living with a guy you just met and slinging beer at a dive bar," Sydney said when she finished.

"I wouldn't call it a dive bar. And I remember hot days here when I was a kid, so I know summer will come eventually."

"When's your Gran coming back?"

"I'm not sure. At least another month if not a little more, I think."

"Okay," Sydney said, and Lucy could hear the click of her nails as she drummed her fingers on a hard surface. It made her think of Lavinia, and she smiled. "So I'll expect you in two to three months, then? I mean, I assume you'll want to visit with your grandmother for a while."

For a few seconds, as relief flooded her body and washed out the tension, Lucy wasn't sure she could speak. She nodded, but Sydney couldn't hear that, obviously, so she did her best to swallow the knot of emotion. "Yeah, but I'll let you know when things start winding down up here."

"We'll have the guest room ready for you. I'm so excited to see you again!"

A tear slid over Lucy's cheek even though she was smiling. It was good to have somebody who *wanted* her. "Me, too. I'll talk to you soon!"

She'd done it, she thought as she slid her phone back into her pocket.

The dream life in Miami was still waiting for her.

"Since you're rarely in a good mood, it can be hard to tell, but I'm pretty sure you're in a really foul mood today," Gray said, leaning against Helen's garden shed.

They'd just finished reframing the doorway and installing new hinges because the shed was getting old and the door wasn't closing properly anymore. All that was left was to hang the new door, but it was a two-man job and Gray had drawn the short straw.

"My mood is fine. I just want to get this door hung before you have to leave to meet those people about the addition."

"Why am I taking the meeting again?"

The question irked Nick because he'd rather they talked and worked at the same time, but it was a valid one. Nick usually took the meetings with prospective clients. "Because I went to high school with the guy—and, sure, we're all adults now—but let's just say we weren't friends and leave it at that."

"It's probably for the best," his brother said, lifting the new door so it stood on end. "You're definitely in a bad mood."

Nick didn't bother denying it again. Mostly because Gray wasn't wrong. He'd been in a mood since Lucy got home from work last night, though he thought he'd been doing a good job of hiding it.

He couldn't have missed the joy and pride radiating from Lucy when she walked through the door, but he'd assumed the shots she made for the private party were a success. Then she told him about calling her friend in Miami.

The first hit had been realizing Lucy still intended to go.

The second came when he realized, on some level, he'd started to believe she might not.

Oh, he'd smiled. He congratulated her, both for the party and for having called Sydney. He admired the photos she'd taken. He said all the right things, but he was sulking on the inside.

They'd just finished hanging the door and making sure the hinges and clasps and locks all aligned when they heard a car pull into the drive out front.

"Is that Lucy?"

Nick frowned. "It shouldn't be, but it sounds like her car."

Gray checked the time on his phone. "I hope she didn't block me in because I have to run. I'll let you know how it goes."

Nick started picking up his tools, and a few minutes passed before the fact he hadn't heard Gray's truck start stole his attention from thoughts about how much he hated Miami considering he'd never been there.

He was just starting around the corner of the house when he heard the truck start, and Nick reached the front just in time to see Lucy wave as Gray pulled into the road.

Of course she was wearing his hoodie over whatever shirt she'd worn to work. Between the air conditioning inside and the evening breeze right off the water outside, she was always cold when she left the Keel.

"Why aren't you at work?"

"Because it was super dead and Billy said I looked tired, which might have been an insult or might have been an expression of concern. Or, knowing Billy, a little of both. But anyway, here I am."

"He cut your shift because you look tired?"

She laughed. "No, he cut my shift because there weren't many customers and it didn't seem right to make Mattie split the tips when the Keel is her entire livelihood. And I actually *am* tired because I didn't sleep well last night."

She was probably too excited to sleep and lay awake dreaming of Miami, he thought sourly.

"Anyway," she said. "Why didn't you tell me this is your favorite hoodie and that it's the last one of this kind you have?"

He shrugged, making a mental note to make Gray's life miserable for a while. "It's just a sweatshirt."

"No, it's not. It's your *favorite* sweatshirt, and it means enough to you so your brothers are aware of that fact. You can take this one back and I'll take one of the others. Or, you know, find a hoodie of my own."

"Don't worry about it. I'm getting used to these," he lied.

Seeing Lucy in a random Slater & Sons sweatshirt pulled from the stack of new ones wouldn't make him feel the same as he did when he saw her in *his* sweatshirt. And that would probably be a good thing, but he couldn't make himself agree she should find another one to wear.

"Did you eat yet?" she asked as she walked inside. "I hadn't had my dinner break yet and I could have eaten something before I left, but I decided to come home and eat with you. Of course, now that I'm here it's obvious I should have grabbed takeout for both of us because then there's no cooking or washing dishes."

There was a moment when Nick felt as if this was his life—life in this little cottage. Lucy coming home to eat with him. Talking about their days. Cooking together. It felt so incredibly right.

But it wasn't real. And she had plans that didn't include him.

The cottage felt too small all of a sudden, and he was afraid of what he might be tempted to do if he didn't put some space between them. Something like kissing her until she couldn't breathe and forgot all about Miami.

"You want to go out for a bite tonight instead of cooking?" he asked instead.

She thought about it for a moment and then gave him that smile and shrug combo that was Lucy shorthand for, "Sure, I'll roll with it." As a person who didn't roll well with things, Nick liked that about her.

Five minutes later, she climbed up into the passenger seat of his truck and fastened her seat belt. "Where are we going?"

"Probably Jenna's."

"Jenna's Diner? I saw it while I was out recently and thought it looked like a decent place to eat, but I wasn't hungry at the time."

"Really good food. Good prices. It's my usual supper spot if I don't cook at home during the summer, though, because the Keel usually has a wait for a table then."

"Pete's Place. Jenna's Diner." She chuckled. "They really went all out on coming up with names, huh? And they clearly missed the nautical pun memo."

"Well, Jenna's used to be called Laytons' Diner, owned by Pete and Jenna Layton."

"Wait, they're married?"

"Hard to say."

"How is that hard to say?"

"Look. I know you've been away a long time, but around here, if you want to know something, you have to be prepared to listen to the story."

"You could give me an abridged version." When he just glanced over at her, waiting, she sighed. "Fine. I'd like to hear the story, please."

"So, maybe twenty years ago or more, Laytons' needed some upgrades, and Jenna wanted to go full retro fifties diner because the summer people love that kind of stuff. Pete was not having it. So Jenna threw Pete out and redid the diner the way she wanted it. She even paid the money to have the name changed to Jenna's Diner. So Pete went and opened his own place, just the way *he* wanted it, and called it Pete's Place."

"So they're divorced and run rival restaurants?"

"Well, it's hard to say."

"Isn't that the whole point of the story?"

"Are they rival restaurants? Maybe. They fill pretty different needs in the community." Nick shrugged. "Also, nobody's really sure if they're divorced or not."

"Do they live together?"

"Nope. I don't think they get along well enough to live together. But neither of them has been with anybody else—publicly, anyway—and they've been known to spend time together now and then."

"Isn't that public record, though? Surely somebody could find out if they're divorced."

He shrugged. "Nobody's business but theirs."

Lucy laughed. "Zero chance you can convince me the people in this town are big on minding their own business."

"There's gossiping over coffee or a meal, and then there's going digging for documents. There's a line."

He pulled into the parking lot, thankful there weren't a lot of other vehicles there, and threw the truck in Park. It occurred to him as they got out that people would talk about them being seen having dinner together, but since everybody all knew they were sharing Helen's cottage, it didn't seem like a big deal.

Like the Keel, it wasn't busy, so they grabbed a booth in the back. It didn't take them long to order because he knew he was having the chicken tenders and fries, and when it came to anything except sandwiches, Lucy tended to trust his taste in food.

Their dinner conversations usually started with the topic of

Helen. A day rarely passed without Lucy and her grandmother at least exchanging a few text messages. But now Helen was on the cruise and had chosen not to pay the very large fee for service. When she started doing regular excursions, she promised to look for places with Wi-Fi and give updates.

Nick didn't really have anything to talk about because his entire life revolved around work, but he listened while Lucy related a conversation she'd had with Willow Brown. Nick knew Willow, of course, but he'd been surprised to know that she and Lucy had been summer friends as kids.

She paused while the server set down their meals, but then resumed talking about mixed-up spices or something to do with a ghost. He was struggling to pay attention because he kept thinking about how it was going to feel when Lucy wasn't a part of his life anymore.

"How come you haven't taken a football coaching job in this area?"

He almost choked on the bite of chicken tender he'd just taken. Somehow, he managed to swallow it, and then he took a long drink of water to thoroughly wash it down.

"Sorry," he said when he could breathe again. "Where did *that* question come from?"

"You told me a while back that you'd accepted a job in the Boston area as a high school football coach, but you had to pass on it when your mother got sick."

"I *chose* to pass on it." Maybe it wasn't much of a distinction, but he always made it because he didn't want his brothers to think he resented the decision.

"Of course you did, because that's the kind of guy you are. You work hard so the company succeeds, which means your brothers succeed. When you're not working, you help out other people. But your brothers are adult men, back on their feet, and you could do something for yourself now."

Every muscle in Nick's body tensed, and it was good he didn't have food in his mouth anymore because, with the way his jaw clenched, it would have been mush. "I think it's pretty clear I wasn't meant to be involved with football."

"Wait." She leaned across the table and lowered her voice, her brow furrowed. "You don't think, if you try to coach again, that something bad will happen to one of your brothers, do you?"

"Of course not." The fact he'd lost a parent each time he'd dedicated his time to the sport didn't mean the universe was trying to keep him from it just out of spite. "I'm busy, and coaching is a big commitment. If something goes wrong, either with the company or something else, do I let down my brothers or do I let down the kids?"

"I think you and your brothers would figure it out together." She sighed. "Maybe you could volunteer with football clinics or something. Just be a little bit in it."

"Maybe," he said, just to close out the subject. Just the idea of another responsibility added to his plate threatened to kill his appetite, and he liked Jenna's chicken tenders too much to risk that.

"So how many ghosts does Willow think she has?" he asked to change the subject back to one he knew she would go on about.

Lucy could think whatever she wanted about how he ran his life and his business. She was going to leave soon, and she'd probably never think about him again.

Chapter Eleven

A "rescued lost dog" has been released back into the wild by the Maine Warden Service after it was confirmed to be a coyote. Officials would like to remind residents to call local authorities to report potential lost dog sightings.

—Local news post shared to Wayward Harbor Online Community Group

Lucy had gotten in the habit of stopping at the Scuttlebutt before work to top up on caffeine and some baked goods, but mostly to visit with Willow.

She missed having somebody to chat with. Over the last couple of weeks since starting at the Keel, she hadn't gotten to see much of Nick. Most days he'd already left for work when she got up, and he went to bed about an hour after she got home. Even if he showed up at the bar for supper, it was different talking while people were looking at them.

Today was Tuesday, so Lucy had the day off. But she'd still driven into town just to have the company of a friend. And when Willow was busy with a customer, brewing more coffee or checking on things back in the kitchen, she would pull her notebook out of her tote and work on ideas for fun cocktails and shots.

Movement beyond the glass snagged her attention—a tall woman with curly red hair pulled back into a loose ponytail. For a second, Lucy thought she'd caught her own reflection in the window at a weird angle, but then the reflection turned and looked over her shoulder, and she realized it was a woman on the sidewalk. And Lucy would have bet the cranberry orange scone sitting in front of her that this was the woman people kept confusing her with.

When the door opened and the woman stepped in, Lucy looked down at her notebook, though she watched the woman in her peripheral vision. They really did look a lot alike, though the other woman was a few years older and her hair was a more subtle shade of red.

She listened to Willow taking her order—just a coffee—and was about to take a bite of her scone when the woman walked directly to where she was sitting.

"You're Iris Macauley's daughter, right?"

"Yes. Helen's granddaughter." Lucy tried to keep her voice light, but the Iris thing was getting old.

Though, it *was* better than the Fairee thing, she had to admit.

"I'm Taylor Perkins."

"I'm guessing you're the woman people keep mistaking me for."

Taylor smiled, but her lips were tight and the smile didn't reach her eyes. "My hair's a little darker than yours, but it's hard to miss, I guess. Do you mind if I sit with you for a minute?"

Lucy wasn't getting the friendly extrovert who wanted to make a new friend vibe, but she nodded and tucked her notebook away in her bag. Taylor set her coffee and napkin down on the table before pulling out a chair. Her body was stiff, and she immediately started smoothing the napkin as though trying to decide what to say.

"How old are you?" she blurted out.

Lucy sat up straight, frowning. It was kind of a personal question, even for a getting-to-know-you conversation, but especially asked in such an abrupt way. "I'll be thirty in three weeks."

Taylor nodded, and then inhaled sharply as if steeling herself to do something unpleasant. "And who's your father?"

Oh no. No, no, no. "I don't know. He's not on my birth certificate, and my mother does *not* talk about it."

"I'm sorry." She picked up the napkin, twisting it nervously. "This is so awkward."

"It's been awkward for a bit now, so we may as well keep going," Lucy said, because she needed to know exactly what Taylor was fishing for.

"I remember, when I was four or five, my parents fought a lot. I know it's normal for most parents to argue, but not mine. They were really quiet people. And these were *bad* fights. I don't know if they actually split up for a while, but I do remember my dad not being around a lot and my mom crying."

Lucy's skin prickled, and her fingers tightened around the handle of her coffee mug. She knew she should say something because Taylor was obviously struggling to come up with the next step in the conversation, but she couldn't find words that made sense.

Does my father live here in Wayward Harbor?

Does Helen know?

Does Nick know?

"My dad passed away about five years ago, from a heart attack," Taylor said softly.

Emotions flashed through Lucy's mind.

Mourning a man she'd never met. Sorrow for Taylor. Anger

at Iris. At the man who might have been her father and didn't claim her. At Helen, if she knew and kept it from her. Loss.

So much loss.

"But I think you might be my sister," Taylor said, and from the way she dropped the napkin and exhaled, Lucy knew that was what she'd come to say.

But she couldn't be done talking. All she'd done was bury Lucy in questions she may never get answers to.

"What was his name?" she asked, because that, at least, she should know.

"John Perkins, but he was a junior, so everybody called him Jack."

Jack Perkins. It didn't ring any bells. She couldn't remember either her mother or grandmother ever saying the name.

"I was born in Rhode Island," Lucy said quietly. "There's no father on my birth certificate, and Iris said I didn't need one and refused to say more."

"I remember once, when I was a teenager, my mom and I came here—well, it was her aunt's then—and I was super bored. You and Willow were getting snacks to take to the beach, and I wanted to go. Willow's younger than me, but we used to hang out sometimes because it's not a big town, you know? But my mom—she was so angry and dragged me out of there. Said I had stuff to do at home."

When she paused, Lucy knew she should say something. But her mind was spinning and her heart ached, and there didn't seem to be any words left inside of her.

"There's been a weird vibe since you came to town," Taylor said, and that was something Lucy could agree with. "More sneaky gossip than usual. At first I thought it was because of that whole thing in Las Vegas, but my mom's been… Well, she's been angry again."

"Do you have a photo of her on your phone?" Lucy didn't

know why it mattered, but Taylor pulled up a photo of a dark-haired woman taken at some kind of cookout. Sure enough, it was the judgy woman from the Keel. "Oh, yeah. She does *not* like me. At least now I know why, I guess."

"I'm so sorry to just spring this on you." Tears glittered in Taylor's eyes. "It's just been so hard knowing you're in Wayward Harbor, and then I saw you sitting in the window. It was a little spur-of-the-moment."

"It's a lot," Lucy said in the understatement of the year. "But I'm glad you told me. It's explains a lot about how I haven't found this warm and welcoming small town so warm and welcoming."

"I don't think that many people know, actually. Your mom—I'm sorry, but your mom made a lot of wives and girlfriends angry, if you know what I mean."

Lucy knew exactly what she meant, and it didn't surprise her to hear it. But she wasn't going to trash her own mother to a stranger, so she kept her mouth shut.

Taylor dug in her purse and pulled out an old receipt and a pen. After scrawling her number on it, she slid it over to Lucy. "I'd love to talk more after you've had some time to process things. I'll be honest—my mom would lose her mind if she knew I was doing this, but…it's about me. And you. If you want to know for sure, I think we can do the DNA thing really easily through the mail, but I'd just really like to have a sister."

A tear slid over Lucy's cheek as she stared into eyes that were hazel instead of blue, but still looked similar to hers. "I think I'd like that, too."

Taylor picked up her coffee and left without saying another word. Lucy had lost her appetite for the scone, but she picked up Taylor's number. After taking a photo with her phone to ensure she couldn't lose it, she tucked the receipt into her notebook.

Willow, who was busy putting a fresh batch of cookies into the pastry case, must have heard it all because concern was written all over her face. “Are you okay?”

“Not really,” she said. “I need to go.”

“I’m here if you need me.”

During the entire drive back to the cottage, the only thought pounding through her brain was that her grandmother *had* to know.

She knew Helen was on her cruise, and she glanced at the list of her planned excursions on the fridge as she walked to the couch. Maybe she wouldn’t be able to get hold of her. If not, she wouldn’t leave a voicemail because it would only worry Gran. She’d try a video call, and if Helen picked up, good. If not, she’d have to wait.

She got lucky, though. Her grandmother was smiling when she accepted the call, but as soon as she registered Lucy’s face on her screen, the smile faded. “Honey, what’s wrong? Did something happen?”

“I had coffee with my *sister* today.”

Helen was speechless for a few seconds, her lips parted, but she rallied quickly. “Okay, honey. Just let me find a quiet bench and dig my ear things out of my bag.”

Lucy usually would have smiled at the use of “ear things” but she didn’t have it in her at the moment. She just waited silently while Helen found a relatively private spot and located her AirPods. In hindsight, blindsiding her grandmother with this call hadn’t been a great idea, but she hadn’t thought to text her and ask for a return call when she was alone. Even if she had, Helen probably would have ended up on the same bench, worried and unable to wait.

“Did Taylor tell you?” Helen asked once her AirPods were connected.

“Yes, Taylor told me. And I got my entire life turned upside down at a haunted scone shop because nobody else *ever* told me. Not Iris. Not Nick. And not you. I was literally the only person in this town who didn't know."

"Actually, Iris is literally the *only* person who knows *anything* for sure. Even I don't know the truth of it, though I suspected. There were rumors, of course, but were they true or, as Iris told me, was Kim just bent out of shape because she chose to believe the rumors?" She paused, her eyes sad. "Of course, the older Taylor got and the older you got, the more it looked like Kim was bent out of shape because she was right and her husband actually got Iris pregnant."

"Why didn't you tell me?"

Tears slid down Helen's cheeks, but Lucy wasn't sorry for the accusatory question or the bite in her tone. Gran should have told her.

"To what end?" Helen said. "You already have a mother who cares more about herself than you. Would knowing you have a father who didn't want you and refused to claim you as his daughter have made your life better?"

No, Lucy admitted, if only to herself. "But I have a *sister.*"

"Kim Perkins wouldn't have tolerated you in Taylor's life when you were younger. And you haven't been on this side of the country for fifteen years, so I had no reason to ever think you and Taylor would cross paths. She's never approached me. And once you got here, well… Kim hasn't spoken to me in thirty years. I thought they'd *both* avoid contact with you, and, with Jack already gone, it could only hurt you. And you were already in a rough place. I never expected Taylor to seek you out, and I'm sorry you found out this way."

"I don't know what to feel," she confessed.

"Of course you don't, honey. It's a shock." Helen wiped the tears from her cheeks and sniffled before managing a smile. "Is Nick with you?"

"No. He's at work, though he'll be home soon, I'm sure."

"Okay. Have him make you a nice soup or some hot chocolate. It'll help you feel better. You haven't called Iris, have you?"

"No." She'd thought about it, but hadn't had the strength. "She'll just lie, and if I push, she'll feel cornered and that can make her mean."

"I wish that wasn't true, but I know it is. There's no reason you need to call her because the one thing it won't do is bring you clarity and comfort." Helen looked directly into the camera with eyes that were still brimming with tears. "I should come home. I don't know how, but they must have some way of getting people off this ship when stuff comes up at home. I'm on an excursion now and this little coffee shop has Wi-Fi, which is why you got me. Maybe they can just get my things off the ship and—"

"No!" Lucy forced herself to brighten her expression. "No, you don't need to come home. I shouldn't have called you while you were on the cruise, anyway. Even if you came home, there's really nothing you can do."

"I could hug you. Really tightly."

"We'll just stockpile all the hugs, and when you get home—*after* your cruise and your visit in South Carolina because I promise I'm okay—we'll just have one massive squeeze hug when you get here."

"Okay, sweetheart. Let Nick take care of you, and I'll be home soon."

Once they disconnected the call, Lucy sighed and flopped over on the couch. Dragging a blanket over herself, she thought about her grandmother's words and felt a flash of anger. No, she was *not* going to let him take care of her.

Because she remembered the look on Nick's face the first time somebody mistook her for Taylor. He had to have known, too. And he didn't tell her.

* * *

Nick had a pounding headache, and all he wanted to do was sink down on the couch and close his eyes.

Theo had gotten called out for a garage fire early in the day, so Nick had to drop what he was doing and finish framing the laundry room his youngest brother had been working on so it would be done for the plumbers. Plumbing was one of the very few jobs they had to outsource, and delays took a chunk out of the Slater & Sons bottom line.

Then the landscaper had shown up to get an idea of the homeowner's plans and the timetable. Nick hadn't had time for him, but the guy was hard to get hold of, so he made the time.

It was one of those days, and he walked through the door thankful it was over. He was going to take something for the headache, relax for a few minutes, and then he'd get to have supper with Lucy. He missed doing that, and it was her day off, so it was the *one* thing he'd been looking forward to.

And then he saw her on the couch, under the blankets again.

"What happened?" he asked, the question coming out of his mouth harshly because all he could think of was somebody from that Fairee fandom thing finding her again.

She sat up, her face flushed and her eyes red from crying. Pushing the blankets aside, she stood and walked toward him. And her face did *not* light up the way it usually did when he walked through the door.

"Since you know everybody in Wayward Harbor, I assume you knew Jack Perkins?"

Nick's stomach tightened and the headache upped the intensity. "I did."

"So you know Taylor."

"I do."

"And did the utterly invasive, overgrown weed that is the Wayward Harbor gossip grapevine tell you that Taylor came into the Scuttlebutt while I was there to tell me she's my sister? Did you know *that*?"

No, he hadn't known about that. He hadn't stopped in town at all after work, and he'd put his phone on Do Not Disturb mode during the meeting with the landscaper and had forgotten about it.

"Lucy, I—"

"You knew. All this time, you knew. Gran knew. And neither of you told me."

He winced at the pain in her voice, but he couldn't deny the accusation. While he hadn't felt good about it, it hadn't been his place to tell her.

Lucy wasn't done yet. "There's been this customer at the Keel who obviously hates me, and I thought it was ridiculous because glaring at me because she didn't like my mother or because of the Fairee thing seemed so petty. But it turns out I'm her dead husband's secret love child, so yeah. I'd glare at me, too."

"She shouldn't be throwing hostility your way when none of this is your fault."

"It would have been nice to know what I was walking into. I know a woman was murdered because a man liked her whoopie pies, and I know Bones choked on a chicken bone in third grade, and I know Pete and Jenna may or may not be married, but I did *not* know my mother slept with a married man and this town isn't going to forgive *me* for it."

"And what would you have done?" he demanded, the incessant headache feeding his temper. "You would either have run away and Helen would have been heartbroken, or you would have stirred up all kinds of trouble with our neighbors."

"Right. The warm and welcoming neighbors."

"I'm not going to blow up my community for a woman who's just passing through."

As soon as he said the words, Nick wished desperately that he could take them back.

It wouldn't have mattered because Lucy was already gone. She stormed past him, pausing only to shove her feet into her shoes before she was out the door.

Nick waited a few minutes, cursing his headache and himself and this entire crap day, but he didn't hear Lucy's car door or the engine starting.

Telling himself she was taking a walk to cool down, he went in the bathroom and took the strongest stuff he could find for his headache. Then he drank an entire glass of water with it because he'd been busy all day and there was a possibility dehydration was partly responsible for the throbbing temples.

Then he sat on the couch, resting his head against the back, and closed his eyes to wait for Lucy to return while he replayed the situation over and over in his mind.

Two hours later, Nick found her sitting at the end of the small dock that extended into the water a little way down the shore from the cottage's property line. Technically, it belonged to the neighbors, and it probably should have been used for bonfire kindling years ago.

Lucy's knees were drawn up, with her heels resting on the edge of the dock and her arms wrapped around her legs. Her chin rested on her knees, and she didn't seem to mind the wind pulling wisps of her hair free from its bun as she stared over the open water. And a thick blue cardigan he recognized as Helen's was keeping her warm.

She wasn't wearing his sweatshirt.

The dock swayed slightly as he walked down the length, trying to avoid the boards that looked most at risk for caving in under his weight. And he cringed as he gingerly sat down next to her, letting his legs dangle over the edge, afraid both of them were about to end up in the water.

"I'm sorry, Lucy."

She didn't look at him, or even move. "How could you keep something so big to yourself? How could you know I have a sister right across town and not tell me?"

"I didn't *know* Taylor is your sister. What I *knew* was I've heard years of whispers and hints about Iris Macauley. And yes, I heard some whispers about Iris and Jack, but whispers and facts are two different things."

"But you knew they were all talking about it again—talking about *me*—and you just let me go around Wayward Harbor and talk to people with no idea what they were saying as soon as I left the room."

"I should have told you," he said. "I absolutely should have told you, and I'm sorry I didn't."

"But *why* didn't you? You can't say it was because you were protecting the community from the woman just passing through because they were already all up in it. I was the only one in the dark."

"When you came here, you were hiding. You were hiding from all the awful stuff people were saying about you, as anybody would. And it took you a little bit, but you came out from under the blankets. You were reclaiming yourself. You were enjoying Wayward Harbor and making friends, and I was afraid if you knew some of them were gossiping about you—about something so big—it wouldn't feel safe to you anymore and you'd go back under the blankets."

After what felt to Nick like a lifetime of silence, Lucy let go of her legs and let them dangle off the edge next to his. Shoving her windblown hair out of her face, she turned to face him.

"I guess I can understand that," she said softly.

"I'm still sorry. No matter why I did it, it was wrong."

"I appreciate you saying that." She sighed, looking back toward the horizon. "I made Gran cry."

"You *made* her cry? Or did she happen to cry during a highly emotional conversation with her upset granddaughter?"

She smiled. "You know, you're very kind under that grumpy exterior. Your brothers are lucky to have you."

"You have me, too," he said, and the words fell heavy between them, clunky and undefined. He didn't know exactly how he meant them, and he was afraid of how she'd take them. "I'm almost as good a friend as I am a brother."

Lucy gave him a weak smile, but those words didn't feel right to him, either. Were they friends? Were they something else? If Miami wasn't in her future, would he be a part of it?

"I'm just a woman passing through," she reminded him.

"I didn't mean that. You're a lot more than that."

"Not really. I *am* just passing through, even if it's taking me a long time to actually do it."

The thought of Lucy leaving Wayward Harbor made his stomach hurt, and it threatened to resurrect the fading headache, so he shoved it out of his mind. He definitely didn't want to think about why that bothered him so much.

"What are you going to do?" he asked softly.

"I *won't* be hiding under the blankets again. I don't know if I'm toughening up or if spring is finally doing its spring thing here, but I got too hot under there." She laughed. "As for having a sister… I don't know how that works. We'll do a test to make sure, I guess. And then, I'd like to have a sister, I think."

"It's good to have siblings. Even the ones I got stuck with."

"I'm not sure how that works, considering everybody in Wayward Harbor will know, and Kim Perkins keeps trying to set me on fire with her eyeballs even *before* Taylor talked to me."

"Let Taylor navigate her mother," he suggested. "You just hold your head up and keep doing what you've been doing because you haven't done a single thing wrong."

She smiled then—a genuine one—and the knot in his chest loosened. "Do you think that pizza place would deliver a Hawaiian pizza?"

That was too far. "No. Lucy, I know I owe you, but I can't do pineapple on a pizza."

"It's apology pizza. You kind of have to."

"How about half pepperoni and half Hawaiian. And I'll buy, including the delivery fee."

"Okay. Assuming we both make it off this dock without it collapsing and drowning us, you're forgiven."

Chapter Twelve

Whoever took my wooden cow from the end of my driveway on Windward Avenue, please bring it back. No questions asked.

First comment: Is there a reward?

Original poster: The reward of being a good neighbor.

Second comment: There's a wooden cow on the roof of the police station. I don't think it was there yesterday? Maybe it's yours?

Original poster: I doubt there are multiple wooden cows.

Third comment: Get there fast before it starts moo-ving around.

Fourth comment: How do I delete this app?

Original poster: That isn't the search bar, Colleen.

—Wayward Harbor Online Community Group

"I think maybe your head is on crooked."

Lucy laughed, even though Nick's tone implied he might not have been totally joking. "That looks straight to me."

He sighed, dropping his forehead to the piece of deck railing he was holding in place. "If you'd just go get the level out of my truck, that would be great."

"Fine. What does it look like?"

The growl that rumbled out of him would have driven bears back into hibernation. "It… I don't know. It looks like a level. A long wooden tool with windows in it, and air bubbles that you set between the lines to see if something's level when your helper's head is crooked and she wouldn't know straight if it bit her in the ass."

"I should start a union and invite your brothers to join," Lucy called over her shoulder as she walked around the cottage to Nick's truck.

She had no trouble finding the level because of course she knew what it looked like. She just really liked the sounds Nick made when he was thoroughly exasperated with her.

It had been three weeks since the day Taylor sought her out at the Scuttlebutt, and so much had changed.

She was only working Friday through Sunday at the Keel now. Billy had been cleared to work the bar again, and though there were already tourists in town, it wouldn't be busy enough for two of them until school let out. Of course, Nicole—the teacher—would be available by then, and it would be almost time for Gran to come home. But for now, she was working weekends at the Keel and helping Nick with the deck after his regular workday was over during the week.

And she might have a sister. Taylor had gotten a sibling DNA test with mail-in cheek swabs and stopped by the cottage on her lunch break. Now all they could do was wait for the results that would tell them if they were undeniably sisters. It would be a crushing blow if the results had been negative, since they'd already developed quite the text history by talking every day and learning everything they could about each other in a way that nobody could see.

She learned that, assuming the test was positive, she'd have a brother-in-law soon, and also—though it was early days to be talking about it—become an aunt. Taylor's fiancé, Carson, managed the bank next to the post office, where Taylor worked. It was hard building a relationship in secret, but it was worth the effort.

Walking back around the house with the level, she chuckled when she remembered the last text message from Taylor.

If Carson and I have a Halloween wedding, you can come in a costume and my mother will never even know you were there.

"What's so funny?" Nick asked when she handed him the level, so she told him about the text from her sister while he set the level along the railing and peered at the bubble.

"Not making any progress with Kim, I gather?"

"I'm not sure she's even told her mom she talked to me yet, and I can't really blame her. It's going to be a mess, and she's already got a wedding to plan and a baby on the way."

When Nick's head whipped around, Lucy realized her mistake and clapped her hand over her mouth. "Dammit. I'm not good at being a sister yet."

"I won't tell a soul," he promised, and she believed him.

"I talked to Gran earlier," she said, changing the subject.

"Come over here and hold the level, please. How's Helen doing?"

"Great. She's gotten a lot of sun. Or it could just be the joy radiating off of her. It's hard to tell through a phone screen." Lucy took over holding the level while Nick grabbed his drill and stuck a screw on the end of the magnetic tip. "She offered to cut her time in South Carolina short so she can be home by my birthday, but I know one of the reasons she was staying down there was her friend's fiftieth wedding anniversary, and she was the maid of honor. I told her we'd grab a cake from Willow when she gets home."

He pressed the tip of the screw against the wood. "Is that level?"

"Looks it."

She was rewarded with another exasperated sigh. "Is the bubble in the center of the sight?"

"Yes." She turned her face away while he put the first screw in. "Did I ever tell you my mother's first husband—the one whose last name I got—made extra cash by stealing tools?"

"Um. No."

"Yeah. One of them was a level—a small torpedo level if you want to get all builder technical vocab about it—and Iris said I spent an entire day seeing if anything in the apartment was level before he threw it back in the box to take to the pawn shop."

He snorted. "So you're tormenting me *why*?"

"For my own amusement, mostly. It's fun when you're grumpy."

"*Anyway*, it was kind of you to delay your birthday for Helen, considering it's a big milestone for you."

"Thirty. Yay." She laughed. "I don't mind turning thirty, to be honest, but I think being married fifty years is a much bigger deal. And so many of her friends have moved south where it's warmer—and who could blame them—but she must really miss them. Also, my birthday is in two days, and I'd rather she not be racing to get here in time."

"Is that still level?" he asked as he prepped another screw.

"Dead center," she confirmed.

When he bent to drive the screw in, Nick was so close to her, Lucy's body tingled with the awareness if she just leaned a little to one side, they'd be touching.

She didn't because she knew just enough about building

things to know you didn't startle a man running a power tool, but she wanted to.

Nick hadn't tried to kiss her again since the night he'd finished the smaller bedroom and given her the tree that, outside of her notebook, was probably her most prized possession. And she hadn't tried to kiss him.

But judging by how often she caught him looking at her, his gaze dropping to her mouth, he thought about it a lot. Maybe even as much as she thought about it.

Things were so good between them, though, that she was afraid to reach for more. If things blew up between them, she'd have to leave. She'd promised Gran she wouldn't leave Wayward Harbor before she got home, but she certainly couldn't stay with her sister without blowing up Taylor's life. She knew Willow would take her in, but it would be hard in the studio apartment she'd made over the bakery.

"You can let go of that, you know."

Startled out of her thoughts, Lucy realized Nick had not only finished fastening the railing, but he was about five feet away. She laughed and stood, stretching her back.

"I just wanted to make sure your workmanship would hold up," she teased.

"My work speaks for itself," he said, and then he looked up at the sky. "It's going to rain soon, so I guess it's time to quit for the night."

"Do you think it'll be done before Gran gets home?"

"It'll be done," he said, but his jaw was tight again.

As she helped gather up the tools they'd managed to strew around the entire backyard, Lucy wondered what had triggered his inner grump again. He had to know Gran wouldn't care if the deck wasn't totally finished when she got back.

But then she caught him watching her from across the yard, seriousness of his mood apparent in his expression and the way he held his body. Once Helen came home, there would be no place for Nick here.

Lucy wanted to see her grandmother so badly. She wanted that squeeze hug, and she imagined them sitting on the porch wrapped in blankets, catching up on everything that had happened while they were apart.

Now the reality set in that, when that happened, this would end. Nick wouldn't be the first person she saw in the morning and the last person she spoke to before bed anymore.

Was Nick just wondering where he was going to sleep once Helen returned, and going through lists of people with comfortable couches? Or was he also remembering this life they'd made together was only temporary?

And the clock was ticking.

Nick had gotten three weeks of blessed peace, not having to keep a secret from Lucy anymore. And now here he was, keeping another one.

On Saturday, Beck and the kids had moved back into their own house. Nick could have gone home two days ago, but he'd said nothing about it to Lucy.

Nick didn't want to go.

He knew he'd have to soon. Helen would be home in less than two weeks, if everything stayed according to plan, and she was going to want to sleep in her own bed. Short of sleeping on the couch, which would be uncomfortable and also very hard to explain, he'd have to go home.

While it would be nice in a lot of ways, especially considering his mattress was a lot firmer than Helen's, he was going to miss this. He would miss this bubble he and Lucy had been living in together, and he couldn't bring himself to pop it.

They made it inside mere moments before the sky released a deluge of rain, and Nick left his tools by the door. He'd put them back in his truck later, though he pulled the battery from his drill to recharge.

Since the rain derailed their plans for the grill, they made BLTs for supper, cheating and using precooked microwave bacon. They both loved bacon, but they also both hated cleaning up bacon grease, so he hadn't protested when she brought it home from the market. It wasn't bacon like Pete made it, but it got the job done.

"We really need to get started on that shenanigans list," Lucy announced while they were eating, and he glanced at the note on the fridge.

Sunrise on Cadillac Mountain.
Go out on a boat.
Visit Dinghy Doodads.
Play football on the beach.

"When did we decide we want to play football on the beach? And I use *we* lightly because that's definitely not a shenanigan I've wanted to get up to. It's a good way to mess up an ankle. Or a knee."

"I want to see you throw a football."

"I wasn't a quarterback."

She rolled her eyes. "Even I know you still spent a lot of time throwing footballs, especially when you were growing up."

"And you were just overcome by a need to play catch on the beach?"

"The list looked sad with only three things on it, so I came up with a fourth thing."

He sighed, shaking his head. "See, to me, it would make more sense to check off at least one of the preexisting items before adding to it."

"Okay. Which one are we doing first?"

He'd walked right into that one. "Unfortunately, neither one is easy. For one thing, I don't own a boat."

"I bet you know people who have a boat."

"Of course I do, but borrowing a boat isn't a small ask."

"Okay, so Cadillac Mountain. Let's do that one."

An image of the two of them—sitting with his arm around her, wrapped in a blanket—watching the sun come up flashed through his mind, filling Nick with a want he hadn't felt in a very long time. "Well, we're in season now, so we'd have to get a reservation. And we'd have to hope the weather was good. And, also, we'd have to leave here at like two in the morning."

"Okay." When he gave her a skeptical look, she held up her hands. "I may not have been here very long, but I've learned that it's best to do things midweek, when tourists are at a minimum. So, like a Wednesday. You take the day off and we'll go to bed early, or at least try to nap until two in the morning. And we'll go do it."

"It's not that easy."

"It's not going to get easier, so we'll just figure it out."

"I can't take a day off like that."

"Nick." She so rarely used a sharp tone like that, he almost dropped his water glass. "You *can* just take a day off because your brothers are fully capable of working for one day without your presence."

She was right, of course, but he couldn't make himself admit it out loud. Keeping Slater & Sons going and making sure his brothers would have that steady work and steady income had been his driving force since their father passed away. He'd relaxed once and his mother had gotten sick. It had been even harder to get them back on track and keep them there when she passed.

Nick wasn't sure what he had left if he set that baggage down.

"I'll look into it," he muttered.

"I will nag you incessantly about it until you make a reservation," she said, and the way he believed her made him laugh. "And I *will* keep adding to that list."

He pushed back from the table so fast, his chair almost fell over. Lucy's eyes widened, but then they narrowed when he picked up the Sharpie from the counter and added an item to their shenanigans list.

Lucy: try a bologna and tomato sandwich.

He put the lid back on the Sharpie with a snap and sat back down while she laughed, shaking her head. "Don't forget I can add to the list, too."

The next morning, he pulled up at the jobsite and was thrilled to see his brothers weren't loitering around their trucks, waiting for him. They were in the final push now, dealing with a lot of fine details, and the sooner they could schedule the final walk-through with the homeowner, the sooner the company could deposit a really fat check.

Gray was the first brother he ran into. He was in the family room, marking a spot on a window with a small piece of blue painter's tape. Since Gray had the most critical eye, he was always the one who went through rooms they'd finished with, looking for flaws. The more things they could address before the walk-through, the fewer things the homeowner could add to the punch list. And until the punch list was addressed, the money would be withheld.

"There's some adhesive left on this pane of glass," Gray explained when Beck walked in.

"And you wonder why you always get picked for this job. You're the only one who'll nitpick the hell out of us."

Gray snorted. "When you pay this much for a view of the water, you don't want to look through gunk leftover from a factory sticker."

"Trust me, I know you're a big reason why we have so many stars on our online reviews."

"Kind of surprised you haven't moved back in yet," Gray said casually, but Nick knew he was fishing by the extra nonchalant way he said it.

Luckily, he'd realized during the drive over this subject would come up, so he was prepared. "I thought about it, but I'm still finishing up that deck, and there's no reason to add driving back and forth to an already long day."

It was a logical—and actually true—explanation, but Gray didn't look convinced. "Got nothing to do with Lucy, huh?"

"What part of it being easier to work on a place in my spare time if my spare time is spent at that place is hard to get?"

Gray only nodded, but Nick could see by the quirk of his lips he wasn't totally buying it. Beck or Theo might have pushed back, but Gray seemed content to let the subject drop for now.

Nick knew they'd talk about him the first time they were together without him, though. And if he cracked at all—gave them even a glimpse of the turmoil that was growing inside of him with every day that passed—he'd never hear the end of it.

So he'd do what he always did. He'd keep his emotions to himself and do his job. And when Helen Griffin came home and he left the cottage, and then Lucy moved on to Miami, nobody would ever guess he'd had his heart broken.

Chapter Thirteen

Now that ice cream season is in full swing, a reminder that Dolly's vet says she shouldn't have ice cream, no matter how much she begs or tries to fight for yours—beware those claws. If Dolly wants to join you, please let us know and we'll provide a little bit of frozen plain yogurt for her to enjoy.

–Schooner Scoops in Wayward Harbor Online Community Group

Lucy shuffled out of her bedroom before seven the next morning, rubbing her face because she did *not* want to be out of bed yet. She was rewarded with a chuckle from Nick. He was leaning against the counter, fully dressed and ready for work, while he finished off his coffee.

"Did you have a bad dream?" he asked. "Like maybe you were battling somebody and woke up all twisted in blankets?"

"I know what I look like, thank you." She also didn't care. "I got a text, and my brain went straight to something being wrong with Gran."

He straightened "Is she okay?"

"Yeah." She poured coffee into a mug. "It was Taylor, but that burst of fear woke me right up and I couldn't go back to sleep."

"Kinda early for conversational texts."

She took a sip of the coffee and sighed. “Right? I usually use the Do Not Disturb stuff on my phone so I’m not used to being woken up by texts, but I turned that off because Gran’s running amok and I have a little anxiety about it.”

“Understandable. I have mine set so my brothers can call me if they need me, but Theo can’t wake me up sharing memes he thinks are hilarious. And Beck sends a lot of pictures of the kids, and I treasure them, but they can wait until I’ve had coffee.”

“I guess she wanted to text me before she left for work, but she wants me to go to the bank at eleven thirty.”

Nick chuckled, and then turned to wash out his empty cup. “That doesn’t sound suspicious at all. Maybe it’s a heist, and she’s going to seduce Carson into opening the vault and then have you run out with the money while she distracts him.”

Thankfully, Lucy had swallowed her mouthful of coffee or she might have spit it out. “I think you watch too many movies.”

“You think she got the results?”

“Probably. I’m afraid it’s bad news because why wouldn’t she just forward me the email or send me a text?”

Nick looked at the clock on the stove and winced. “Maybe it’s not even the results. Try not to worry about it all morning.”

“I’ll try not to. And you should go. I know you hate to be late.”

He nodded and started for the door, but then he turned back. “Let me know, okay?”

“I will,” she promised, and the concern in his eyes warmed her as much as the coffee. It was nice having somebody care enough to want her to check in.

A few hours later, Lucy walked into the bank with her stomach in knots. Over the course of the morning, she’d managed to convince herself this *had* to be about the DNA test results. And until she actually faced the possibility Taylor wasn't her sister, she hadn't realized how desperately she wanted her to be.

A man was standing near the center island, where people could fill out deposit slips and such. He was wearing a shirt and tie, and his dark hair was cut very short. A perfect banker type, she thought as he stepped toward her and extended his hand. "I'm Carson. Let's go to my office."

There were two offices separated from the lobby, but they had massive glass windows, so they weren't exactly private. But Carson led her down a short hallway and up a flight of stairs to a longer hallway. At the end, on the right, a heavy wooden door stood open.

"My office," he told her, gesturing for her to go ahead. "Sorry for the subterfuge, but Taylor's lunch breaks are short and she didn't want to wait until after work."

"People are going to think I bounced a really large check," she said, and he laughed. "It's nice to meet you, though."

"The door we just passed is a storage room, and I'm going to go rifle through some ancient boxes to give you some privacy." He smiled sheepishly. "I'd go downstairs, but I can't come up with a good explanation for leaving you alone in my office."

"Don't people know Taylor's up here?" Maybe none of them were as sneaky as they thought.

"I let her in the back door. I do it all the time if she comes over for lunch, and honestly I don't think anybody saw her. They'd have to check the cameras."

Taylor poked her head out into the hall. "I don't have much time."

Carson blew her a kiss, which was adorable, and then turned back toward the storage room. As soon as Lucy was in his office, Taylor closed the door behind her. "The results are in my email."

Lucy's pulse quickened and tears threatened, even though it wasn't time for them yet. "What do they say?"

"I don't know. I wasn't going to read it without you."

"How did you not even peek for *hours*? I don't think I could have resisted."

"It was hard, but…I'm a little scared." Taylor looked at her, with her face and hair that were like Lucy's, and yet not. "No matter what this says, we can still be sisters, you know."

The tears couldn't be contained as Lucy nodded. "Sisters, no matter what."

After they both took deep breaths, Taylor unlocked her phone. They stood with their shoulders pressed together so they could both see the screen as the email opened.

A moment later, the tears ran unchecked as they held each other in the middle of Carson's office. They were officially sisters—forever bound by a man Taylor had loved and lost, and whom Lucy had never known at all.

"I knew it as soon as I met you," Taylor said once they'd taken a minute to breathe and put a serious dent in the box of tissues on Carson's desk.

"When I left Las Vegas, I didn't feel like I had anybody," Lucy said. She'd even felt abandoned by her mother. "And now I have Gran back in my life and I have a sister."

And Nick. She had Nick, too.

"Forever," Taylor whispered. "No matter what. And hopefully we'll be able to tell people someday."

Their laughter put an end to the lingering tears, and by the time Carson knocked on the door and stuck his head in, their eyes were dry. Maybe a little puffy, but they were all smiles.

"From stranger to future sister-in-law," Carson said after they'd broken the news. He gave her a quick awkward hug before giving them a chagrined look. "I hate to break up the party, but I have to resolve an issue downstairs so this meeting has to be cut short."

Lucy laughed and gave her eyes a final swipe with a fresh tissue. "Can you tell I've been crying? They're going to think I bounced a *really* big check."

"Unfortunately, you won't be the first person to leave my office having cried. At least these are happy tears."

After giving her official sister a final hug, Lucy followed Carson down the hallway. She couldn't wait to tell Nick, and she paused before the first step to send him a quick text message.

I have a sister!

He was working and probably wouldn't respond immediately, so she slid her phone into her back pocket and followed Carson into the lobby. He turned to shake her hand, and over his shoulder she saw Nick talking to the teller behind the counter. He gave her a quick smile and, after a few words to the teller, turned to leave.

Lucy finished saying goodbye to Taylor's fiancé, trying to keep up the appearance they were wrapping up some kind of banking-related meeting, and then she went after Nick.

He was waiting for her on the sidewalk, leaning against the brick wall. "Congratulations."

"I'm so happy right now." She held up her hands. "What are you doing here, though?"

"Well, it's my bank. And the company's bank. I come here a lot, actually. They always have good candy in the dishes and not just cheap lollipops." He shrugged. "And I've been worrying about you all morning, so I figured I'd show up so we could either get ice cream to cheer you up or to celebrate. And this is great because celebratory ice cream tastes better than consolation ice cream."

It was a good thing Lucy was cried out, so she was able to smile and nod without blubbering into his shirt in public. "That's science. And when I passed Schooner Scoops while looking for parking, it might have triggered an ice cream craving."

"Let's go, then," he said, and then he chuckled. "You really are a sucker for nautical puns."

By the time Nick gave up on what he was looking for, the garage and the shed were trashed, and he'd done a pretty good job tossing the basement, too. But he'd come up empty.

How was it possible his life now included living in a house with no footballs in it?

Sure, there were several plastic bins of football memorabilia in the basement, including at least three game balls he could think of off the top of his head. A touchdown he'd run in to win the Maine Shrine Lobster Bowl Classic his senior year of high school. His first college touchdown. The ball he'd run into the endzone in a college championship. But they were older now and probably wouldn't be holding air worth a damn.

Also, he didn't want to open those bins. He hadn't been able to throw the memories away, and he never would. But after his mom's cancer was diagnosed, putting his football history away had been one of his personal stages of grief. His family had said nothing, but he'd seen the sorrow and guilt they felt, so he tried to pretend it wasn't a big deal. It had been, though. He couldn't look at it all anymore—the reminders of how long and hard he'd worked to be mere months from achieving his goal—and closing those bins had been a way of accepting that football was over for him.

But lately he'd been itching to hold a ball again, and it was 100 percent Lucy's fault.

It wasn't as if he'd totally avoided football. He watched the Patriots with his brothers or friends at the Keel, and there would be jokes made. People still liked to reminisce with him about some big play he made back in the day. Football was a part of life.

But with Lucy, it had been different. His brothers occasionally made jokes about it as if it was just something he'd done when he was younger, like Beck's unfortunate but blessedly brief electric guitar phase. They didn't seem to acknowledge—or didn't want to face—that Nick had given up a part of himself. A lot of other people talked about what plays had meant to *them*. Nick had never talked to anybody about what football had meant to *him*.

And then she'd gone and added playing football on the beach to their shenanigans list.

The first thing he'd done after parting ways with Lucy once they'd finished their ice cream—including a little treat for Dolly, who joined them while they were ordering—was send a text to his brothers letting them know something came up and he was taking the afternoon off. Gray and Beck just hit the thumbs-up reaction to the text, but Theo wanted to know if he was sick. Or maybe possibly dying because Nick *never* blew off work. Nick just said something had come up that he had to take care of.

That something turned out to be driving three towns over to buy a football. And then driving back to the cottage, where Lucy was standing on a kitchen chair, washing the top of the refrigerator.

"Didn't you do that last week?" he asked, stepping out of his boots by the door.

"I'm bored and I have way too much energy after finding

out I have a sister and then eating ice cream. But everything's clean, and I don't know what enough flowers are to work in the garden. And why aren't you at work? Again."

"We're going to go burn through some of that energy." When she stopped wiping and looked at him with arched eyebrows, he rubbed the back of his neck. "Do you have sweatpants and sneakers?"

"I have leggings and sneakers." Did she sound a little disappointed the burning of energy required clothing, or was that his imagination?

"We're going to the beach, but not in the water."

He thought she'd ask a million more questions, but she jumped off the chair and returned it to its spot before disappearing into her room. He changed into a clean T-shirt and navy sweats—good ones with a strong drawstring this time—before putting his sneakers on.

"Uh-oh," she said when she emerged from her bedroom. "If you're wearing sneakers, we're doing something athletic because you wear your boots for *everything.* Have I mentioned I'm not very good at sports?"

He snorted, and then looked over her outfit. The leggings clinging to her long legs were distracting, but the long crewneck sweatshirt and sneakers would work. Her hair was in a thick, curly ponytail, and it looked as if she'd just put a fresh coat of sunscreen on her face.

"Grab a couple water bottles and let's go," he told her.

It took almost twenty minutes to drive the network of back roads to get to the tiny slice of secluded beach he'd chosen. It had more sand than rocks, and it wasn't on the tourists' radar. With a few days left of school and it being work hours, he'd hoped they'd be alone and he'd gotten lucky.

After grabbing the water bottles, Lucy hopped out of the truck and immediately headed for the shoreline. Nick opened the back door of the truck and grabbed the football. It felt good to have a ball in his hand again, and when she turned back to see what was taking him so long, she caught him smiling.

"Why are you grinning like that?" she demanded. "You look like a man keeping a juicy secret. Wait, are you hiding something behind your back? It better not be a fishing pole, Nick."

He was actually keeping a couple of secrets, but he shook his head and showed her the football. She actually bounced a few times on her toes, clapping her hands.

Then he tossed the ball to her, and she put her hands over her eyes as the ball sailed past her.

"This is going to be a short game," he said as she ran after it.

"No, I can do this!" she called back. "I wasn't ready."

Nick wasn't sure what ready looked like for Lucy, because an hour later, she'd managed to catch barely half the passes he threw to her. Of course, his reception rate wasn't much higher, but that was because she had the aim of a blindfolded drunk.

When she started to look less like she was having fun and more like she was discouraged, he lobbed an easy one to her. She caught it easily, and then started running toward him. Because they didn't have flags to grab—he hadn't thought full-contact tackling was a good idea—they'd decided on a rule that if the defender was able to touch the ball, it counted as a tackle.

"What is it they yell on the TV when somebody runs?" she said as she ran across the sand, determined to get by him this time. "She. Might. Go. All. The. Way."

Laughing, Nick reached out and easily slapped the ball. It slipped out of her grasp and hit the sand, so he scooped it up. "Fumble!"

He tucked the ball securely in his arm and ran, the muscle memory kicking in as though it had been days and not years since he'd played the game. It felt good, but when he reached the driftwood marking the goal line and turned, Lucy was still standing at the spot of the fumble recovery, hands on her hips.

She was clearly peeved. “You could let me have a little win here and there, you know.”

He grinned, tossing the ball up in the air and catching it easily in one hand. “Is there anything about me that made you think I wouldn’t be competitive when it comes to football? You’re the one who wanted to play against the former golden boy of Wayward Harbor.”

She blew at a wisp of hair in her face. “Fine. Throw it again. I’m going to get a point, dammit.”

Laughing, he tossed her the ball again, putting it right into her hands. She didn’t try to tuck it under her arm this time, but just ran straight toward him. He started toward her, but before he could reach out for the ball, she stuffed it under her sweatshirt and crossed her arms over the fabric to keep it from falling out.

“You can’t touch it now!” she said, trying to fake to her right to get past him.

“Penalty,” he said, and then he wrapped his arms around her and tackled her to the ground, ball and all.

He twisted as they went down, so his back took the brunt of the impact. There were enough rocks mixed in with the sand so he knew he’d have a few bruises to show for it, but he didn’t care. Lucy in his arms, laughing so hard she couldn’t escape him, was worth a few black and blue marks.

“You cheated,” she squealed, trying to wrangle the ball that was trapped under her sweatshirt.

“No, *you* cheated.”

“I never heard any rule banning me from putting the ball under my shirt,” she argued, smiling down at him. Her entire body was pressed along the length of his, but she shifted so one of her knees was in the sand. “But there was definitely a no tackling rule.”

They were both smiling and slightly breathless, and her sun-kissed cheeks were pink with exertion. He brushed a wisp of hair back from her face, and her gaze softened, dropping to his mouth.

Then she lowered her head, and everything but the need to kiss her faded away. Her lips were gentle, almost tentative, but he cupped the back of her neck and let her feel every bit of the hunger he'd suffered since the last time he'd kissed her. She moaned against his mouth, the delicious weight of her body relaxing onto him.

Letting go of her neck, he slid his hands under the sweatshirt, skimming over the warm skin of her back. His right hand brushed the football, and he closed his hand around it, while the other stroked her back. His fingertips ran over the closure of her bra strap, and his body tightened as he imagined freeing her breasts. Pulling her sweatshirt up and—

She pulled back, resting her cheek against his for a moment before lifting her head so she could look down at him. "There might be people in those houses. They might be looking out their windows."

"I got caught making out with a girl on this very beach when I was sixteen. The lady who lives in that blue house down to the left? She called the police, and the chief followed me home so he could tell my parents all about it. I don't recommend it."

She laughed. "And even I know there's no second base in football, Nick."

He grinned and tightened his fingers around the ball, his fingertips denting the leather, before yanking it free of her sweatshirt. She gasped and tried to reach for it, but he held it just beyond her reach.

"Interception," he said, and then he kissed her again—hard and fast—before rolling out from under her and pushing to his feet, the football secured.

Chapter Fourteen

Reminder: Any parking signs reading Reserved For Locals Only are neither sanctioned by the town nor enforceable. Any person caught installing one of these signs in any manner will be subject to fines and/or arrest.

—Callie Devens, Town Manager

It's not worth the risk because tourists ignore them, anyway. —Harold Rollins, Chief of Police

—Wayward Harbor Online Community Group

The next day, Nick got home a half hour after Lucy expected him and told her to put her shoes on. While she had no idea what was going on, she was always up for going somewhere.

"Where are we going?"

"Errands," he said. "You can help me carry stuff."

Not exactly the most fun activity to celebrate turning thirty, but Lucy was pretty sure Nick had forgotten. That was fine, since she was putting off cake until Gran got home, and when you reached a certain age, cake was really the only thing worth celebrating. Gran had sent her a text message early that morning, wishing her a happy birthday, and she'd gotten a funny video from Sydney, singing the song to her with the Miami skyline in the background.

She hadn't heard from Iris, but she rarely did on her birthdays.

Lucy was confused when he drove by the hardware store, and then the market. She wondered briefly if he was going to surprise her with the boat trip she'd put on their shenanigans list, but she trusted he would have warned her to dress warmer and to secure her hair a little better. It was always windy on the water, according to Billy.

"No, really, where are we going?" she asked when she couldn't stand it anymore. "It's not outside, like yesterday, is it?"

"You're the one who wanted to play football on the beach."

She sighed. "I really thought that would be more fun."

"It *can* be more fun, if you have actual teams and play actual football, with hitting each other and everything. What we played was a glorified game of catch until you tripped and threw my football in the water and wouldn't go get it."

"You still crossed it off the list," she pointed out. "And I thought the waves would wash the ball back to shore."

"Eventually, but you've got a pretty good arm on you when you're in the process of falling on your face."

Lucy laughed. "You had a good time and you know it."

He smiled, and she knew he was thinking about that kiss. "I did."

"So did I, but where are we going now?"

"We just have to run by the scone shop really quick."

"It's more fun if you call it the Scuttlebutt. Also, Willow closes at two, Nick."

"Yeah." He cleared his throat. "She hid a check under the mat for me. A deposit for some work she needs done."

"She could have given it to me when I was here earlier *today*." It made no sense to her that it hadn't even come up in conversation, considering Willow knew she lived with the man. "And leaving a check under a mat is weird."

"Small towns are like that," Nick muttered. "We can grab it easy enough."

"We? It's going to take both of us to get a check from under a mat?"

"It's a nice night. Actually, I'm just going to park here and we can walk. It's easier."

Lucy wasn't sure why it was easier to park down and across the street and walk rather than parking right across from the building, but she didn't care enough to push. And then, when she was climbing down out of the truck, she almost fell on her face when Nick accidentally laid on the horn with his elbow while getting out his side.

"Are you okay?" she asked when she reached him at the curb. "You're acting odd tonight."

"Sure."

"Sure you're okay or sure you're acting odd?"

He shrugged. "Two things can be true at the same time."

They were almost to the Scuttlebutt when the inside of the bakery lit up and she saw Willow and Mattie grinning in the window, holding up a sign that said Lucy's the Big 3-0! Happy Birthday! in huge letters.

Lucy laughed and shoved at Nick's arm. "What did you do?"

"I'm just an accomplice whose only job was to get you here without giving away the surprise. If they'd known how bad I am at lying, though, they might have fired me."

"Or at least given you a script," she teased. "A check under the mat?"

"Hey, I got you here," he reminded her as he pushed open the door.

Immediately, Lucy was pulled into a round of hugs. Willow first, and then Mattie. And then Willow again.

"Aren't you supposed to be at work?" she asked Mattie.

Mattie shrugged. "It's Wednesday night. Billy said he'd cover me for an hour and to tell you happy birthday even though you didn't tell anybody. And Sasha is bummed she couldn't be here, but Billy can't cook worth a damn. She said we'll have ice cream after close the next time you're in."

"Okay, Nick. You're up again," Willow said, gesturing toward a mound of fabric on one of the tables.

Lucy watched Nick lift the cute valances down from their brackets so the windows were bare. And then he replaced each one with long drapes pre-hung on different curtain rods. They blocked out the daylight, and the bakery's soft lighting and the fairy lights hung around the crown molding gave the place a festive air.

Lucy looked at Willow, confused. "I'm almost afraid to ask what we'll be doing that we don't want anybody to be able to see."

In answer, Willow turned to the door to the kitchen. "All clear!"

The door opened and Taylor burst through, a huge grin lighting up her face. "Surprise!"

Carson was with her, and Lucy got a little weepy as Taylor pulled her in for a hug. She'd had friends who were up for going out for drinks with her on her birthday, but she couldn't remember the last time she'd had a proper birthday party. With actual friends.

And her sister.

"I'm going to get the cake," Willow said. "I hope everybody's ready to sing."

"Oh no," Carson whispered, and everybody laughed.

"Back when we were in school, Carson was always just asked to mouth the words when we'd sing for the Christmas program," Taylor explained.

Carson's face was a vivid red, but he was grinning. "I did

karaoke once at the Keel because I lost a bet, and Billy had to comp everybody a drink to keep them from walking out."

"You can sing as loud as you want because it's my party," Lucy said. "I have to ask, though, what song did you sing at karaoke?"

"That Titanic song by Celine Dion," he said. "'My Heart Will Go On.'"

"Ouch. *Really?*"

"Again, I lost a bet."

"I guess it's better than having to shave your head."

Carson and Taylor shook their heads in unison, making her laugh. Then Carson asked Nick how business was and they started a side conversation while Taylor moved closer to Lucy.

"I know covering the windows was silly, but I hope it's okay," Taylor said. "We could have had the party on the deck at the Keel, but…you know. I know I'm a grown woman and it's ridiculous, but she *is* my mom, and rubbing a celebration of your birth in her face seemed like a step too far."

"I get it, and I'm just glad you're here. Plus, if we were at the Keel, Lavinia couldn't come and I'd be down three guests."

Maybe the thumping noise was Nick shifting the chairs so Willow would be able to set down the cake, but that wouldn't explain why they all looked down at the floor.

"Sorry, Jacob," Lucy yelled toward her feet, just in case. "Down *four* guests."

"Okay, everybody," Willow said as she pushed through the door with the cake in her hand. In the center was a single candle that looked like a chunky thirty, and the flame flickered as she started to sing.

They all sang, even Carson, who was a truly awful singer. But he sang with enthusiasm and Lucy loved it. Nick, she noticed, had a rather nice voice. He might not have made it as a professional, but she'd bet he'd be a hit at karaoke.

She wondered what song he'd sing.

"Okay, make a wish and blow out your candle," Willow told her when the singing was over.

Lucy's birthday wish was easy—and thankfully a secret because it involved her and Nick and zero clothes. She leaned close to the cake and inhaled deeply.

But before she could blow, the candle went out.

"Must be a draft," Mattie said as she took a lighter from Willow and relit it.

Lucy made her wish and was drawing in another breath when the candle went out again. She laughed and looked at Willow. "Does this seem more like Lavinia or Jacob to you?"

"Definitely Lavinia. Jacob likes to stomp up and down the stairs and clink glass bottles in the cellar, but he doesn't really come upstairs. Lavinia, though? She likes to be a part of things."

"So do you think she doesn't like my wish?" Lucy asked. "Does she want to be part of the fun or does she not like open flames?"

"Or there's a draft," Nick muttered.

Lucy waved a hand at him. "Don't be grumpy."

He snorted. "At this point, I'm not even sure what you think grumpy means."

"Well, I tried to look it up in the dictionary, but it was just a picture of you," she shot back, and everybody groaned. Possibly even Lavinia and Jacob. "Okay, that was bad. *Old* and bad. I deserved that."

"Okay, one more time," Mattie said, relighting the candle. "Maybe wish for something else this time."

In that moment, Lucy's only wish was that she could have friends like these in her life forever. And this time, the candle didn't go out.

* * *

It was tight quarters in the tiny scone shop, and it was getting warm. But Nick was the reason they were here in the first place, so he wasn't about to complain.

They should have hosted the party at his house. It was far enough from the center of town so Taylor and Carson wouldn't have had to sneak in like burglars trying to avoid cameras. There was plenty of space, and they wouldn't have had to come up with a ridiculous plan for how to cover the windows.

But if they'd had it at his house, his brothers would have been there. There was almost no chance they'd get through the entire party without one of them revealing Nick's bedroom had been sitting empty for a few days.

He *probably* could have skated by on the same excuse he gave Gray, but he'd rather not take the chance he'd be forced to confess to Lucy that he couldn't bring himself to leave her.

"The cake was amazing," Lucy said, setting her empty plate on the table with a sigh. "As was the ice cream. I don't think I've ever had vanilla ice cream that was so creamy."

The rich chocolate cake with raspberry filling and frosting, as well as the ice cream, were excellent. And Nick was glad they'd had big servings because as he was taking his first bite, he realized his hasty plan for getting Lucy to the party hadn't included getting supper into her first. He'd gotten hung up on the jobsite and was running late, but cake and ice cream was a good supper.

"Making ice cream is one of Carson's hobbies," Taylor said. "He loves to try fun flavors that people wouldn't expect, but vanilla's always best for a party."

"Okay, we have to do presents before Mattie has to go," Willow said, clapping her hands. "Mine first!"

"Presents?" Lucy sounded as if she was going to cry. "This is too much."

Willow scoffed as she pulled a stack of gifts from behind the counter. Nick recognized his gift as the one on the bottom, making the base of the stack. He'd dropped it off that morning on his way to work because he didn't see any way to smuggle it in with Lucy in tow. And he hadn't wanted to forget it.

She opened Willow's first because Willow was handing them out and she thrust it into Lucy's hands. Inside the wrapped box was a photo frame, and both women got a little weepy.

Nick didn't think to bring a pocket pack of tissues to a birthday party but, knowing Lucy, he probably should have.

The photo showed two girls, maybe twelve or thirteen, holding hands as they leaped off a floating dock into the water. Judging by the cloud of red hair in the photo and the way the two women hugged now, it was them, back during one of Lucy's visits to town.

When they'd used napkins to mop their faces, Willow tried to hand her the next gift, but Taylor snatched it away, startling all of them.

"No," she said, clutching it to her chest. "I changed my mind. It's too corny, but I'll get you something else tomorrow."

"I love corny gifts," Lucy said. "Please?"

Taylor tipped her head back and heaved such a dramatic sigh, Nick had a flashback to middle school when she was a Drama Club darling. "Fine."

Lucy took her time with the ribbons and paper, clearly enjoying Taylor's suffering. They all craned their necks to see when she lifted the lid, but the elegant gold bangle bracelet didn't look all that corny to Nick.

"It's gorgeous," Lucy said, clearly as confused as everybody else.

Taylor sighed again. "There's an inscription on the inside."

Lucy lifted out the bracelet and held it to the light so she could read the words inside. "It says Little Sister."

Taylor held up her wrist, showing off an identical bracelet. "Mine say Big Sister."

The ribbons, paper and jeweler's box fell to the floor when Lucy stood to wrap her arms around her sister.

"What if—" Lucy couldn't even bring herself to say it.

"I was giving it to you no matter what."

Yeah, he *really* should have brought tissues.

Everybody laughed, though, when Mattie took her gift from Willow to hand it off to Lucy. "I hate to follow these two, but this is from Sasha and me. And Billy, too, I guess. I'll tell you right up front, you're not going to cry."

Lucy pushed the bracelet from Taylor onto her wrist and took the present from Mattie. Inside was a frosted glass with the logo for the Uneven Keel etched into it—the same logo that was on the sign and the aprons.

"I've never seen one of these," Lucy said, holding it up so everybody could see.

"Those were the original glasses, but Billy went to generic, plain glasses sometime when Sasha was a teenager because those were too expensive to replace when they got broken. But he's got a couple of boxes tucked away, and sometimes we'll give one to somebody who's pretty special."

Lucy held the glass to her face, and Nick could tell by the sniffling and the way her shoulders shook that she was crying again.

"Crap," Mattie said. "Why is there so much crying at this party?"

Everybody laughed, including Lucy, but Nick knew. Six weeks or so ago, Lucy felt alone in the world. Hell, she *was* alone in the world, except for a grandmother she hadn't seen in a decade and a half. And now here she was, surrounded by friends and a sister who obviously cared about her.

Then Willow handed Lucy the gift from him, and on one hand, he hoped she wasn't going to cry again. But on the other, he knew there was a chance he might feel bad if his was the only gift that *didn't* make her cry.

She smiled at him before she opened it, the wetness of her eyes doing nothing to dim the sparkle. And she looked so damn happy, he couldn't help but smile back at her. Their gazes were locked, and he could have looked into her blue eyes all night, if somebody—probably Willow—hadn't given a dreamy sigh.

"I'm feeling some pressure here," he told her and was rewarded with her laugh.

She tore the paper from his gift, flinging it away. And then she went still, looking at the notebook he'd chosen for her for a few moments before flipping through the pages to the middle. Then she ran her hand over the paper, feeling the creamy blank pages for sketching cocktails and notes. It had a soft cover, in graduated hues from tan at the bottom to beige to light blue to a darker blue, like sand, sea and sky.

"This is beautiful," she whispered.

"I was watching you write in yours recently and it looked almost full. And the cover looks like the shots you made for that party, which is what you really want in life."

Tears trickled down her cheeks as she skimmed her fingers over the cover. "It's perfect. Thank you."

"Happy birthday, Lucy."

The other guests started moving around, picking up wrapping paper and gathering the cake plates, but because Nick was still watching Lucy, he saw her open the notebook and run her hand over the creamy paper again and smile.

She was going to fill that notebook with ideas that would make her dreams come true. And he was going to be happy for her, even if it killed him.

Chapter Fifteen

It's the last week of school! The library and town hall both have a list of fun—and free—things to do this summer. And if you need a little help with lunches, message me to be put on the brown bag list. Your community is here for you!

—Wayward Harbor Online Community Group

By the time they got home from the party, Lucy's stomach hurt from laughing, her throat was already sore from so much talking, and the sugar was coursing through her body like an energy drink.

But she didn't care. "That was the best birthday party I've ever had."

Nick set the Scuttlebutt bag with her presents in it on the table and put the box of leftover cake in the fridge. "I'm glad you had a good time."

"You had a good time, too."

He nodded reluctantly, but then chuckled. "Yes, I did."

"I bet Lavinia enjoyed it, too."

He laughed. "Is that the same ghost you claim was blowing out your birthday candles or a different one?"

"Your skepticism is really showing. But anyway, that was definitely Lavinia. Jacob never goes upstairs, according to Willow, but Lavinia was definitely judging my birthday wish."

"What did you wish for?"

Lucy froze, her mind blank except for desperately wishing she could take her words back. All she needed to come up with was something that a woman who died in 1932 would judge, and that had to be a big list. "If I tell you, it won't come true."

"You're blushing, so now you're going to have to tell me." His grin was wicked, and a shiver went through her body. "What did you ask for that a ghost would find sinful, Lucy?"

"I didn't say it was sinful," she shot back, pointing at him. "I just said Lavinia was judging me. Maybe I was wishing for a gluten-free whoopie pie with dairy-free filling. That's going to make a ghost baker from almost a century ago roll over in her grave."

"There's *zero* chance you were wishing for a whoopie pie with no gluten or dairy."

She had to admit that wasn't one of her better attempts at stretching the truth. "It was just an example of the kind of wish Lavinia might judge me for."

Was it her imagination or was Nick closer? The man was slowly advancing toward her, and that had to be why it was so hard to breathe all of a sudden.

"Okay," she said. "Do you remember when we kissed after I sat on the sidewalk with Dolly and we agreed it was a bad idea?"

"I remember it very well."

"And do you remember when we kissed the night you gave me my sparkly tree and we agreed it was a *really* bad idea?"

"Vividly." His cheeks and neck looked a little rosy, too, so at least she wasn't the only one suffering.

"And do you remember when we kissed yesterday and we didn't talk about it being a bad idea, but we both knew it was."

He nodded. "Lavinia might have been trying to keep me from

wishing for something that's a very, *very* bad idea. Possibly the worst idea ever."

Nick was close enough now to rest his hand on her waist, but he didn't pull her closer. Instead, he waited until she took the final step to close the distance between them. With her body pressed to his, she wrapped her arms around his neck.

"It's your birthday," he said, his voice low and rough. "It's a great day for worst ever ideas."

It *was* her birthday, and she wanted to unwrap this man like a gift—slowly, and treasuring every moment.

He smiled, as though reading her thoughts in her eyes. "And since you haven't actually told me what you wished for—specifically—it can still come true."

Lucy cupped her hand behind his neck and pulled his lips to hers. The kiss was gentle at first, but Nick's mouth grew more demanding, and she moaned into it.

Then he stopped, putting his finger under her chin so he could see her face. "I have a wish for your birthday."

"Oh, I bet you do."

"Take that thing out of your hair."

It wasn't easy, but Lucy finally tugged the oversize scrunchie out of her hair so it was free. Running her fingers through it to look for knots, she shook it to loosen up the curls.

Then Nick was kissing her again, hard and hungry, and a groan came out of him when he buried his hands in her hair.

"Your room or mine," he whispered against her mouth.

"Definitely mine." Nick might be sleeping in that bed, but it wasn't his.

She gasped when he lifted her off her feet. There was a moment when he had to brace himself and she thought they were both going to fall. Laughing, she wrapped her arms around his neck.

Then he steadied himself and carried her to her bed, kicking the door closed behind him and plunging the room into darkness. She reached out and hit the switch on her metal tree. A warm glow filled the room, and she saw him tugging at the hem of his shirt.

"No," she told him, pushing up to her knees on the mattress so she could reach him. "I want to do that."

And in the twinkling light of her little tree, Lucy unwrapped her gift. Her hands on his naked body might have been the worst idea ever, but it was a birthday she'd never forget.

Nick was glad this morning was limited to the final walk-through with the homeowner and getting a check because there was no way he could be trusted with power tools today.

His body was tired, though for an admittedly good reason. After making love, he and Lucy had gotten out of bed and eaten more of the delicious cake. Then they made love again before lying awake in the dark, talking about how chocolate and sugar at well past bedtime wasn't a great idea. But they both confessed to having no regrets.

It was Nick's mind spinning that was causing him problems. Spending the night in Lucy's bed had been the best thing that ever happened to him. Allowing himself to do it was one of the worst ideas he'd ever had.

He already wanted to do it again, and resisting the urge wasn't going to be easy.

Lucy had still been asleep when he'd left for work. After sliding as silently as possible out of her bed, he'd gone to his own room to get ready. Deciding whether or not to leave her a note had eaten up five minutes of his prework morning routine.

On the one hand, being gone when she woke up didn't feel right. On the other, what would he say? It didn't make sense to tell her he'd call her later. He'd be coming home later. She knew she'd see him. And a quick thank-you note felt *really* wrong.

In the end, realizing he was going to be late to the jobsite had made the decision for him, and he'd tried not to overthink it while following the very picky homeowner around the finished house.

Finally, large check in hand, Nick was able to get in his truck and leave that job behind him. They'd be starting a new one tomorrow, but for now—thanks to Gray's meticulous attention to detail keeping the homeowner from coming up with a punch list of his own—they all got the rest of the day off.

Since Lucy was only working weekends at the Keel now, her car was in the driveway when he pulled in. He wasn't sure what to expect when he went inside, and he was dreading the possibility she was upset he'd left without saying goodbye or at least leaving a note.

Lucy was sitting sideways on the couch, with only one light blanket over her legs. When he walked through the door, she looked up and smiled. Then, putting her pen between the pages to hold her place, she closed the notebook she'd been writing in and set it on the table.

"How did it go?" she asked, sounding totally like herself and not at all upset.

"Good. We got paid and now it's on to the next job." He stepped out of his boots and walked to the fridge. Going straight to the food seemed a better play than hovering in the doorway, unsure of whether she'd expect him to go over and kiss her hello or not. "I'm starving and we have the rest of the day off, so I came home for lunch."

"You probably won't be surprised to hear that I ate the rest of the cake for breakfast."

He chuckled, opening the deli meat drawer. "I was pretty

sure you would, so I didn't get my heart set on it. You want a sandwich?"

"It was a *big* slice of cake."

Nick shook his head and then grabbed a beefsteak tomato out of the crisper drawer. His parents used to argue about whether or not tomatoes were meant to be kept in the fridge, but he kept them there because that was where he always found them when he was a kid. He still didn't know if his mom was right, but she'd clearly won all of the arguments.

After he'd made himself a couple of bologna and tomato sandwiches—with extra mayo, of course—he pulled out a chair and sat at the table. Lucy joined him, sitting in her usual seat, and sifted idly through the mail he'd grabbed on his way in.

Because he was trying not to stare at her while his brain tried to navigate how to handle last night, Nick looked around the kitchen at anything but her. And then he spotted the list on the fridge.

"You should have a bite of this," he said, holding up half of one of the sandwiches.

She looked up from a sales flyer and wrinkled her nose. "No thanks."

"It's on our shenanigans list," he reminded her. "One bite, so we can cross it off."

"Oh," she said, pointing at him. "So now it's *we* and *our*, but I never agreed to it going on the list in the first place."

"One bite."

"Fine." She got up and walked around to his side of the table, plopping down in the chair next to him.

When he extended the sandwich, he thought Lucy would take it from him. Instead, she leaned closer and took a decent-sized bite while he held it. Initially, her nose wrinkled again, but after chewing it thoroughly and swallowing, she didn't look disgusted by it at all.

"It's good, isn't it?"

She sighed. "Yes, okay? It's actually very good."

And then she took an unbitten half off his plate and went back to her own seat. He laughed and slid one of the extra napkins he'd grabbed down the table to her. The extra mayo and the juices from the tomatoes got really messy, which was part of why they were so tasty.

"You know what's even better?" he asked while she jumped up to cross the item out on the list before going back to the stolen sandwich. "If you put potato chips on top of the tomatoes. Good salty ones."

She laughed. "You're just messing with me now."

"Nope. It's delicious. Then the sandwich is juicy and crunchy and salty and… Trust me."

"I forbid you to add any more food-related items to the list," she said sternly. "Take the win."

They lapsed into a comfortable silence while they ate. She flipped through the sales flyers and he watched her, trying to come up with some way to broach the subject of where they stood now when it came to bad ideas.

"So we should talk about last night," she said when he'd finished eating and was about to stand up.

"Okay." He wiped his hands the best he could on the napkins, not wanting to look like he was disinterested by going to the sink to wash his hands.

"Lavinia probably had the right idea," she said, and he sighed. "Don't make your grumpy face at me."

"You started off the serious conversation we need to have with a ghost."

"Real or not, I like Lavinia. Or I like the idea of Lavinia.

Either way, you're the one who's making this a 'serious conversation' with your grumpy face. I just wanted to talk."

"Okay. So you agree with the woman who died almost a hundred years ago that you shouldn't have made that wish?"

"I think all three of us agree it was a bad idea."

The obvious effort Lucy was putting into not smiling confirmed she was deliberately pushing his buttons, so he let that slide. "I'm not sorry last night happened. But it's complicated. You're leaving soon. Before that, Helen will be coming home and you and I will go our separate ways."

"Exactly," she said, telling him nothing about where she stood.

"So…?"

She hesitated, clearly disappointed he hadn't exactly voiced where *he* stood going forward, either. "So all of that makes anything more happening between us a super bad idea."

Disappointment flooded through him, even though she was right. "Yes, it does."

"But since we *know* that, we know ahead of time it's just a summer fling—or a half-a-summer fling—and then we'll part ways again with no harm done, so then keeping on doing what we've been doing isn't such a bad idea, right?"

"Oh." He definitely wanted to keep on doing what they'd done last night. "Right."

"But we should keep it to ourselves, behind closed doors," she added. "So the people in our lives don't get the wrong idea."

He'd managed to hide how he felt about her for this long. He could keep doing it in public if it meant he got to put his hands on her privately. "Agreed."

"Good." She smiled brightly and then slid one of the flyers across the table to him. "Tomatoes are on sale. We should go buy more."

Chapter Sixteen

The JV and varsity football teams need assistant coaches for the upcoming season! This is a volunteer position, but background checks and agreeing to the Code of Conduct are nonnegotiable. Ideally, we're looking for three to five people with not only a passion for, but actual knowledge of the game. Contact Coach through the school's athletics page if you're interested!

—Wayward Harbor Online Community Group

"How do you add the colors, though?" Taylor asked, looking at the sketch in Lucy's notebook.

It was an idea she was working on for gender reveal parties, with a clear shot, and then guests would use an opaque dropper to add blue or pink tinted Bailey's Irish Cream. The color would then disperse through the clear alcohol.

Her problem was that using the necessary clear liquors needed for the base was boring. But if she added stars or some other fun confetti, it interfered with the dispersal of the thicker liqueur.

"You can tint Bailey's Irish Cream with food coloring," Lucy said. "Just not too much because it'll make it thin and it won't create the right effect. It's just years of knowing the different ingredients and how they layer and interact with each other."

"I bet they'd love that up at the resort," Willow said. "They host so many events there."

Lucy nodded, though she didn't take the bait. The resort a little way up the coastline might host a lot of events, but it wasn't Miami. It would be seasonal work, and it wouldn't be nearly as much. Also, it wasn't in Florida.

The bell over the door rang, and Willow sighed. "Be right back."

On the one hand, the fact Willow had cleaned off a small table in the back of the kitchen so Taylor could sneak in the back door and they could all have coffee together was ridiculous. On the other hand, they all got to have coffee together, which was the important part.

"Lucy, it's for you," she heard Willow call.

"That's odd," she said, closing her notebook and getting up. The only people who could be looking for her were Nick and Mattie, and either of them would have sent her a text message. Or called.

It wasn't until she was already pushing open the door that she thought of the online trolls. It had been a while since she let them take up space in her head. But she was already committed, and if it was one of them, they'd just follow her into the kitchen anyway, Employees Only sign be damned.

Then she saw the woman who'd come in and squealed with excitement.

"Gran!" As tempting as it was to try to leap onto and over the pastry counter like an action movie star, Lucy recognized her limitations and took the time to walk around it. "You're home!"

Very few things in Lucy's life had ever felt as good as Helen's arms wrapping around her and squeezing did. "Oh my goodness, sweetheart, it is so good to see you."

"I didn't know you'd be home today. You didn't even tell me you left!"

"I wanted to surprise you the way you tried to surprise me, and I thought I'd be later, but I took the highway instead of the scenic route and made good time."

Lucy wanted to reply, but all she could do was nod. While she'd talked to Gran so many times since she'd arrived, and felt the love and support, there was nothing like a good squeeze hug.

"Lucy, are you crying into my hair?"

"Of course not," she said, sniffling as she lifted her head. She tried to swipe away her tears before she stepped back, but she was absolutely busted.

But Helen was crying, and she was wiping away a few tears, too.

"Have you been home yet?"

"Not yet. I saw your car wasn't in the driveway and thought you might be here. I can use a coffee and a sweet snack after all that driving."

"This will probably sound weird, but we're actually having coffee and sweets in the back of the kitchen right now."

Gran looked around the empty shop, clearly confused. "Does somebody have the tables all reserved?"

"Actually, it's because Taylor joins us, and it's better for business than covering the windows so nobody can see her and rat her out to Kim."

"I have to go anyway," Taylor said, and they turned to see her face barely peeking out through the door. "My break's over, but I'll call you later, Lucy. It's good to see you, Mrs. Griffin."

"It's good to see you, too, Taylor."

After grabbing their mugs and plates, as well as Lucy's notebook, they joined Helen at a table in the front of the shop.

It worked out for the best, as customers began trickling in for a midafternoon pick-me-up, so Willow was up and down.

They talked about Helen's adventures until well after their mugs were empty. She had a ton of photos, of course, but they saved those for when they could sit side by side on the couch.

When Helen excused herself to use the restroom, Lucy realized with a start that she hadn't even thought about Nick. She needed to tell him her grandmother was back because it was going to change everything.

She pulled out her phone and typed in a quick message. Gran is back in town. She wanted to surprise me. We're at the Scuttlebutt but I wanted you to know.

Helen was sliding back into her chair when Lucy's phone dinged with his reply. I had to make a run to the hardware store and heard her car had been spotted. I probably won't beat you back to the cottage, but I'll be there shortly.

Lucy realized he'd said *the cottage* and not *home*, and a pang of sadness took a little of the joy out of the day.

"Is everything okay?"

"Of course," Lucy said brightly, dropping the phone into her bag. "I was telling Nick you came early to surprise me, but, of course, he'd already heard you were back in town."

"It's not easy keeping a secret in this town, that's for sure," Gran said as they gathered their things to leave. She must have caught Lucy's wry look, because she gave her a sheepish smile. "Well, small ones, anyway."

Because they were in separate cars, Lucy had the drive home to wrap her head around the fact her life was about to look very different again. With Nick giving the primary bedroom back to Gran, he wasn't going to have any place to stay.

And Lucy couldn't very well invite him to share *her* bed because, one, she had no idea how Gran would feel about that.

But secondly, they'd agreed not to share that part of their lives with anybody.

Nick had actually beat them to the cottage because his truck was next to Helen's car in the driveway. Lucy pulled up behind her grandmother's car and walked slowly up the stairs to the porch.

She'd known this day was coming, but she thought she had more time.

The first thing she saw when she walked through the door were Nick's duffel bags, sitting on the floor by the kitchen table. Miscellaneous other things, like his sneakers and extra sweatshirts, were set next to them. She stared at them for too long, willing herself to put a smile on her face, but she couldn't quite manage it.

"Lucy?" It was Nick, and she turned to find him standing in the bedroom doorway. "You want to help me remake this bed?"

"You don't have to do that," Helen protested. She'd had her back to Lucy, sifting through a large tote bag, so she'd missed her granddaughter's reaction to seeing Nick's bags packed.

"You know I'm going to make that bed," Nick said, his voice warm with affection. "The bedding that was on it is already in the wash. It'll just need to go in the dryer when it's done."

"I think I left my other glasses in the car. I'll be right back."

Left alone, Lucy watched Nick go back into the bedroom. She followed him and took the corner of the sheet he handed her. "You don't have to go."

"Of course I do. We talked about this. Helen's back and it's her bedroom, so it's time for me to leave."

But she didn't want him to go. "Of course Gran should sleep in her own bed, especially after two months of traveling. But you can sleep in the second bedroom and I'll crash on the couch again. It'll be like old times."

"No, Lucy. We're not doing that."

"What are you going to do?"

Was that guilt that flashed across his face? "I'll head home and sleep in my own bed, I guess."

"What about your brother and the kids?"

"They're back in their own place, actually."

Well, that was certainly news to her. "When did that happen?"

Nick scrubbed his hand over the back of his neck, not meeting her eyes. "A couple of weeks ago now, I guess."

"Oh." She wasn't sure what to do with that information.

"Didn't make sense to drive back and forth to work on the deck," he said, and she could see that. But he was rubbing his hand over the back of his neck, which was a sure sign there was something else he didn't want to admit.

"That doesn't really explain why you didn't tell me. You could have said Beck and the kids went home, but you were going to stay until the deck was done."

"And I know the quiet gets to you at night, so I thought maybe you wouldn't want to be alone."

That was very sweet, but it still didn't explain why he hadn't shared the good news. But she could see the reserve creeping in—the grumpy mask sliding into place—and decided to let it go.

"Well, I'm belatedly happy for them. The kids must love being back in their own home."

He shrugged, smoothing his hand over the top sheet. "I think so. They like hanging out with their uncles, but having all of their toys back and their own rooms probably makes up for it."

"Found them," Lucy heard Gran say, and she blinked away a tear. "It's going to take me days to sort that mess of a car."

"I'll carry in your bags," Nick called back to her. He gave Lucy a sad smile before walking into the living room. "But the crumbs between the seats are all you."

Helen laughed, and Lucy made sure to rearrange her expression into a happy one before joining her in the living room. It seemed like no time at all before Nick had brought everything in from the car. Then, while Lucy and Gran started dealing with that, he carried his own stuff out to his truck.

Rather than follow them around like a lost puppy, Lucy made herself busy in the kitchen while Nick showed her the work he'd done. The smaller bedroom and the deck were the biggest things, along with the shed door. But he'd done a lot of little things, too, some with Lucy's help. When they came back in, Gran looked as if she'd gotten a little weepy, but she was smiling.

Lucy knew the feeling. When it came time to say goodbye to Nick as if he was nothing more than a friend who'd stopped by for a visit, she was weeping on the inside. But she kept a smile on her face.

Nick dropped his duffel bags on his bed and looked around at the bedroom he hadn't slept in since mid-April. It was immaculate, of course, right down to the fresh bedding, because Beck had given it a thorough cleaning after vacating it.

He couldn't help wondering what Lucy would think of it. It wasn't until he'd lived in Helen's cottage temporarily that he realized there was a serious lack of color in this room. The oak furnishings were plain, but solid. The walls were beige. A throw rug with neutral shades of beige and gray partially covered the hardwood floor. And a gray comforter covered the bed. He didn't have any throw pillows or accent items, and now he was very aware there was nothing hung on the walls. The only color in the room was the sage green of the armchair and ottoman in the corner.

Nick found it all soothing, but now he understood why Beck had told him he appreciated the use of the bedroom, but he'd been in bank lobbies with more personality.

The mattress was nice, though. If there was one good thing about being home again, it was the firmness of his mattress.

"Hey," he heard Theo bellow up the stairs.

Nick walked down the hall to look over the railing at his youngest brother. "What?"

"I heard footsteps up there and didn't know you were home."

"Did you think somebody stole my truck and drove it here so they could rob us?"

Theo shrugged. "I mean, if somebody took your truck keys, they'd also have your house key, so it's not that far-fetched. But I was out back with my headphones on, so I didn't hear you pull in, and I didn't see the truck."

"What was the plan if I didn't answer?" Nick asked, walking down the stairs.

"I probably would have yelled it again, but louder." Theo shrugged. "Then? A bridge I didn't have to cross, I guess. So Helen's back?"

"Yeah. She came home early to surprise Lucy. I'd just wrapped up the last thing I wanted to get done for her, so it worked out well." Except for the part where he was once again living with Gray and Theo, instead of with Lucy.

"I was getting ready to throw some kielbasa on the grill. You in?"

"Sure. Where's Gray?"

"He said something about Cory, but I missed what, exactly, they were doing. Cory's been pretty needy since the split."

Nick snorted. "Then he shouldn't have been so needy with that brunette from Pennsylvania at the Keel."

"Right?" Theo pulled a package of kielbasa from the fridge. "The Keel? How did he think Brooke wouldn't find out about that?"

"Pretty sure he wasn't on his first drink of the night."

"Lucy must be happy Helen's home," Theo said, and Nick was glad his brother's focus was on the knife block because his flinch might have shown on the outside.

It didn't matter they'd talked about this—that Helen would come home and it would change everything. It still sucked.

They'd finished eating and were sitting in the lounge chairs, talking about sports, when Nick's phone vibrated in his pocket. He pulled it out, which Theo took as permission to take his own phone out and immediately dive into whatever social media app was popular this week.

The preview showed it was a text message from Lucy, and he almost sprained his thumb swiping to get to the entire thing so fast.

I'm sad we didn't get to everything on our shenanigans list.

Nick chuckled. He couldn't help it, even though it earned a questioning look from Theo. But he shrugged, and his brother went back to minding his own screen.

I'm not dead, Lucy. I'm just across town.

I bet Lavinia wouldn't mind if you died. I think Jacob was a little young for her.

This time he laughed loudly, and Theo wasn't put off with a shrug. "Who are you talking to?"

"None of your business."

"So Lucy then," his brother said, and then he smirked and went back to his phone.

Stop trying to hook me up with the dead whoopie pie lady. What's left on our list?

Sunrise on Cadillac Mountain and going out on a boat.

So the two hard things, then. The initial burst of hope because he had a reason to see her again faded as he realized the only things left on their list were things he might not be able to pull off.

I'll see what I can do, but don't hold your breath or you might have to get up to shenanigans with Jacob.

She sent back what looked like every different laughing emoji the keyboard offered, but then that was it.

He wasn't ready to be done, though.

There's supposed to be quite a storm day after tomorrow, so you should put the cushions and umbrella for the patio set back in the shed.

I will.

You should write it on the to-do list on the fridge.

Don't be bossy or I'll come up with something else to put on our shenanigans list.

He could think of a couple shenanigans he'd like to get up to with her, but he just sent her back one smiley face emoji.

It helped, he thought, laughing with Lucy, even by text. It helped him get over the shock he'd felt earlier when he stopped by the hardware store and Don told him Helen was back in town.

In some ways, her earlier than expected arrival was for the best. He'd have longer to wean himself away from craving Lucy's company before she packed up her car and headed to Miami.

But he thought he'd have at least a couple more nights in her bed before he went back to sleeping alone. He thought there would be time for them to talk about whether they'd have bad ideas together once her grandmother returned—though somewhere else, of course. He hadn't figured out where exactly that somewhere else would be, since he didn't want his brothers making assumptions.

His hand covered the phone sitting on his thigh. For right now, though, Lucy wasn't gone. And he'd probably be able to sleep tonight.

Chapter Seventeen

The morning forecast warned about the storm coming in and the potential for lightning and damaging windows, but so you know, Dolly was seen meowing on Edna's porch until she was let in. It's going to be a bad one, folks. Secure your garbage bin lids.

—Wayward Harbor Online Community Group

Storms were a lot more fun when Lucy was a child.

When she was a kid, thunderstorms and wind buffeting the house were exciting, like an adventure she was caught up in. As an adult who owned things, understood the potential for damage, and knew dealing with insurance companies wasn't a fun way to pass the time, she wasn't a fan.

And yet, there was something hypnotic about watching a storm over the ocean. It was gorgeous and terrifying, and she wanted nothing more than to be curled up on the porch next to Nick, watching the lightning strikes in the distance.

Unfortunately, the winds were driving the rain almost sideways, and everything on the porch was soaked. And Nick didn't live there anymore.

Lucy missed him so much. She'd known it would be a little sad when the temporary little life they'd built was over, but she hadn't anticipated feeling the lack of him in the cottage so deeply.

"I can hear you sighing over the wind," Gran said from her seat at the kitchen table. She'd decided to take the stormy day to sort through the mail that had accumulated while she was away, which mostly meant flipping through the magazines she subscribed to.

And Lucy was taking the day to do nothing after Billy had told her not to bother coming in because nobody else would. She moved away from the window, sighing again. "I was thinking about how storms are fun when you're a kid, but not as fun when you're adult."

"That's a fact." She closed her magazine, giving Lucy one of those face-searching looks mothers and grandmothers did so well. "They don't sound like nostalgia sighs, though."

What Lucy did *not* want to do was confess she was feeling down because Gran had come home, and she was thrilled to see her, but it meant she didn't have Nick around anymore.

"Just thinking about how daunting it will be to get in my car and just drive to Miami without much of a plan."

Gran laughed. "You've driven farther than that without a plan."

"That's valid," Lucy admitted, pulling out the chair across from Helen's and dropping into it. "But this was a visit—like a time-out. Going to Miami is starting my actual life over. It's what I've wanted for a while, but it feels…huge."

"It *is* huge. Chasing a dream is no small thing, and it shouldn't be."

"What if it doesn't work out?"

"Then you'll come back here and figure out a new plan."

Lucy smiled sadly. "I can't keep running back to you every time life gets hard."

Gran laughed. "Of course you can. You come back here, you get a hug and lots of love, and you regroup."

"Thank you, Gran."

"Life is like a house, honey. You have to build the *life* you want the same way you build a house—with a solid foundation—before you can live in it." Gran reached across the table to cover her hand. "This home and I are your foundation, Lucy. We're not going anywhere. We won't shift with the tides. No matter where you go or what you do, we're right here if you need us."

For what was possibly the first time in her life, Lucy felt as though, if she fell, there was somebody there to catch her. To soothe her and help her get back on her feet. She could feel that unconditional love in Gran. She heard it in Nick's voice when he talked about his brothers.

"I'm sorry I didn't come visit," Lucy said softly.

"And I'm sorry I didn't encourage you to." Helen closed her magazine. "It wasn't easy for me to tell Iris I didn't want to see her anymore. She's my only child and I do love her, but…"

"Was it Jack?"

"No, not specifically. I never knew for sure if those rumors were true, or any of them, really. Because there were a lot. She'd disappear, but then she'd come back when she needed money. And while she was here, she'd stir things up again. She always wanted more—more excitement, more attention, more money. And she was beautiful, so men liked to give her those things—even the ones who weren't single. She left a trail of heartbreak and anger every time she came through Wayward Harbor."

"I'm sorry, Gran. She still…she still looks for men to take care of her."

"I hoped she'd grow up and change—especially after she had you. But when your grandfather passed, when you were just a baby, she got worse. He'd always been tighter with the money, and she thought I'd be more vulnerable. And I was, for a while. The last summer you were here, the bank called me because she'd tried to use one of my checks to buy a car. And I told her she could leave and not come back, or I'd press charges. Losing you about killed me, sweetheart, but I couldn't do it anymore."

Lucy nodded sadly. "When I called to tell her I'd driven all the way here because I felt like she should know where I was, her first thought was for me to convince you to sell this place and move into a retirement home."

Gran snorted. "I wish I could say that shocks me, but I would have expected nothing less from that girl."

Her phone rang, startling both of them, and Helen laughed as she pressed her hand to her chest. Lucy picked it up, certain it was going to be Nick, checking on them. He'd already sent a text that morning, warning her to check the weather forecast and reminding her to put the cushions and umbrella way, which she had. Because him thinking about her gave her all kinds of mushy feelings, she'd sent back a heart.

She'd been overthinking that emoji choice ever since.

But when she looked at the screen, she saw her mother's name. Frowning, she turned the phone so Gran could see it. "It's Iris. Did we summon her somehow? Did she feel a disturbance when her daughter was given love and support?"

Sorrow flashed across Helen's face before she hid it behind her usual loving expression. "You can answer it, sweetheart. It won't bother me."

Even though she hated the idea of her mother being in the room with Helen, even over the phone, Iris rarely called her. Maybe her boyfriend dumped her and she needed Lucy to pay the deposit on a new place to live, but there was a chance something was actually wrong. After taking a breath, she swiped to accept the call. "Hi, Mom."

"Hello, Lucy. I haven't heard from you at all, so I wanted to check and see how things are going there."

"Everything's fine. And with you?"

"Same," Iris said, and Lucy could tell by the way she practically spit the word out that her boyfriend still hadn't proposed. But at least she didn't need money for a new apartment yet. "And how is my mother?"

"She's doing well." Lucy had no intention of offering more than that.

"Oh, that's good." Sure, that sounded totally sincere. "I've been looking into property values in the Wayward Harbor area, and it really would be foolish for her not to sell and move into a retirement condo somewhere. She'd have a *very* tidy nest egg."

Lucy watched her grandmother moving around the kitchen—a woman who was kind and generous and loving—and felt a surge of protective outrage. There was one woman in Lucy's life who loved her unconditionally, and it wasn't her mother.

"Lucy, did you hear me? You need to talk to your grandmother and—"

"Mom, stop." Years of tangled emotions and resentment fell away until all that remained was clarity and resolve. "Gran's life is none of your business."

"Of course it is! She's my mother."

"What does that mean to you, though? Because you're *my* mother, and when my entire life fell apart, you let your boyfriend throw me out with nowhere to go."

"He owns the house, Lucy."

"You've always chased men to take care of you. Including Jack Perkins. Do you remember him?" There was silence on the other end. "I met my sister, and she's wonderful. But I didn't get a chance to meet my father because he passed away. You're selfish and you ruin lives."

"He didn't want us."

Lucy closed her eyes briefly. "He was married, and you

knew it. You don't care who you hurt as long as you get what you want."

"I don't have to listen to this. I just wanted to see how you were doing and check on my mother."

"Gran doesn't need you to check on her. And her property is none of your business. I don't know what she intends to do with the cottage because it's also none of *my* business, but I do know you won't be inheriting a single dime. There is nothing for you here in Maine."

"Lucy Macauley, don't you dare—"

"That includes me. Don't contact either of us again, Iris." She disconnected the call and set the phone on the table. Then she exhaled a long, shaky breath.

"I'm sorry, honey."

Lucy looked up at her grandmother. "I'm sorry, too."

"Maybe Iris was the trial I had to get through in order to have you."

"So we could have each other." Helen nodded, and tears filled Lucy's eyes. "I'm going to miss you when I go to Miami, Gran."

"I'll miss you, too, but we'll talk all the time. And I'll come visit you for the holidays, since you might actually freeze to death here with how you are. And you can come in the summer, when the weather's perfect here, to visit with me and Taylor. I'll see you twice a year."

"At least twice. I promise."

"Good." Gran slapped her hand on the table. "Now I'm going to make us some tea and we're going to ride out the rest of the weather with a good jigsaw puzzle."

Lucy cleared the table while her grandmother brewed the tea. She kept the sorted mail piles intact as she transferred them to the counter, and then did the same with the magazines she'd read and the ones to be read.

What would it be like to visit Wayward Harbor once a year? If she spent a week, it would be so full visiting Gran and Taylor. She'd visit Willow at the Scuttlebutt and stop by the Keel.

Would she even get to see Nick? Would each visit be like a snapshot of his life since she left? A girlfriend. A wife. His first child. Another child. Gray at his temples. Or maybe she wouldn't even run into him, and Nick Slater would fade into a fond memory that resurfaced when she came back to Maine.

Her heart ached at the thought, but she refused to allow herself to cry. Gran's heart also had to be aching right now, and Lucy didn't want to make it worse. She would drink tea she didn't really like, except for the warmth it spread through her, and do jigsaw puzzles while the storm raged outside.

Nick couldn't stay away.

He pulled into the Keel's parking lot the night after the storm and was lucky enough to find a spot his truck would fit in. Since he'd told himself if the lot was full and he had to park on the street, he'd just go home and send her a text with his news instead, he took it as a sign.

He'd see Lucy. He'd have a meal. And that would be enough to get him through until tomorrow. It wouldn't take long for him to get used to not having her around. Hopefully. But he had good news and, rather than add to their rapidly growing text message thread, he decided to tell her in person.

And when he walked in, their eyes met and her face lit up, and he knew it was well worth what the meal was going to cost him.

"Hey, stranger," she said when he'd grabbed a seat. It was the corner seat at the end and had the worst view of the television hung over the shelves in the center, so it was rarely used. It had the benefit of leaving three stools empty between him and the next guy.

"Did you guys do okay in the storm?" he asked her, wishing he could reach across the bar and kiss her instead of asking benign questions about the weather.

"All good. We lost power for a couple of hours, like everybody else, but no damage. You?"

"All good."

"Well, I wouldn't say *no* damage," Lucy said as she put a coaster with the Keel's logo on the bar in front of her, and he tensed. "I officially cut ties with Iris."

"I'm sorry," he said automatically. It couldn't have been easy. "It's definitely her loss."

"She was actually researching the cottage's value, and I realized…well, anyway. That's done."

"It must be nice to have Helen in person, finally."

"It's great. She took *so* many pictures, and we've done so much talking. And I have to build a house."

"That sounds drastic. And expensive." He cocked an eyebrow at her. "Plus I've seen you swing a hammer. Have you considered just renting an apartment somewhere?"

Like somewhere nearby so you're still in my life?

"No, it's like a metaphorical house. Or something. It's hard to explain. But Gran's my foundation and now I need to build the life I want to live in, like a house."

Maybe it was because building houses had been a part of Nick's life since he was old enough for his father to trust him with snapping a chalk line, but he thought it was a shaky analogy. Building houses wasn't a sure thing. A lot of people built houses and then realized the floor plan that looked good on paper didn't actually work for their families. They built houses they couldn't afford and eventually had to sell or lose to the bank. They cut corners and had bad rooflines and leaky basements.

"You just keeping that stool warm?" Billy asked in a rough voice as he stepped up behind Lucy.

"Hey, Billy. Having some trouble deciding what I want tonight."

He snorted and nudged Lucy's arm with his elbow. "He'll have the meat loaf with mashed, extra gravy. No veg. Two rolls, extra butter. And a ginger ale."

When Lucy arched an eyebrow at him, Nick shrugged. "Sounds good."

Billy barked out a laugh. "This one's got a habit of showing up when meat loaf's on the special board."

After he walked away, Lucy put her hands on her hips. "And here I thought you'd come to see me."

He had—he hadn't even looked at their Facebook page or at the specials board outside—but the meat loaf gave him an excuse for being there other than not being able to stay away from her for a full two days.

She had to tend to some other customers after she set a ginger ale in front of him, so he pulled out his phone and scanned through the news in his sports app. He didn't really care, but it gave him something to look at other than Lucy laughing with her other customers.

But when she brought out his meal, she leaned her elbows on the bar like she had time to visit for a few minutes.

"You know," he said, "if you build a house, you need to make sure you build with the good quality materials. And you have to be prepared for the house not working out for you, after all."

"So, I should build an RV?"

He snorted. "No. Nothing that temporary. But the house you build doesn't have to be the house you stay in forever if you're not as happy there as you thought you'd be."

For a moment, the words hung between them—heavy with

a meaning neither of them were sure he meant—and then she smiled. "You'd be a great life coach."

"Absolutely not." The last thing he needed was more people looking to him for answers, even if they were writing him checks for the advice.

"Okay, maybe not a great life coach, but a great coach." She gave him a falsely innocent smile. "I'm just saying."

She had no way of knowing he'd been thinking the same thing lately. Maybe it was just being able to talk openly about what football meant to him again. Or the feel of the ball in his arms as he ran down the beach. Probably both. But he'd seen the school was looking for volunteer assistant coaches and, unlike in the past, he was thinking about it.

So far he hadn't done anything *but* think, but he was starting to think it might be a good idea. Between moving back into the house and Lucy leaving, he knew he was in danger of going back into the small bubble of work and his brothers that he'd been living in.

Coaching could never fill the hole Lucy was going to leave in his life, but he could try to grab a little happiness for himself. And the busier he kept himself, the less time he'd have to miss her.

He wasn't ready to talk about it yet, to anybody. Not until he'd talked to Coach and made a decision.

"Where's Mattie?" he asked, making a show of looking around. "She's such a great bartender. Just gives me what I ask for and minds her own business."

"Hey, don't be a rude customer on my last night."

Nick froze, not sure he'd heard her correctly. "What?"

She nodded. "Nicole's going to be here next weekend, so I'm all done. I'm a little sad about it, to be honest. This has been one of my favorite places to work."

Then don't go. The words were on the tip of his tongue, but he bit them back. Even if she did stay in town, she couldn't take the job away from Nicole. And this wasn't her dream.

First Helen had come home. Now Lucy was working her last shift at the Keel. It was the next step in her plan to get in her car and leave Wayward Harbor behind.

To leave *him* behind.

He cleared his throat. "So what are you doing early Tuesday morning?"

"I don't know. How early?"

"Like two o'clock in the morning early?"

Lucy recoiled, but then understanding dawned and she grinned. "Did you get a reservation? Are we doing it?"

"I *did* get one. I know it's short notice, but it has to do with how they release the reservations to try to make it fair for tourists already in the area. So sunrise on Cadillac Mountain on Tuesday?"

"Definitely." She wrinkled her nose. "The logistics, though. Maybe it would make the most sense if I just stayed at your place since we have to get up and leave in the middle of the night."

Maybe it *did* make sense, but Nick's brain short-circuited at the idea of Lucy sleeping in his bed. Of course, she might have been implying she was going to crash on his couch, but he hoped not with every misguided fiber of his being.

"We're too old for all-nighters, so you might want to cut off the coffee tomorrow earlier than usual," he warned. "We'll have to sleep before that drive."

"I'll work in the yard all morning so I'm tired from the fresh air," she said.

"Good idea. I took tomorrow and Tuesday off, but I have some stuff to do in the morning, so I'll be home by early afternoon." He paused in spreading butter on his roll to give her a stern look. "Dress warm. And then bring something warmer to put on when we get there."

"Got it," she said as a guy down the bar called her name. "I guess I should see what he wants. It would suck to get fired on my last day."

Nick let himself watch her walk away before going back to buttering his dinner rolls before they got cold. He'd come here to get just a little taste of Lucy's company. And now she was coming for a sleepover at his place.

He wasn't sure that was progress, but he wasn't turning her down.

Chapter Eighteen

Good morning, Wayward Harbor! You'll notice extra donation jars at many of our local businesses for the foreseeable future. Dolly's fine! But there was a close call earlier this week when a very kind tourist tried to "rescue" her. Luckily, as those of us who've taken a turn transporting Dolly to the vet have learned, Dolly isn't a fan of car rides and was fairly vicious in rejecting the attempted adoption. We're raising money to make cute, funny signs for the windows in town and for lodging establishments introducing our Dolly and asking visitors not to rescue her.

First comment: An attempted adoption? More like a cat burgling!

*Next twenty-two comments: *groan**

Twenty-fourth comment: Meow, meow, everybody. Don't get your whiskers in a bunch!

—Wayward Harbor Online Community Group

On Monday morning, Lucy went into town with a plan to buy small bins for repacking her belongings. It would all be going back into her car, and then she'd be in Sydney's guest room temporarily. Her wardrobe needs in Maine had been simple, but she'd want easy access to *all* of her belongings in Florida, so reorganizing everything was on her to-do list.

But somehow she ended up at the Scuttlebutt instead. Business had definitely picked up for Willow over the summer—which was why Lucy was parked two blocks away—but she was able to grab an empty table. It was the smallest one, with only two chairs, and didn't have a window view so it was the seating of last resort for visitors.

It was nearly twenty minutes before a lull allowed Willow to sit down with her, and Lucy knew she might get two minutes or she might get an hour, so she started with the important stuff.

"Nick scored a sunrise reservation for Cadillac Mountain," she said. "For tomorrow."

"That explains the decaf," Willow said. "It confused me, but I heard that woman complaining about the raisins in her oatmeal raisin cookie and couldn't think straight. You have to leave really early for that."

"I have to get up at two in the morning, apparently."

"Oh, that's fun."

"Yeah. I'm going to stay at Nick's tonight so it's easier. We won't disturb Gran, plus I can sleep the extra ten or fifteen minutes I'll save by not having to drive over."

"I really can't figure out what you and Nick are," Willow said.

"What do you mean?"

"You're obviously friends. And you did live together."

Lucy laughed. "We didn't *live together* live together. Not like that. We both needed to stay at Gran's, and it happened to be at the same time."

"Okay, sure. But the way you look at him and talk about him." She shrugged. "I feel like there's more, and yet, nobody's ever talked about seeing you two touch or hold hands or anything. It's hard to explain. Like a vibe, I guess."

Lucy took a sip of her drink, trying to buy herself some time to think. It didn't help, so she took another.

"I guess it wouldn't make sense for you to get together, anyway," Willow continued. "I can't really see him moving to Miami, and long-distance relationships are hard. Plus, usually the long-distance thing has an end date—like there's a plan to live in the same place eventually. You're actually *moving* to Miami."

"Yeah."

"I'm so excited for you. I mean, *Miami*. I don't think I've ever met anybody who's lived there."

"I'll text you and Taylor photos all the time." She checked the time on her phone. "I should go. I promised Gran I'd pick up a few things at the market, and then I need to pack some warm clothes for tomorrow."

"I hope it's a clear morning. I've always wanted to go up there, but I never have."

"I'll let you know if it's worth getting up in the middle of the night for."

Willow laughed. "If you go up when the days are shorter, you don't have to get up so early. But then, it's *really* cold."

"No, thanks." After swiping her card in the machine, Lucy gave Willow a quick hug. "I won't see you tomorrow, but I'll let you know how it goes."

She got waylaid by Dolly on her way to the market and lost some time to petting the cat. She didn't sit on the sidewalk this time, though, because Nick had things he needed to do this morning and she didn't want him interrupted by somebody worried about her again.

Then, just as she was getting out of her car at home, her phone chimed. The high of thinking it might be Nick to the low of seeing Iris's name was quite a swing, but she leaned her hip against her front fender and read the text message.

Are you over your tantrum yet?

She deleted the message and went into her contacts. She blocked Iris Macauley without batting an eye, and then went into the house.

"I found you something today," Gran told her as soon as she walked through the door.

"Hi," she said as she toed off her shoes. "Is it a good thing or a bad thing?"

"I guess that depends on how you feel about wearing somebody else's wool underwear."

Lucy froze in the act of setting her tote bag and the two bags from the market on the kitchen table. "I can honestly say I've never given that a lot of thought. Whose underwear are they? And have they been washed? Why did you find me used underwear and why are they wool? I have so many questions."

Helen's laughter filled the cottage. "Fair enough. They're not underwear in the way you're thinking. They're long underwear, but a fine wool so you won't get too hot, but you'll be nice and toasty, even if you get wet."

"Oh. Like a base layer for skiing."

"Exactly. I didn't know you skied!"

"I don't. I just watch a lot of television, but I guess I missed the shows with the wool underwear." Lucy stopped, frowning. "You mean like those things they wore in the old Westerns, with the flap on the butt?"

"No, although they do make those. Here, just look at them."

Lucy caught the bundle of clothes her grandmother tossed to her and was pleasantly surprised to find a separate top and bottom—not a flap on the butt—made of a fine, smooth wool. They were black and wouldn't add any bulk under her clothes.

"These could probably pass for leggings and a long-sleeved shirt if I put a cardigan or tunic over them," she said.

"Maybe where you come from, you could," Gran agreed. "But around here, people would know you're running around in your wool underwear. To answer your question, they're mine, but I rarely wear them because they're too long for me and bunch up and I found a shorter pair from a different company. And yes, they've been washed. They're yours if you want them."

"Thank you, Gran. I probably won't have a lot of use for them in Miami, but I'll be grateful for them tomorrow morning, for sure."

"You can leave them in the dresser drawer in there with some dryer sheets to keep them fresh. You'll have them when you come visit because Miami's definitely not going to help you acclimate to coastal Maine."

"Thanks, Gran."

"Did you get those bins you were after?"

"No, I didn't," Lucy confessed as a guilty flush spread over her cheeks, as if Gran cared if she bought the bins or not. "I visited Willow instead."

"I get so much joy from you two girls finding each other again. You drank a lot of coffee while you were there, did you?"

"Decaf only," she said. "And I walked from the Scuttlebutt to the market and back, hoping to tire myself out."

"Good thinking. I'll put those groceries away while you start getting your stuff together. And mine won't fit you, so you make sure you ask Nick to borrow a good pair of his wool socks. Nothing ruins a day faster than cold feet. He works outside, so he'll have some good ones."

"I won't forget, though knowing Nick, he'll probably have a pair set out for me before I even get there."

"That's the truth. He's such a good man, that one."

Lucy glanced at her grandmother to see if she might be hinting around at something, but Gran had her back to her, putting the butter in the fridge.

Rather than responding to that, Lucy grabbed her tote bag and went into her room. Gran had already helped her pick out the clothes that would be comfortable, but also warm. They included a thick sweater with a hood, and then a windbreaker Gran had picked up for her in a thrift shop in South Carolina. She packed it all into a bag, along with the wool underwear. Then she debated on what she should bring to sleep in.

They'd never really nailed down *where* she would be sleeping. She might end up on his couch, and he lived with two of his brothers, so she threw a pair of leggings and a long T-shirt into the bag.

She'd bring them, and then just secretly hope she ended up not needing them.

"It's good to see you, Nick."

"You, too, Coach."

And it was. Nick missed hanging out with the man who'd coached and mentored him from a kid with nothing going on to a guy accepted to a D1 school on scholarship. It was a big thing for a football coach in a small regional high school to have one of his guys go all the way, and Nick had been on his way. Coach McCabe had cried the day Nick told him he was dropping out and coming home to Wayward Harbor.

"I reach out to you every year about this time," Coach said, leaning back in his creaky chair. "What brought you in this time?"

"I feel like I'm in a good place."

"You know I'll be glad to have you. Hell, don't tell Andy, but I wish my assistant coach spot was open."

Nick laughed, shaking his head. "I can't make that kind of commitment. I have a lot on my plate, and even though I want to make time for something that makes me happy, I want to do something nonessential. I'm happy to help out and coach and mentor wherever I'm needed, but I don't want anybody in a position to be let down if I drop the ball."

"I understand," Coach said. "You've got a lot to teach those boys, and I'll be grateful for whatever time you can give us."

"I'm the grateful one, Coach."

They shook hands, and then Coach had a meeting with a teacher about a player's grades, so Nick headed back to town. He'd only had one cup of coffee that morning, but he was riding so high after the meeting, he didn't even need the caffeine.

By the time he heard Lucy's car pull into the driveway, he was practically vibrating with nerves. Going to bed early was already going to be a challenge. He wasn't looking for a full night of sleep, but he'd need about a solid four hours before he made the drive. And that meant being asleep by ten o'clock at the latest.

Because the big door was open to let in the breeze, Lucy saw him through the screen door when he was on his way to greet her. She smiled and let herself in, meeting him in the living room.

Nick was so happy to see her, he didn't even think about whether he should—he leaned and gave her a quick kiss hello.

Of course, in the next breath he panicked. That wasn't a thing they usually did, but she didn't seem to mind. She just smiled and held up her bag. "So, where should I put this?"

"I'll take it," he said, mostly because he'd been raised not to stand around with empty hands while a woman carried a bag.

Then he realized his mistake because he had no idea what he should do with it. "So, where should I put this?"

To his relief, Lucy laughed and rested her hand on his arm. "We didn't talk about that part."

"I realized that *after* the conversation was over and couldn't think of a not-awkward way to bring it up." He shrugged. "But I did put clean sheets on my bed, just in case."

The way her hand went from resting on his upper arm to stroking down his forearm, her nails skimming his skin, took his breath away. "We definitely don't want clean sheets to go to waste."

"I'll be right back, then. Go ahead in the kitchen and poke around to see what we have if you want. We'll have to eat early so we can go to bed early, I guess."

"Oh, Gran told me to ask you for wool socks," she called up the stairs after him. "My feet are a lot bigger than hers."

"I've got some set out on my dresser for you. Wool underwear, too, though they'll be baggy on you."

"She gave me the set that was baggy on her, so I only need the socks."

After setting her bag on the chair in his room, Nick took a moment to breathe. He needed to calm down. It was Lucy. He didn't have to try so hard with her. He could relax and just be himself.

When he found her in the kitchen, she was leaning against the counter with a glass of water. "Oh good, you found the glasses."

"I did. I figured I'd just look in the cabinet where most people keep their glassware."

"Smart-ass." He loved her laugh. "Are you excited about this upcoming adventure?"

"Upcoming shenanigan, thank you very much. And yes. I'm a little worried about you doing all the driving on so little sleep. I've never driven a pickup truck, but it can't be that hard. Gas. Brake. Steering wheel. Keep all four tires between the yellow line and the white line."

"Pretty much. But I'm hoping to get at least a few hours of sleep. If I tell myself it's a nap and not stress about it, maybe it'll work."

Lucy's mouth curved into a naughty smile. "You might need some help relaxing when we get in bed."

He rested his hand on her hip, but then he heard a truck door slam, so he didn't move in for the kiss. "That'll be Theo."

"Can you tell by the sounds of their truck engines?"

"Sometimes, but I can always tell when it's Theo because he slams that damn door."

Sure enough, seconds later, Theo walked into the kitchen with his face in his phone. "Hey, Nick, did you hear Reese Noonan and Faith Lincoln reconciled and they're doing a joint interview on prime-time TV?"

Nick watched Lucy's entire body tense, and he was afraid she'd drop her glass, but she was gripping it so tightly that wasn't possible. After setting it very carefully on the counter, she tried to take a steadying breath, but it caught in her chest and came out in a hiccupped sound of distress.

Theo looked up from his phone at the sound. "Oh damn. Sorry, Lucy. I didn't know you were here."

"No, it's fine," Lucy assured him, but Nick could hear the slight tremor in her voice, even if his brother couldn't. "I hadn't heard the news, so it just took me by surprise is all."

"I told you both Lucy's crashing here since we have to get up in the middle of the might to beat the sunrise."

"Oh right. Cool. Makes sense." Then he went to the fridge to grab a soda and went out to the backyard as if a woman staying over with Nick was an everyday occurrence.

It definitely was not.

"You okay?"

"Of course," she said. "The names kind of blindsided me, I guess. Until I heard them, I hadn't realized how little I thought about the Fairee debacle anymore."

"That's a good thing." And then he thought about kissing her again.

The slider opened and Theo was back. "Hey, I heard you went to the high school today and met with Coach McCabe."

Lucy's eyes widened, but Nick just glared at his brother. "How the hell did that get around?"

Theo shrugged. "I don't know. I heard it at the fire station. You finally going to join the team?"

"I'm going to volunteer to help out some," he said. "When I can. But I'm not officially on staff."

Lucy's hand gripped his arm, and Nick looked into her eyes to see them gleaming with excitement. "That's wonderful! I'm so excited for you!"

And then she threw her arms around his neck, and he didn't care if the entire population of Wayward Harbor was watching. He was helpless to do anything but hug her back, lifting her off her feet a little.

Beyond the cloud of her hair, he saw Theo's eyebrows arch. Nick narrowed his eyes. Theo smiled. Nick gave him his best threatening big brother look.

Theo's smile grew into a grin, but he went back outside and closed the slider.

Chapter Nineteen

I lost my phone! Can somebody who has my number call it, please? Maybe somebody will find it!

First comment: What ring tone are we listening for?

Original poster: I don't know what the ring tone is. I always keep it silenced.

—Wayward Harbor Online Community Group

While there'd been plenty of nights in her younger days Lucy wasn't coming in and going to bed until two o'clock, she thought this might be the first time she'd gotten out of bed to go out at that obscene hour.

But she rolled out when Nick nudged her because his alarm was going off. She'd stretched, naked and aching in all the right places, and he'd dropped his head back to his pillow and reached for her.

"Nope. We'll fall back to sleep after, and we have shenanigans to get up to."

There was creeping through the house and silently drinking a mug of coffee while Nick filled two large tumblers with the remainder of the carafe. After brewing another pot, he poured it into a thermos and, because he was a good guy, he took the time to set up a fresh carafe to brew at its usual time for his brothers.

Then there was what felt like forever of driving in the dark. Luckily, Nick knew the roads and was a confident driver, but Lucy felt some pressure to keep up the small talk so he'd stay awake. She was down to sharing her favorite internet conspiracy theories—not involving quarterbacks and actresses—when he turned into the national park.

When they reached the intersection where they scanned his reservation and he started driving up a narrow, windy road, through what looked in the dark to be very rugged terrain, she started getting nervous. Did this road even go all the way to the top?

"Wait. Does this shenanigan require actual hiking? Because I appreciate that this is something you've always wanted to do, but I'm not really dressed for it. Also, it's very dark."

"So if you had the proper footwear, a good coat and a flashlight, you'd want to go for a hike?"

She narrowed her eyes at him. "I would say yes just so you don't feel bad, but I'm afraid you've hidden women's hiking boots and some headlamps somewhere in this truck so…no. Hiking isn't really my thing."

"Obviously, it's too dark right now, but on the way down you'll be able to see the views from this road. They're pretty amazing."

"I thought you've never been up here," she said. "Did I get up in the middle of the night to do something you've already done?"

"If I'd been up here, I wouldn't have told you it was something I've always wanted to do and never have. I've seen pictures online, so I know what it looks like."

Lucy was relieved when they reached the parking lot and she could see that they were at the top. She would have hiked a little bit for Nick's sake, if she had to, but she'd rather not.

There were other vehicles in the lot and people roaming

around, but Nick found a parking spot and turned off the truck. Once the headlights went out, it was dark again, though she could see the headlights of another vehicle coming up the hill bouncing in the trees.

As soon as she opened the door, she was rocked by a cold wind. “Oh, this is fun.”

She thought she’d muttered it under her breath, but on the other side of the truck, Nick laughed. “You were warned.”

He pulled out a big bundle that she’d noticed in the back seat earlier. It was held closed by a bungee cord, and she’d just assumed it was something for work.

“Okay, let’s find our spot,” he said, and after pulling up the hood of her sweater, grabbing their almost empty coffee tumblers and the thermos with more coffee, she followed him.

Lucy had no idea where they were or what direction they were facing, but she had faith that Nick knew in which direction the sun would appear. Plus, as she looked around, she realized most of the other visitors who’d already picked a spot were facing the same direction. There was one guy who was facing the opposite way, but there was a possibility he was sleeping against a boulder.

“This is good,” Nick said, standing next to a flat slab of rock.

Lucy was pretty sure her butt wasn’t going to appreciate that, and it also looked very cold, but she kept her mouth shut. This was something Nick had always wanted to experience, and if she ended up with an aching, hypothermic butt, so be it.

After taking off the cord, Nick unrolled the bundle. He put down what looked like a blanket made of aluminum foil. Then a flannel-backed blanket. She laughed when she realized the next thing he unrolled was a cushion from one of their patio loungers. And then he spread a heavy blanket over that.

“Okay,” he said. “Get comfortable.”

He'd chosen the rock well because it sloped in the front, so she wasn't forced to cross her legs. And after she'd settled on the cushion with the coffee supplies in front of her, he sat next to her. The last step was a wool blanket he draped over their shoulders.

"You warm enough?"

"It's perfect," she said, and it was true. She would have told him she was warm enough regardless, but with the layers she was wearing and the wool cocoon they were wrapped in, she was toasty.

"Look at that sky."

The awe in his voice made her throat tight with emotion as she looked around. Even though the sun wouldn't break the horizon for a while yet, the shifting colors in the dark sky were stunning.

After a few minutes, he poured the coffee from the thermos into the tumblers and handed one to her. It was surprisingly warm, and she wrapped her hands around it.

"Should I set up my phone to video it or take pictures or anything?" she asked after taking a sip.

"No." He turned his head to look at her, his smile gleaming in the darkness. "I just want to experience it with you."

Lucy would gladly get up in the middle of the night anytime to see that look on his face. It was so worth it.

Nick watched the sun glimmer on the horizon and knew this moment was rare. As the dawn broke, Lucy was snuggled against his side with his arm and the blanket wrapped around her. They were quiet, watching the day begin together, and he hoped there would never come a time in his life he couldn't remember the way this moment felt.

They sat there even after others began moving, packing up things or exploring the top of the mountain. Some of them would be hiking, others were already starting their cars to move on to the next item on their vacation list.

"Was it everything you hoped it would be?" Lucy asked after he'd pointed out things they could see now. The ocean. Islands. It was going to be a gorgeous day.

"It was." He squeezed her shoulders. "Thank you for helping me make the time to do this. I maybe could have just gone the rest of my life thinking this was a thing I'd really like to do someday."

She laughed and it carried in the crisp air. "You might be onto something with making lists, you know."

"Now, the big challenge. Can I get up?"

"So is now a good time to tell you I *really* have to pee? That was a lot of coffee."

"Follow that crowd of women over there and get in line. I'll put all this away."

"Why isn't there a crowd of men?"

Nick gestured around the mountain. "So many trees."

"Gross."

He chuckled and watched her pick her way back over the rocks to the main path. Then he packed away the thermos and empty tumblers and rewrapped the cushion and blankets. By the time he had it all back in the truck, Lucy was walking back toward him, though she kept stopping to take pictures with her phone.

Even though the wind was fairly wicked on the summit, they explored for a few minutes. Lucy wanted to take a selfie of them with the view spanning behind them, and Nick laughed. "Another first."

"You've never taken a selfie?"

"Nope. I take pictures. Others have taken pictures of me, but I've never taken one of myself with my phone. Why would I?"

"I'll show you why."

And Nick patiently suffered through Lucy's process of taking the perfect selfie. First there was finding just the right backdrop. The right angles. Then waiting for a family to wander out of her shot. Then making him lean into her—which he didn't mind—and framing it just the way she wanted.

Then she realized she looked like a gnome with the hood of her sweater up and pushed it down. With her hair in the wind becoming part of the process, he wasn't sure if they'd still be there, deleting bad selfies until the sun went down again.

But then she got one and handed him her phone to see it. When he looked at the screen and saw them laughing together, her hair blowing across their faces with the mountain behind them and the ocean beyond that, he understood the selfie thing.

"Send me that," he told her, and she grinned.

By the time that was over, she had to pee again, but once they were in his truck, she dug through her bag until she found a stronger hair tie. "What now?"

"You got anywhere to be today?"

She shook her head, so he smiled and backed out of the parking space. He didn't have anywhere to be, either, so they might as well see the rest of the park. Of course, once they reached the bottom of the summit road, they were back with all of the tourists who hadn't gotten a reservation. Even though it was midweek, the weather was gorgeous, so he pulled into the slow-moving traffic.

They hit all of the tourist hot spots, and Lucy had to dig out her phone charger because she took so many photos with her phone.

"I can't believe you've never come here," she said after they'd stopped at a little picnic spot where she could explore the rocks and find shells.

He hoped she found all the treasures she'd hidden in his truck, or it was going to smell pretty bad after a few hot days.

He shrugged, letting a car pull out in front of him even though the car behind him was clearly impatient. "I think when you're from a place, you don't do all the tourist stuff."

"Well, you should have. It's the most gorgeous place I've ever seen."

"I'm glad I didn't," he said, taking her hand and clasping their fingers over the center console. "Because I got to do it with you."

She gave him a warm smile before being distracted by a huge sailboat out in the far distance. "It must be pretty in the fall, too."

"Probably fewer people," he grumbled as they crept down the road, but she just laughed and kept watching for the next thing that would take her breath away.

Nick didn't mind sitting in traffic because Lucy was beside him. And nothing could get to him right now, because he was having the greatest day of his life.

Chapter Twenty

Why can't we put little seasonal outfits on Cricket's statue like Boston does for the ducklings? He could be wearing a little Red Sox hat right now!

First comment: Go Yankees!

Admin: Stop messaging me. I can't ban a member of the group for having terrible taste in sports teams.

—Wayward Harbor Online Community

"I should just get in my car and go," Lucy said, though her words were muffled because her forehead was resting on the kitchen table.

Next to her head was the phone still open to the screenshot of a social media post Taylor had sent to her with an accompanying message of eleven exclamation points.

Hey, Fairee lovers! Did you hear that Faith Lincoln and Reese Noonan are back together and ready to talk? Everybody will be watching, but my friends and I are on our way to a little seaside town in Maine for a little vacation. That's right! We're going to "run into" the other woman and convince her to serve up some tea! More soon!

"You don't need to leave until you're good and ready to

go," Gran told her, and she actually sounded a little amused, though Lucy didn't lift her head to see if she was smiling.

"What if they stake out the cottage, trying to get pictures?"

"There's no way for them to be safely off the road without pulling onto my property, and either way, Chief Rollins will run them off. They're not welcome here, and we certainly won't be giving them any tea."

Lucy lifted her head. "You know that doesn't mean actual tea, right?"

Helen gave her a stern look that made Lucy's cheeks flush. "Yes, I know what it means. I think I spend more time online than you do, young lady. And you need to be done hiding from what other people say about you. Put your chin up, square your shoulders and live your damn life."

"Yes, ma'am," Lucy said, sitting up straighter, and Helen smiled.

"And you can't go running off to Miami with everything you own strewn around like a tornado dropped down and only tore up that bedroom."

She definitely had a point there. The plan to organize and repack her stuff for the car trip was taking longer than she thought it would. Maybe because, other than bringing it all in the bedroom and sorting it into something very loosely resembling piles, she hadn't touched it. She also hadn't messaged Sydney to make plans for her arrival.

"I never did buy those bins. I ended up visiting with Willow instead. And I also met Taylor out on the walking trail so we could take a walk together. Oh, and Cadillac Mountain with Nick. I keep forgetting, but I'm going to buy them right now." She stood, determined to get moving.

"Can you run into the market for me? We're almost out of sugar."

She stilled, not because she minded doing errands for her

grandmother, but because the hardware store was slightly away from the heavy tourist traffic, whereas the market was more visible. She'd been planning to sneak in the back way to Smith's, and then sneak back out.

"Don't let them stop you from living your life," Helen said again, more sternly this time. "If you let them in your head, you're going to end up on the couch with a blanket over your head."

Lucy turned to face her grandmother. "Did Nick tell you?"

"Did Nick tell me what?" she asked, looking genuinely confused.

"Never mind. So, sugar. Anything else?"

An hour later, Lucy had found some plastic storage bins she liked at the hardware store and was in the market's baking aisle, trying to talk herself out of buying an entire bag of dark chocolate chips, when she heard her name called in the next aisle.

"Oh, sorry," the voice continued. "I thought you were somebody else."

"That happens all the time," she heard Taylor respond. "Actually a lot of people tell me I look just like that woman who got harassed because of that actress and her cheating jerk boyfriend."

"Are you from here?"

"Yes, and it's so annoying. Tourists have been confusing me with her since it happened."

Lucy didn't hear if anything else was said because she was already at the end of the baking aisle and turning away from where Taylor had been loudly speaking. She thought about making a run for the front doors, but she was halfway down the last aisle when she saw a woman holding up her cell phone as though filming.

And Kim Perkins, who looked right at Lucy.

Cursing under her breath, she ducked into an alcove that had several doors. The restrooms, which would be dead ends with no way to escape. And one that was marked for employees only. She had no idea where it went, but she was afraid it was just a break room with no exits.

"Lucy Macauley?" Lucy heard Kim ask, and she closed her eyes. She was about to go viral again. "Never heard of her."

Lucy's eyes flew open and she let out her breath in a ragged sigh of relief.

"Her car is in the parking lot. She's a redhead and hard to miss."

"We're a tourist town. There are always cars I don't recognize in the parking lot. As a matter of fact, most of them park in this lot because it's easy, and then walk down the street to the arcade as if the people who live in this town don't have groceries to lug out to our cars."

"Arcade?"

"It's quite the hangout spot. So whatever her name is might have parked here, but she's probably not in the market."

Calling the pizza place with three pinball machines and two Skee-Ball machines an arcade was a stretch, but Lucy appreciated the effort.

A few seconds later, Kim joined her in the alcove and didn't look pleased about it. "You still have Nevada plates? And your car's out front?"

"Yes."

Kim Perkins probably couldn't have looked more unhappy if she tried. "Go through that door behind you. Don't follow it all the way back to the loading dock because they might be watching that exit. There's a door to the left that leads to the break room, and it has an exit door into the alley between the buildings. You can't really see it from the sidewalk. I'll meet you at the end of the alley in two minutes. You can figure out how to come back for your car later."

Before she could ask any questions—like *why?*—Kim was gone.

She did as she was told, and a few minutes later she was on her way out of town in the passenger seat of Kim's SUV. She took a winding path out of town, down back roads Lucy hadn't even seen, checking her rearview mirror constantly. Finally satisfied, she navigated back to the main road that would take Lucy home.

"I really appreciate this," Lucy said, because the silence was *incredibly* awkward. "I'm sorry to put you out. Did you leave Taylor at the market?"

"No, she has her own vehicle. The two of us being there at the same time was purely coincidence."

"Oh, good." They'd already been pulling away from the market when Lucy realized Taylor wasn't in the back seat, but there wasn't a lot she could do about it.

The older woman sighed. "Taylor's an only child. Obviously my marriage was pretty rough for a while, and by the time we'd moved past it as best we could, it felt like it was too late to have more kids."

Lucy kept her mouth closed, determined not to apologize for her mother's actions, no matter how bad she felt for Kim.

"You're Taylor's sister." The words sounded dragged out of her. "She's getting married and she's going to have a baby. And she should have her sister."

"I'm going to Miami," she said out loud. But *I'm going to be an aunt* was echoing in her mind, as it so often did.

"I know you're leaving, but she'll still have you to talk to." Kim hit her turn signal and pulled into Helen's driveway. "It's not easy for me. I know it's not your fault, but..."

"I understand."

"I'm going to try, for Taylor's sake. It might take me a little time, but you won't need to smuggle her into secret birthday parties at closed bakeries in the future."

"You knew?"

"Of course I knew. It's Wayward Harbor."

"For the record, it was a surprise party. I neither aided nor abetted the smuggling."

Kim actually laughed as she came to a stop and immediately put the vehicle in Reverse to indicate she wouldn't be staying. "Good luck with that Fairee mess. We'll all do what we can."

"Thank you. For everything."

As she got out of the SUV, the screen door opened and Nick stepped out onto the porch. He gave a half-hearted wave to Kim as she drove off, but kept his eyes on Lucy.

"Are you okay?" he demanded. With his jaw clenched and eyes narrowed, Nick was drawn up to his full height and scanning the driveway and tree line, as if searching for a threat among the leaves.

Lucy had never seen him look like that, and it was a little scary. And also very hot.

"Some paparazzi or just random people wanting to go viral were looking for me, and Kim told them she'd never heard of me and told them to check the pizza place," Lucy explained. "And then she told me how to get out to the side alley, where she picked me up. I couldn't go out the front without being seen. Plus my car still has Nevada plates, so even with all the tourists in town, it still stands out."

"Come on inside," he said, but there was a tension in his voice that made her hesitate. He was probably thinking about the possibility of strangers taking photos through their windows.

"I should go stay at a motel because Gran—"

"She's not worried about them. She's worried about *you*. Get inside."

As soon as she stepped through the door, Gran pulled her into a strong hug, holding her until her breathing calmed. "I shouldn't have sent you to the market."

"No, you were right, Gran. I can't not live my life. And honestly, I shouldn't have run from them. I should have let them take pictures or videos of whatever they wanted and just told them I had no comment."

"After what the internet did to you, nobody blames you for hiding," Nick said.

"Why are you here and not at work?" she asked, just then realizing Nick being in the cottage wasn't everyday life anymore.

"Taylor called me, and I guess I beat you here."

"Kim took a lot of back roads leaving town. It was like being in an action movie, except, you know, a lot less fun."

"Well, I don't know," Gran said as she poured Lucy a glass of ice water and gestured for her to sit. "Watching an action movie is fun, but it's probably not fun for the characters *in* the movie."

Once she was settled at the kitchen table and had a few sips of water, Lucy finally started to relax. It was hard not to with the two people who made her feel safe sitting at the table with her.

"So Kim Perkins, huh?" Nick said. "Didn't see that coming, because Taylor didn't mention her mom's part in it. She just said people were in town looking for you and you were on your way home."

"Trust me, I didn't believe it, either."

She filled them in on her entire conversation with Taylor's mother, and it didn't sound any less believable coming out of her mouth than it had from Kim's. They just listened, eyes wide until she was done.

"Well, this has certainly been quite a day," Helen said after a moment.

Lucy sighed. "Well, I did get the bins I wanted for packing. They're in my car, which is still in the market's parking lot, but at least I got them. Oh! Oh, Gran. I didn't get the sugar."

"Considering you snuck out the back alley and there are no registers out there, it's probably for the best you didn't have the sugar yet," she replied, and they all laughed.

With the tension eased, Lucy looked at her grandmother, taking comfort from the steadiness of her gaze. Even though it had turned into a mess, Gran hadn't been wrong. Lucy needed to live her life. She had a strong foundation, and now she needed to build the life she wanted to live without hiding from people who wanted a say in it.

"I'll get one of my brothers and we'll grab your car," he told Lucy before smiling at Helen. "And some sugar."

"You're so sweet, Nick," Helen said. "What would we do without you?"

And then Lucy wanted to cry again because she was going to find out the answer to that question very soon.

What would she do without him?

Nick was so disgusted with himself, he didn't even look in the mirror once while brushing his teeth before bed.

He was a horrible person. There was no way around that, and he knew he was going to toss and turn all night, but he didn't care. He deserved it.

When Lucy had told him about the Fairee crowd finding her, his first thought was for her safety. But his second thought was about all the people in her life who'd turned their backs on her rather than deal with the hassle.

And how maybe it would cost her Miami.

If her friend in Miami decided to team up with a cocktail artist who came with less baggage, maybe Lucy would decide to stay in Wayward Harbor.

With him.

What kind of jerk hoped a woman's dreams would be crushed so she'd give up and spend her life with him?

Nick didn't deserve her.

After rinsing his brush, he finished up in the bathroom and yanked the door open. Gray was in the hallway, on his way to the stairs, but he stopped when he saw Nick's face.

"You good?"

He was very much not good, actually. "Sure. Just tired."

"I've seen you so tired you fell asleep at the kitchen table and you looked better than you do right now." His brother jerked his head toward the stairs. "Want to sit on the porch and talk about it? Have a beer?"

"I just brushed my teeth."

"That is such a *you* thing to say. Come on and keep me company."

Nick knew he *should* go to bed, but he also knew he was just going to toss and turn half the damn night. He didn't think a beer would help, but it probably wouldn't hurt. And he probably wasn't going to be very good company, but Gray already knew that, so it was on him.

"Why do we do this on the front porch?" Nick asked once they were settled into the comfortably padded chairs. "The whole backyard is set up for sitting around, talking."

"I don't know why. But remember how Mom and Dad always sat out here when they wanted quiet time? I think the backyard was always about cookouts and kids playing and adults socializing, and I don't remember them ever sitting out here with friends. That was always out back. So, I think this is just the quiet family place."

Nick nodded, because as he sifted through old memories, Gray was right. The front porch had always been for quiet, private conversation.

"How's Lucy doing?" Gray asked, popping the bubble of warm, fuzzy nostalgia.

"Okay, I guess. And thanks again for your help getting her car back home."

He'd driven Lucy's car back to Helen's while Gray drove Nick's truck, and the first thing he'd noticed were the bins in the back seat. And when he'd set the bag of sugar on the passenger seat, it had rested on top of a shiny new road atlas, on which she'd probably map her route to Miami.

He'd made the drive surrounded by the evidence of Lucy preparing to leave town, and he'd had to fake every smile he'd given the two women for the few minutes he'd been in Helen's house. He'd handed over the keys and the sugar. And he'd turned down the invitation to stay for dinner on the pretext Gray had somewhere he had to be.

"Have you even asked her to stay?" Gray asked, snatching his attention back.

"What?"

"Have you even asked her to stay?" he repeated patiently. "And save me your stoic big brother act, please."

"What's that supposed to mean?"

"You might be putting on a whole just-friends-who-were-roomies-for-a-bit act around town, but we know you, Nick. You're into her in a way we've never seen you into a woman before."

"She's going to Miami. That's always been her plan."

"Plans change."

"It's none of your business."

Gray made a humming sound. "It kind of is."

"It's definitely not."

"We live with the fact you gave up your dream of playing pro ball because Dad died and we weren't old enough to do the work. And Mom hadn't had a job outside of doing Dad's paperwork for years. She couldn't have earned enough to keep this roof over our heads and feed three teen boys. And we know you gave up a dream coaching job when Mom got sick. And yes, you did it for Mom, but you also did it for us."

"I don't have *any* regrets," Nick shot back. "I would make the same choices every single time."

"And that's fine, but what we're *not* going to do is let you give up Lucy because of—" he stopped and waved his hand around "—any of this. Us. The house. The company. If you want to go to Miami with her, go. We can run the business without you. We don't want to, but we *can*. And if you're telling yourself anything different, you're not only screwing yourself over, but you're insulting the hell out of us."

"I would hate Miami."

"Maybe. Maybe not, especially if Lucy's there. Or, again, you could ask her to stay. I assume you haven't because, well, you're you. Putting yourself last."

"I'm not putting myself last. I'm putting her first, and yes, there's a difference. She's wanted to do this thing in Miami for a long time. It's her dream, and she has a friend there who's already in the business. It's a perfect opportunity for her."

"I still think you should ask her," Gray said. "Nick, you know better than anybody that dreams change. But they don't always change because something bad happens. Sometimes they change for good reasons."

"If her dream had changed, I doubt she'd be in the process of packing her car up, with a brand-new Rand McNally on the passenger seat."

"You'll regret not asking."

"I'll live with it."

"Hey," Theo yelled out of his open second-floor window. "Since we're having all the serious conversations tonight, Beck and I have been talking, and we think it's time to change the name of the company to Slater Brothers Construction."

"Do you know how much it would cost to redo everything?" Nick shouted back.

"Beck and I never really got to work with Dad, you know. To you and maybe to Gray, maybe this is a legacy you're carrying on, but to Beck and me, it's been us. The four of us, working together."

"He's got a point," Gray said. "Dad was a builder and we learned the ropes with him, doing jobs around town. He kept a roof over our heads and we learned to pound nails. He was a good man and a good provider. But this…this company with the excellent reputation—the company that's known throughout New England as the guys you want if you have a summer place in this area—that's us. You came in and you kept it going as we came up, and together we've built something Dad would be damn proud of. But *we* did it."

Nick swallowed the lump of emotion in his throat and had to blink a couple of times to clear his vision. "We did."

"Plus, you don't look old enough to be our dad, and the name really confuses people," Theo yelled down.

Nick laughed while Gray tried not to choke on the mouthful of beer he'd been in the process of swallowing. There was a time, when Theo was very young, that he'd actually thought his middle name was *you're too much.*

"Theo, you're too much," was something almost every single resident of Wayward Harbor had said to the youngest Slater at some point in his life.

"We'll need new hoodies," Nick yelled back. "And if we

can spend money rebranding the company, we sure as hell can afford to get the original supplier back."

"Done," Theo called, and then they heard his window slam closed.

Gray snorted. "Remember the time he leaned too far out the window, trying to eavesdrop on our parents, and he fell out of the window, rolled down the porch roof and fell into the rosebush?"

"I remember it took Mom, like, an hour to pick the thorns out of him with tweezers because he wouldn't sit still."

They sat in silence for a few minutes, listening to the night sounds, and then Nick pushed himself out of the chair. "It's been a long day, so I'm heading up."

"Don't forget to brush your teeth again."

"Funny."

"And Nick," Gray said as he was pulling open the screen door, "we all know we can lean on you. Do all of us a favor and figure out you can lean on *us*, too, okay? And if there's something you want, go after it. We've got you."

That lump in his throat was back, so he just nodded and went back inside.

Chapter Twenty-One

Did anybody else get a scone from Scuttlebutt, Spirits & Scones this morning? Mine tasted weird.

First comment: Mine, too, and they're usually so delicious!

Willow Brown: I'm so sorry! My shelves got moved around and I accidentally used the wrong ingredient. Please stop by anytime and have a delicious one on the house!

Third comment: Did you make Lavinia mad again?

—Wayward Harbor Online Community Group

"I just want to say that woman in the pictures did nothing wrong. I knew she didn't recognize me, and I gave her my middle name. I deliberately misled her, and even though drinking that coffee in public was our only interaction, I know she was harassed online. I can only apologize for the harm my actions caused her."

Lucy snorted and handed Taylor's phone back to her. Reese Noonan's public statement was too little and too late.

"It won't change anything that happened, but maybe it'll help going forward," Willow said. "Trolls are bored by personal responsibility, so they'll move on to somebody else, and you'll be free to start over in Miami."

Miami.

At some point during the night, while watching her tree twinkle away the darkness instead of sleeping, Lucy had finally admitted to herself why barely half of her stuff was packed and she still hadn't messaged Sydney to ask her to get the spare room ready and give her an ETA.

Once she left Wayward Harbor, her relationship with Nick would be over. And maybe he'd never held her hand in public or put a label on what was between them, but that didn't change the fact it was real.

She loved him. And she didn't want to leave him.

But she couldn't stay if he didn't feel the same. It would hurt too much.

The one thing Lucy knew for sure was that if Nick asked her to stay in Wayward Harbor, she would.

"Lucy?" Taylor touched her arm, dragging her away from her thoughts of what if. "What's going on?"

"That was not the face I expected you to make when I mentioned Miami," Willow added.

Thankfully, the Scuttlebutt was empty but for the three of them, because Lucy burst into tears. Napkins were shoved into her hands, and she buried her face in them as Willow and Taylor took turns rubbing her back.

When the crying jag passed and she'd dried her face with a fresh wad of napkins, Lucy took a shuddering breath. Then she sipped the water Willow brought her.

"What's going on?" Taylor asked again.

She wanted so badly to tell them everything. They were her friends—Taylor was her *sister*—but that was exactly the problem. If she told them the truth of how she felt about Nick and how it would hurt to leave him, but he hadn't even hinted at not wanting her to go, they'd be upset on her behalf. And he lived in this town. With them.

And even though he hadn't done anything wrong, Willow and Taylor might hold it against him.

"I'm going to miss you both so much," she finally settled. And it was the truth, even if it wasn't the whole of it.

As expected, they buried her in promises to call and text and FaceTime constantly. And they talked about how Lucy would have to come back when the baby was born. Plus, when the baby was a little older, they could all come visit her in Florida.

A lot of promises were made, though Lucy knew traveling from Maine to Florida wasn't cheap.

She smiled and nodded along with everything they said because they wanted her to feel better. But they didn't know there was only one person who could do that.

After parting ways with them, Lucy went home and found the driveway and cottage empty. It took her a moment to remember it was one of Helen's club meetings at the library—book club, knitting club, or maybe a talking about books while knitting club—and they usually went to Jenna's for supper after.

Since she was going to be alone for at least a few hours, Lucy dug out her Bluetooth speaker and plugged it in so she could blast a fun, upbeat playlist and get to work.

The first thing on her list was emptying the dryer. It had buzzed before she left for the Scuttlebutt, but she'd just popped the door and left it for later. It was a load she'd thrown in of heavier items—jeans, sweatshirts and cardigans that probably should be hand-washed, but she couldn't say because she deliberately didn't read care labels—and the last thing she pulled out was Nick's favorite hoodie.

Sitting back on her heels, Lucy pressed it to her face and

inhaled. It didn't smell like Nick, of course, but there was still some comfort in picturing him wearing it. And that was the problem.

If she was going to embrace a fresh start, she couldn't take it with her. There was no denying she was going to miss Nick painfully, and she could see herself sitting in her car with the air conditioning on blast so she could wallow in his hoodie. It would be the same as hiding under Gran's blankets, and she wasn't going to do that anymore.

After turning off the music, Lucy grabbed her bag and the hoodie, and she was in her car before she could talk herself out of driving to Nick's house. If there was ever a moment he might ask her to stay—to give her even a glimmer of hope Nick didn't want her to leave—it would be when she gave him back the hoodie.

He would know she was in the final stages of getting ready to head south.

But once she was parked in front of his house, she couldn't bring herself to get out of the car. Agreeing that what was between them was only a temporary fling had been a lie, and confessing that to him was daunting. She sat with her hands squeezing the steering wheel until her knuckles ached.

Then Nick stepped out onto the front porch and watched her, his head tilted as if waiting to find out what she was doing.

After taking a deep breath that did nothing to calm her nerves, Lucy grabbed the hoodie from the passenger seat and got out of her car. His gaze dropped to the sweatshirt in her hand as she walked toward him, and his body stiffened.

He didn't come down the steps to meet her, either. Instead, he moved to one side to make room for her to join him, but that grumpy face was back. Nick's spine was rigid and his jaw was tight. She wasn't sure what it meant, but he certainly wasn't happy to see her right now.

"Sorry to just drop in without texting first," she said, in case he'd been in the middle of something.

"It's not a big deal. My brothers and I were out back, but we have cameras and it alerts me when somebody pulls in, so I saw your car."

"Right. Well, I'm sorting through my stuff and I thought I'd give this back," she said, dropping the folded hoodie onto the nearest chair. "Because it's not actually *my* stuff."

"You can keep it if you want," he replied, his voice tense. "We'll be getting more."

"I probably won't need it in Miami."

His jaw tightened even more as he gave a sharp nod. "Probably not."

Lucy resorted to teasing to break through that mask because it had worked for her in the past. "Are you going to miss me?"

Nick didn't respond for so long, she actually thought he was going to ignore the question. But after pressing his lips together and swallowing hard, he looked into her eyes, and Lucy knew that, even though it was clearly hard for him, he was about to admit he didn't want her to go.

And the rest, they could figure out together.

"Will I miss having one more person in my life I have to take care of?"

The words struck her like a slap across the face, and she took a step back, as though putting more space between them could lessen the impact.

"Take *care* of?" Shock, hurt, embarrassment, anger—they were all swirling around her head and they all came out in her tone. "Sure, the night I arrived, I had to ask you to let me stay, and maybe I needed a kick in the ass to get off the couch at first, but I've never asked you to *take care* of me."

"Maybe you haven't technically asked, but you know I will.

You knew from day one that I don't let the people in my life down, and you just kept gravitating back to me."

"I gravitated to you—as you so unflatteringly put it—because we lived in the same house. It was hard not to. But also because I liked you. I enjoyed your company, and I thought the feeling was mutual, but apparently not."

Nick tried to catch her arm as she spun away from him, but she jerked away. "Lucy, wait. I didn't— I'm sorry."

No force on the planet could have made her turn back and face him as she processed that Nick Slater not only didn't return the feelings she'd developed for him, but he thought she was just looking for somebody to take care of her—the way her mother looked for a man to take care of her.

She was nothing to him but a barnacle he was looking to scrape off.

It was a painful way to get an answer, but at least she had one.

Nick wanted to cry. He wanted to throw up, or kick a truck tire until he couldn't move his leg anymore. He wanted to drop to the ground, screaming and kicking like a toddler throwing a tantrum. Instead, he just sat on his front steps, staring down his empty driveway.

He'd done the right thing.

Lucy would never ask him to go to Miami with her. She knew he would hate it there, so she wouldn't put him in the position of having to choose. But he couldn't ask her to stay because he couldn't ask her to give up Miami.

He knew what it felt like to give up what he wanted in his life for love. The love of his mother and his brothers. They were his whole heart, and he'd never lied to them. He would still make the same choices, every time.

But he knew how it hurt. Resentment and loss were like the tiniest of splinters. Not enough to keep him from enjoying life, but there. And ready to catch on something with a zing of pain at times.

How long could Lucy pour beers or scoop ice cream before she remembered she could've been a hot mixologist in a hot city? He did not want to see that regret in her eyes. He loved her too much to ask her to give it up. But he was afraid she might love him enough to do it anyway.

So he'd taken the choice off the table.

She would cry a little. She'd get angry. And she'd probably hate him for a long time. But she'd go to Miami and start her business, and eventually she'd be happier than she would have been with him.

That was what he had to believe.

Nick sat for a long time, trying to will his broken heart back together enough so he could go in the house and pretend he was just fine. But eventually he forced himself to get up, because if there was one thing he'd learned about grief, it was that the world didn't stop for it.

When he reached for the door, he saw it. His favorite hoodie, folded and set on the other chair where Lucy had left it.

He picked it up and buried his face in the fabric, hoping to breathe in the scent of her vanilla bodywash and the cream she used in her hair to fight the frizz. He wanted to inhale the scent of *Lucy*.

It smelled like laundry detergent.

When he went inside, his brothers were still in the backyard. He could hear their voices and their laughter, and he knew they were expecting him to come back. But he couldn't do it. Right now, with Lucy gone and his sweatshirt in his hand, there was no way he could pretend he wasn't falling apart inside.

Instead, he went upstairs and closed the door. Then, still fully clothed, he curled up on his bed, the hoodie in his arms, and hated himself.

Chapter Twenty-Two

We recently received a generous grant from a Maine author earmarked for growing our collection of popular genre fiction. Romance, mystery, horror, science fiction, fantasy! We're taking suggestions, so let us know what you want to be reading during the cold months to come!

First comment: [deleted]

Second comment: We don't ban books in Wayward Harbor, Colleen.

—Wayward Harbor Online Community Group

When Helen got home from her night out, she found Lucy sitting on the floor of her bedroom with her belongings spread all over the bed and the bins sitting, still empty, next to her.

Lucy looked up at her. "I didn't get very far."

Helen chuckled. "You're surprisingly bad at this. I mean, it's all going with you. It's just a matter of making it all fit in your car again."

"I know." A tear slipped down her cheek, and she swiped it away.

"What's really going on, honey?"

"I don't know if I want a fresh start."

"I don't understand. You want to go back to Las Vegas?"

"No. Not Las Vegas." That never even crossed her mind. "I really like it here, Gran."

Saying it out loud broke the logjam of emotion in her mind, and she sobbed into a fistful of tissues until there was nothing left in her but sniffles and hiccups.

Gran brought her a glass of water and then sat quietly on the edge of the bed, letting Lucy sort herself out. It took a while, but her grandmother was patient and waited until it didn't seem like there were any tears left in her.

Then she stood. "Let's go sit on the couch. I'm too old to perch on a bed like this."

Once they were settled on the couch, Helen reached over and covered her hand. "Lucy, if you want to stay here, you're welcome to stay. I hope you know that. As a matter of fact, nothing would make me happier, but I didn't want to say it out loud and influence you. I want what makes *you* happier, and I thought that was being a fancy mixologist in Miami."

"I thought so, too. But this town feels like *home*."

"It is home. And no matter where you live, it can still be home because I'm here. Taylor's here."

"Nick's here," Lucy whispered.

"Ah."

"You know how you told me building a life is like building a home and you're my foundation?" Her grandmother nodded. "You *are* my foundation, but in my heart, the house I was building had Nick in it."

"Did you tell Nick that?"

"No." Lucy shook her head, not wanting to admit she was too afraid.

"Okay. So I guess it's safe to say that Nick's already made some visits to your house. And that he liked being in your house."

Lucy snorted a laugh. "That sounds a little dirty, Gran."

"It really does, but it was too late. I'd committed to the analogy."

"I think Nick liked being in my house. But I think it's because he knew my house isn't permanent. Like maybe visiting my house was okay, but he doesn't want to live in it."

"But you didn't invite him to try, right?"

"It's complicated."

"It always is. But tell me why."

"I've had this dream of Miami for a long time. But even if he agreed to go, he'd be miserable, Gran. Maybe he'd try to hide it, but I know he'd hate Florida. And he'd hate being so far from his brothers. And Beck's kids."

"But you'd have to give up your dream to stay here with him."

"That's the thing, Gran," Lucy said, suddenly unable to sit still. She stood up and threw her arms in the air. "I don't know if that's even what I want. I dreamed about Miami at a time I had nothing but a job serving drinks, friendships that were superficial at best and Iris. Sydney, who was a good friend, said I should go to Miami and work with her, being my own boss doing a thing I'm passionate about."

"And now?"

"Now, my life is full. And my *heart* is full. I have you and Willow. And I have a *sister.* A sister who's getting married and having a baby. I have friends. I live in a community where people care about their neighbors and come together to take care of Dolly. Where a woman who has every reason to hate me will still help me when I need it. But—"

She ran out of steam and plopped back onto the couch, dropping her head into her hands. "But I love Nick, and I don't know if I *can* stay in Wayward Harbor because he thought my house was just a summer rental."

"Do you *believe* he thinks that?"

"I *know* he thinks that."

It was hard, but Lucy told her grandmother what Nick had said to her. About having one less person to take care of. Her voice cracked a couple of times, but she got it all out while her grandmother's expression hardened.

"That was very harsh," Helen whispered, but it was the confusion in her eyes that caught Lucy's attention.

She stilled, remembering the moment Nick broke her heart. But this time she pushed the hurtful words to the back of her mind and focused on his face and his body. His back rigid and his hand curled into fists. The line of his jaw.

His eyes.

"He was lying." Lucy looked at her grandmother and shook her head. "He was lying so I would go to Miami and chase my dream without looking back."

Helen's shoulders sagged with relief. "Okay, that sounds so much more like Nick."

"Yes, it does." The shock and pain of what he'd said had been so overwhelming in the moment, she hadn't seen it.

"What are you going to do?"

"Nothing." And she meant it. "Whether he thought he was doing the right thing or not, Nick hurt me. So if he wants back in my house, he's going to have to come knock on *my* door."

The next morning was brutal. Nick was usually the first one up, so he got to enjoy a cup of coffee before the others came down. But after one of the most miserable nights of his life, he'd overslept. Not only were Gray and Theo already sitting at the island with their coffee mugs, but Beck was there, too.

"Was about to go up and start vacuuming outside your door like Mom used to do," Beck said when he walked into the kitchen.

"You didn't come back outside last night, either," Theo added, while Gray just watched him.

"Didn't feel great," he muttered. "A bug or something. There better be coffee left in that pot."

"There was, like, half a cup left," Theo said. "So I poured it in your cup and brewed a fresh pot because you've trained us well."

Nick didn't laugh. He dumped out the half cup of cold coffee and filled it with fresh stuff from the carafe. Then he looked at Beck. "Why are you here? Where are the kids?"

"They're sitting on the back deck," his brother said, pointing to his kids, who were sitting in his line of sight on the other side of the glass. "They're eating the powdered doughnuts they talked me into like we didn't just get back from spending half the night in the urgent care center."

Nick's head jerked up, the idea of sadly staring into the depths of his coffee forgotten. "What happened? Why didn't you call?"

"We're fine. Jeremy's been coughing a lot lately, and it got so bad in the middle of the night I was afraid it was something awful, so I took him in. I was going to call one of you to sit with Sierra, but she was awake and refused to stay home." Beck sighed. "Turns out Jeremy has an ear infection and the cough is from fluids draining down the back of his throat. He's on antibiotics and will be fine, but I won't be working today."

Nick nodded. "Good. Though you could have just gone home and called, you know."

Beck grinned. "But then they would have eaten those powdered doughnuts in my house instead of on your back deck."

"The ant population thanks you," Gray said, saluting him with a raised mug.

Nick didn't usually mind his brothers' banter, but he'd

woken up with a headache almost as bad as his heartache and today wasn't the day.

"Are you aware you're actually making a growling sound out loud?" Theo asked, and then he shrugged when all three of them glared at him. "What? Just saying."

"I already mentioned I don't feel great. And I have a headache."

"And I hope I get called out so I don't have to work with you today," Theo grumbled. "Though that means somebody has a fire. Maybe a small fire would be okay. An outdoor garbage bin fire could work."

Nick stood and took his coffee upstairs to his bedroom, where he could drink it in peace. He'd take something for the headache, take a shower. Then he'd get in his truck, go to work, come home, eat, sleep and do it again. Grief had sideswiped him before, and he just had to push through it.

He made it a day and a half. Nick was on a ladder, trying to plan how they would take down a historic home's crown molding and tin ceiling without damaging it, when a question blew through his mind and almost knocked him off.

Is Lucy still in Wayward Harbor?

She'd brought him his hoodie back, and that could only have meant she was wrapping up her stay and saying goodbye. There was a possibility she'd thrown her stuff in her car yesterday and was already driving south.

Feeling shaky, Nick climbed down the ladder before he could fall off. Then he stared blankly at the wall they'd be demolishing soon.

Her last memory of him would be the hurtful lies that had come out of his mouth. And his last memory of her would be the utter devastation in her eyes. He'd burned it down, and everything they'd shared was ashes.

If she was gone, it was what he'd wanted for her. To go to

Miami and not look back. He didn't want her torn between him and what she wanted from her life. But now that she might be gone, the pain and regret couldn't be ignored. Maybe she was okay, but he couldn't live with the possibility she wasn't.

He looked up at Beck, who was standing on top of a ladder at the other end of the crown molding, staring down at him. His brother didn't look confused or annoyed by the interruption. He just looked down at him for a long moment and then smiled. "Go."

Nick didn't need to be told twice. He sprinted through the house, past Gray and Theo in the kitchen, where they were measuring the room to be updated. He left an explanation up to Beck and jumped in his truck. Before turning the key in the ignition, he rested his hand on the hoodie lying folded on the passenger seat, hoping for luck.

When he pulled into Helen's driveway, Nick almost drove into a tree when the relief of seeing Lucy's car parked next to her grandmother's sapped all the strength from his muscles.

She hadn't left yet.

Grabbing the hoodie, he made his way up the porch and knocked on the door. He concentrated on slowing his breathing while he waited for somebody to open it, and trying to prepare himself for the possibility the women inside would ignore him.

He'd deserve that.

When Helen finally opened it, he braced himself for scathing words, or at least anger in her eyes. But her expression was neutral. "Hello, Nick."

"Hi, Helen. Can I talk to Lucy, please?"

"Hold on a second."

Nick noticed she didn't invite him in as she always would have done in the past. Instead, she left him standing on the porch like a guy trying to sell her something, which told him she knew everything.

Through the screen door, he watched her walking toward Lucy's room. And when he looked past her, his heart sank. He could see enough of the smaller bedroom to see that the chaos that was Lucy trying to organize things was gone. The boxes he'd carried in there the night he finished the room were gone.

He hadn't thought to look into her car windows when he walked by, but it looked like, very soon, Lucy would also be gone.

As he watched, Helen nodded and then went into her own bedroom and closed the door. A moment later, Lucy appeared in her place and Nick could finally take a full breath.

She walked slowly toward him, her blue eyes never leaving his face. Anxiety rippled through him because her eyes weren't rimmed with red. Her nose wasn't red, and her face wasn't puffy. Maybe he'd misjudged everything, and she wasn't heartbroken at all.

He had to step out of the way when it became obvious she wasn't going to invite him in, but rather join him out on the porch. He wasn't even living room company now. Just front porch company, and he had nobody to blame but himself.

"Hi, Nick," she said softly when she'd pulled the big door closed behind her and let the screen door swing shut. "What can I do for you?"

There were so many things he wanted to say to her, starting with how sorry he was and ending with how much he loved her, but it was all jammed up in his mind, not making sense. He held out the hoodie. "I want you to take this with you."

"Why?"

Because I won't be able to hold you anymore, but maybe imagining my favorite hoodie wrapped around you will keep me from crying myself to sleep every night. "It gets cold in

Miami, you know. In January and February it can be in the forties. And back in 2010, the temperature actually dropped to thirty-five."

"I thought you established you wouldn't be taking care of me anymore. And I'm pretty sure I established I don't need you to."

"I lied," he blurted out. "Everything I said was a lie."

Lucy didn't look surprised. She simply kept looking at him with her arms crossed. "Why?"

"To drive you away before I could ask you to stay."

She tilted her head, her arms crossed. "Why would that have been so bad?"

"Because you might have stayed. You might have given up your dreams of living in Miami and being your own boss. And I know very well that you can know you made the right choice, but still feel the loss of what you gave up."

"But you didn't let me make a choice at all. You chose to hurt me instead."

"I'm so sorry for that. I was sorry as soon as I said it, and I should have chased you down the road, screaming it."

"Why didn't you?"

"Because I still thought that, even though I did it the wrong way, I did the right thing."

She shook her head. "So why are you here now?"

"Because I couldn't live with myself if you… I don't know. You believing I thought so little of you ate at me, and I didn't want you going off to Miami hurt like that."

"I'm not leaving."

For a moment, he wasn't sure he'd heard her correctly. "What do you mean? You're not leaving today? Or soon?"

"I mean I'm not going to Miami. I'm staying in Wayward Harbor."

The relief that went through Nick was so potent, he sagged

against the porch post. Thankfully, it was one of the repairs he'd done, so it was strong enough to hold his weight.

"But I'm not staying for you," she said. "I'm staying for me. I'm staying because I have friends and family here, and because it's my home."

His vision blurred slightly, and he blinked furiously. "I'm happy for you. I screwed it up in a big way, but I swear that's what I wanted for you. For you to be free to do what makes you happy."

Nick nodded once and then dropped down a step. He should go, before he made it worse. He didn't deserve her forgiveness, and he wouldn't beg her for it now. If she could give it someday, he would be grateful, but he wouldn't push her now.

"Why didn't you ask me to stay?" she said before he could take another step.

"Because I love you, Lucy, and it scares me. The feelings I have for you scare me." He inhaled and then shook his head. "No, it's more. My feelings for you actually *terrify* me."

"Am I that bad a bet?" She laughed, but it wasn't the happy Lucy laugh he adored. "Loving me is *terrifying*?"

"What scares me is knowing I would let everybody in my life down if that's what it took to keep you," he said quietly. "I would let down my brothers. I would walk away from my family's business. I'd let down our customers and the team and every single other person who relies on me if that's what it took to make you happy."

"I would never ask you to turn your back on everybody in your life."

"I know." He scrubbed a hand over his face. "It's not that you would ask it, I guess. It's more just recognizing that I *would*. It's terrifying, honestly. Asking you to stay would have been asking you to give up *your* dreams, and I knew I would walk away from my family if you asked me to go with you."

"So you took the choice away from both of us."

"I did and, again, I'll always be sorry."

"You would *hate* Miami," she said, and she looked as if she *might* smile.

"I absolutely would hate Miami. But I love you more than I would absolutely hate living in Miami. And, as you've said, my brothers are grown men. They can take care of themselves."

"Do you remember when Gran told me to build a house, and you told me not to forget that you can leave a house if it no longer serves you?"

"I do."

"Dreams can change, Nick." She walked to the edge of the stairs, and because he was down a step, they were almost eye level, but now she had the edge. "When I came to return your hoodie and asked if you were going to miss me, that was kind of my way of flirting my way into telling you how I felt."

Nick closed his eyes. The regret so strong, it was like acid in the back of his throat. But he opened them again because every second they were closed was a second he couldn't see her pretty blue eyes.

"I accept your apology," she said, finally giving him a small smile. "Because I know you, and because you're a good man."

The air left his lungs, and he reached out to take her hand. "I don't deserve you."

She scowled, her fingers squeezing his. "Don't you ever say that again, Nick Slater."

"I love you," he said, holding her gaze so she could see how much he meant it.

"Now, *that* you can say a *lot*." Then she leaned in and pressed her mouth to his.

The kiss was warm, like the sun after a cold spring storm, and he lost himself in it. Somehow this amazing, exasperating woman loved him, and everything felt right in his world.

She broke off the kiss and ran her thumb over his bottom lip. “And I love you.”

“Fair warning, I’m going to tell everybody I love you. I’m going to hold your hand everywhere we go. I’m going to kiss you all over this town.” When she laughed, he stepped back onto the porch so he could hold her close. “I might even post about it in the online group.”

“No,” she said, pulling away. “There’s a guy who won’t stop doing cat puns, and I’m honestly starting to be afraid for him.”

“Yeah, everybody wanting to sink their claws into him should give him paws.”

“No, Nick,” she said, and then she leaned against his chest, her body shaking with laughter.

“I can’t wait to see what we build on our foundation,” he whispered against her hair.

Epilogue

Wednesday is the first day of school! And the lunch special at the Uneven Keel, from 11:30 a.m. until 1:00 p.m., will be a sandwich of your choice with fries you don't have to share and a free "fancy shot," as we like to call them. It's called the "Forgotten Backpack." We'll also be offering a nonalcoholic version—they will be getting off that bus in a few hours—so come on down and fuel up for filling out the exact same school forms you filled out last year!

—Post from Lucy Macauley in the Wayward Harbor Online Community Group

"Whose boat is this?" Lucy yelled, trying to be heard over the ancient-sounding motor. "Are you sure it's safe to be on the actual ocean in it? This feels more like a boat for a pond."

Nick laughed and then glanced around before he cut the engine. The sudden silence was a relief, but Lucy wasn't sure how she felt about the small craft just bobbing aimlessly.

"We're not going any further out in it, but it's sound," he told her. "And it belongs to Cory Weston, a friend of Gray's."

"I've met Brooke a few times. So this is her ex-husband's boat?" She frowned, shoving at the hair the wind had torn from her attempt at restraining it in a braid. "Word at the

Scuttlebutt is that it wasn't a very amicable divorce. You're sure she didn't drill any holes in it, right?"

"You know, you can just say, 'Scuttlebutt says it wasn't amicable.'"

"But I heard it at *the* Scuttlebutt, thank you very much, and it sounds more fun." She grinned when exasperation got the better of him and he scowled at her. "Wait, are there sides? Gray is Cory's best friend. You're Gray's brother. I live with you. Does that mean I can't be friends with Brooke? I hope not, because I actually like her a lot."

"You can be friends with Brooke," he assured her. "It's tough on Gray, though. Not you being friends with her, but the relationships in general."

"Oh, he can't really be friends with Brooke anymore, I guess."

"It's messy. He's been friends with both of them since they were kids. He and Brooke were actually a thing in high school, but they split and she ended up with Cory."

"Oh no."

"Gray got over it. But I don't think he's ever gotten over *her*, to be honest."

"That *is* messy. Because marrying your best friend's ex-girlfriend is kinda bad. But hooking up with your best friend's ex-wife is *way* worse."

Nick gave her a stern look. "That is *not* scuttlebutt for *the* Scuttlebutt, by the way."

"Of course not." Lucy sighed and glanced around the vast amount of water they were drifting aimlessly in. "Are you sure this is safe?"

"It's safe," he said patiently. "Especially since you're making both of us wear our life vests instead of just having them at hand if we need them."

"If a whale decides to come up under the boat and toss us in the air, you'll be glad you listened to me."

"At least it's a whale now," he grumbled. "When you were running this scenario by me *very* loudly at the dock, it was a sea monster."

Her cheeks heated. "Yeah, but I saw all the guys laughing at me—okay, at *us*—and I know some of them are already at the Keel, laughing about the city girl being afraid of sea monsters."

"I already got a text from Theo."

"Of course you did." She sighed, wrapping her arms tighter around the bulky life vest. "It's just a very small boat."

"But now you've been out in a boat," he said, opening the waterproof bag at their feet. He pulled out a plastic baggie that had a piece of paper and a Sharpie inside. "Now you can cross it off our list of shenanigans."

Lucy laughed, taking the list and the Sharpie from him. "I can't believe you brought this out here with us."

After drawing a thick black line through *Go out on a boat*, she handed the list to him. "That's it. That's all of them."

Everything under the heading of *Our Shenanigans* was crossed out. He held out his hand for the Sharpie, and she put the cap back on before handing it to him.

"We got up to all the shenanigans," he said, giving her a little shrug.

"I'm sad about it, though. I'll miss that list."

"You know, we can always *add* to the list." He pulled the cap off the Sharpie and turned away so she couldn't see what he was writing.

"That better not involve eating anything adventurous," she warned. "Or hiking. Or fishing. I am very willing to be the only resident of Wayward Harbor who doesn't know how to bait a hook."

He chuckled and recapped the Sharpie. When he handed her the paper, she noticed his hand was trembling slightly, but she assumed it was cold. Not that he would admit it, but it had been warm in town. It was *not* warm out on the water, and it was only September.

Then she looked at the list.

Our Shenanigans:
~~*Sunrise on Cadillac Mountain*~~
~~*Go out on a boat*~~
~~*Visit Dinghy Doodads*~~
~~*Play football on the beach*~~
~~*Lucy: try a bologna and tomato sandwich*~~
Get married? Y/N

Lucy's breath caught, and she held tight to the paper as she looked into Nick's eyes. "Really?"

"Really. I love you, Lucy Macauley, and I want to spend the rest of my life getting up to shenanigans with you."

It was hard to see the list with tears welling up in her eyes, but she yelled out a yes across the water as she carefully circled the *Y*. Then, after showing it to him, she delicately sealed the paper and Sharpie back in the plastic bag. It seemed to take forever for Nick to put it back in the big bag, but she didn't ever want to lose that list.

Finally, he was done, and she launched herself into his arms. The boat rocked wildly, but she didn't care because Nick was holding her. Awkwardly, because they were both wearing life vests, but she was in his arms and that was all that mattered.

"I love you so much," she said against his ear before pulling back so she could kiss him, until a swell shifted the boat too much and she squealed against his lips.

"We're fine," he said. "But I'll fire up the motor so we can start heading back. Now that you're going to be my wife, you should probably know I actually don't love being *on* the ocean all that much."

"Your *wife*," Lucy said, and she grinned before she kissed him—just a quick one because she didn't think she liked being on the ocean all that much, either.

"I have a ring for you, but I left it on dry land," he said. "I was so afraid I'd be one of those guys who dropped the ring in the water, and I would never have lived that one down."

She laughed as he fired up the motor and yelled over the noise. "Let's go get it, then. We've got a lifetime of shenanigans to get up to."

* * * * *